OSLO SPIES

PHYLLIS BOWDEN BOOK 2

SJ SLAGLE

ROUGH
EDGES
PRESS

Oslo Spies
Paperback Edition
© Copyright 2022 (As Revised) SJ Slagle

Rough Edges Press
An Imprint of Wolfpack Publishing
5130 S. Fort Apache Rd. 215-380
Las Vegas, NV 89148

roughedgespress.com

Paperback ISBN 978-1-68549-057-7

OSLO SPIES

PROLOGUE

"Don't be frightened."

The little girl looked from her terrified mother to her father, his face reddened from strain with purple veins bulging at the temple. She clung to her mother wrapped in the man's arms, all three locked in their teary embrace. Fear permeated the room with artillery exploding just outside. When the door flew off the hinges and the windows shattered with the next bomb, he pushed away from them both.

"I have to go. You *know* I have to go. I've stayed too long as it is. My company is loading on the fjord as I speak and if I'm captured...well, let's just say it won't be good."

"Oskar, you promised we could go with you."

"I can't take you, but if I can return some day, I promise I will."

That only made the mother and daughter cry harder. With the war exploding around them, a reunion didn't seem remotely possible. Death was more inevitable.

He scurried into another room returning with something in his hands.

"Take this, liebchen. You've been such a sweet girl and I'll miss you." Pressing his lips to her forehead, he placed the item in her arms before kissing her mother. His kisses were light, meaningful, but final. With that, the man brushed off his green uniform before rushing out the open door. She knew as well as her mother that if he'd looked back, they all would have been done for. It was crushing enough that their life together had fallen apart. And with the British forces invading the south and the Soviets coming in from the north, the girl knew her family would soon be no more. She wasn't sure why, but she knew it.

It had been in her father's lingering looks and the terror on her mother's face. Things were changing around her and these changes weren't going to be good. She looked down at the doll in her arms.

ONE

Oslo was raw and exposed as if someone had sliced open the city's stomach and its contents had spilled out. Driving down a main street, blocks of tall, stout buildings would suddenly devolve into shattered husks of once thriving businesses. A square pile of bricks with the top floors blown away stared straight ahead unblinking with two glassless windows as eyes. Eyes as unbelieving as hers.

Devastation was everywhere, yet long lines of people queued by the open doorway of a soot-covered building that had miraculously survived.

It was a strange kind of nighttime—the kind with daylight instead of darkness. Being this close to the Arctic Circle, it should have been cold. But in July 1945, the weather was almost as warm as in Washington, DC where she'd just come from visiting her family.

Phyllis Bowden's lips stayed firmly closed and she wasn't going to ask, it wasn't her place. She held it in as long as she could, but the words escaped all too soon.

"Please, sir. What happened? I thought the German authorities resided in Oslo. It looks like the place was bombed."

"Ja." The word was pushed out of the Norwegian driver's mouth while he inhaled. "Volcomen Norge."

"Excuse me?" she asked.

"Welcome to Norway."

Not the welcome she expected. She'd just left her Embassy assignment in war-torn London to be assigned to war-torn Oslo. Both cities had bombs falling on them until the end of that horrendous war with Germany, but Phyllis had learned from classified reports that much of Norway's destruction was due to the Norwegian resistance that had wreaked the havoc she witnessed. Unlike other occupied countries, Norway had waged an internal war with the Germans like no other. She needed to know much more to be of any use here.

Phyllis glanced about the bus as it jerked clumsily along the debris-strewn street. The vehicle, along with many others, had been liberated from the Germans and was unlike any she'd seen. It was built with comfort in mind. Every cushioned seat had a table with a reading lamp and telephone. An impeccable lavatory filled with sweet-smelling soaps and soft towels was five feet away. Nubby carpeting covered the floor and the whole inside was spotless. Glancing out the window, beautiful blonde women with golden tans and white shorts rode by on bicycles. Many Norwegians she passed were wearing white and were dressed better than the English she'd just left behind. In London, there had been plenty of clothing to buy, but it was rationed. She wondered how the Norwegians could look so much better since there was not one article of clothing to be purchased in all of Norway.

The five-year German occupation had seen to that. She'd learned the Germans had stripped the country bare of anything of value. They'd closed most of the stores, halted the fishing industry and any exports. Children wore paper or fish scale shoes, wooden clogs if they could make them. Leather was an unheard of luxury. Even though the German occupation had ended, there was still little homegrown food, no clothing, rationed electrical power and no medicine. America and Sweden were sending supplies, she knew, but like starving people, Norwegians would have to limit their diet until stomachs were able to digest the vegetables, meats and macaroni being donated. With an austere diet for five years, any fat in the new foods would make Norwegians sick.

Yet the glorious feeling of the people was a sight to behold, even at night queued in lines with happy smiles on their faces. She could guess the reason for their happiness: Germans were no longer in control.

"What's that?" she called out to the driver.

"A camp for German prisoners," he responded.

"Are they leaving soon?"

"Ja, we hope, but there's thousands who have lived here for years and it will take time."

Phyllis considered what he said until they passed a government building with a Norwegian flag, bright red with a blue cross, waving proudly from a flagpole nearby. Her gaze strayed to the crumpled Nazi flag near a trashcan before she noticed Norwegian policemen escorting a handful of young women. They wore similar dresses, like uniforms.

"Excuse me, driver."

"Yes, miss?"

"What's happening here?"

The driver slowed at a stop sign allowing Phyllis time to take a good look at the small crowd assembled. The young women were really young girls, not even teenagers.

"Those are Quisling girls," he told her in a gruff tone.

"Quisling?" She had read a classified report about Quisling, but wanted the driver's take on the situation.

"Ja. Vidkun Quisling." She heard him spit on the floor. "Scum who tried to take over Norway when Hitler," another spitting sound, "was in charge."

"He's Norwegian."

"And a traitor to his country."

"What will happen to him?"

"He's been arrested and I hope he's shot."

Phyllis was quiet watching the scene play out. One little girl, not eight years old, caught her eye as the driver pulled away. She glanced up to see Phyllis watching her and the fear on her small face was palpable. A policeman herded her with the other girls, but she ventured a brief smile to Phyllis before disappearing into the building.

"And these girls? What will happen to them?"

"Don't care, miss, but if they're shot, it's better than they deserve."

A thought nagged at her until they reached Army Headquarters. What could a seven year-old Norwegian girl have done that was considered so traitorous to her countrymen? She shook off the thought after arriving and being met by a State Department representative. He put her up for the night in an apartment with State Department personnel. There was a kernel of darkness in this newly liberated country. As much as she tried to overlook it, Phyllis knew this kernel would pop into trouble.

But hopefully not tomorrow.

Jay nodded. "I never stood out much as a redhead in London and Scotland, but I must look like an alien here."

Phyllis laughed. "But a pretty alien so I think we're safe enough." She nodded towards the street. "Let's get going. We're burning daylight."

They began walking down a street filled with people hurrying in different directions. A mass of cables crisscrossed overhead with lights hanging down every hundred yards or so. Broken bricks in the street and sidewalk made for treacherous walking.

"Be careful not to muss those saddle shoes. Get those at Harrod's?"

"I did," said Jay, "and it sure looked like a couple of those women on the trolley were ready to rip them off my feet."

The three-story buildings they passed were covered in grime. The occupation hadn't been hard on only the Norwegian people; every vehicle, every bicycle, every building, even the few dogs they saw looked exhausted. Everything needed a thorough wash, a fresh coat of paint, and a good meal. But the people couldn't have been friendlier. Everyone Phyllis and Jay passed smiled at them. Ladies nodded while gentlemen tipped their hats. Halfway into the block, they stopped at a small café for lunch. With a hastily repaired door and tape across cracks in the windows, the café had obviously just reopened. The shy proprietor met them at the doorway and escorted them to a corner table.

"God dag, mine damer. Jeg heter Arne." The timid man with threadbare clothes and frizzy gray hair handed them a thick piece of paper, an unreadable menu. He smiled hopefully, pushing the paper closer. Phyllis and Jay exchanged embarrassed looks.

"How much Norwegian do you know?" Phyllis handed the menu to Jay. "I just got here. You've been here a few weeks. Have a go at it."

Jay shook her head. "I know how to say 'good morning' and 'where's the bathroom'."

Phyllis laughed. "That may not get us any food."

"Well, I can point," added Jay, "but there's no guaranteeing what we'll get."

"Not a linguist?"

"Not even a little."

The man's smile widened. "Engelsk? American?"

They understood that and nodded.

"Ah!" He held up a finger and hurried into the kitchen.

"This isn't like Mick's place back in London, is it?" Phyllis glanced around the bleak interior with few tables and chairs. No one else was in the place. It hadn't been bombed, but showed signs of long disuse with barren walls and few foodstuffs on shelves. The forlorn atmosphere was just this side of desperate.

"No," Jay agreed, "but he's probably happy to be open again. I'm sure there was nothing to sell during the occupation."

Footsteps from the kitchen had Phyllis and Jay turning their heads to see the proprietor propelling a reluctant young boy towards them. His blonde hair stuck up in several places and his shorts were ragged. The frown on his face indicated he wasn't happy to be there.

"Engelsk!" The man proudly pointed to the boy. "Sonn." He placed his hand on his chest.

Phyllis smiled. "Your son?" She extended her hand to the boy. "Nice to meet you."

The man nudged the boy forward to clasp Phyllis' hand.

"Nice...to...meet   du," he   said   hesitantly. "My name...Lars."

"Nice to meet you, Lars. I'm Phyllis."

"Fill...us," said the boy and the man together, looks of wonder on their faces.

She turned to Jay. "This is Jay."

Jay stretched out her hand to the boy who took it and repeated, "Ja-ay." He beamed triumphantly. "Nice to meet...du."

"Same to you, mate." Jay handed the menu to the boy with raised shoulders. "Food?"

His confused expression made Phyllis wonder if they'd

ever get anything to eat. Suddenly, a smile spread across his face and he pointed to an item on the menu. "Farikal... iz...good."

Both Arne and Lars looked so proud that Phyllis and Jay could only smile and nod in return. The man and boy rushed back to the kitchen.

"What did we just order?" asked Phyllis.

"Wait a minute. I think I have a Norwegian language dictionary with me." Jay dug around in her purse and pulled out a small book. She thumbed through a few pages. "Here it is. Farikal: mutton stew."

"Mutton stew? Great." Phyllis spread her paper napkin on her lap and looked toward the kitchen. "Wonder what else is in it."

Jay smiled. "Guess we'll find out soon enough."

Just then the man, with a hastily donned apron, brought out two steaming cups to place before the women. He smiled and left quickly.

Phyllis glanced into the cup, held it up to her nose.

"What is it?" Jay eyed her cup suspiciously.

"Well, it's brown, so I think it's supposed to be coffee."

"Try it and see."

Phyllis snorted. "Want me to be the guinea pig?"

"Yes, ma'am."

She raised the cup to her lips and blew in it before taking a cautious sip. Phyllis swirled it in her mouth. After she swallowed, she glanced over at her friend.

"Well?"

"It's not coffee, but it's hot."

"Just what we needed on a summer day." Jay picked up her cup for a taste. "Not bad, whatever it is."

Phyllis' face scrunched in thought. "In my preparation for this assignment, I remember something about there being no coffee at all in Norway because they weren't allowed to import anything. I think this may be roasted rye."

Jay licked her lips. "It tastes nutty. I bet you're right."

"When in Rome," began Phyllis as she took another sip.

"...do as the Romans do," finished Jay.

They clinked their cups and downed more of the brown liquid.

Arne and Lars brought in two large bowls with towels protecting their hands.

"That looks hot," commented Phyllis.

"Ja," said Lars. "Hot."

After placing the bowls on the table, they stepped back and watched anxiously as Phyllis and Jay picked up their spoons. Phyllis poked around in her bowl.

"Mutton, potatoes and cabbage." She blew softly on a heaping spoonful before putting it in her mouth. Her eyes widened. "Good!"

Jay dug in and they ate happily with Arne and Lars applauding briefly before hurrying back to the safety of the kitchen. Lunch went smoothly and Jay put some bills on the table when Arne brought the check. Phyllis glanced at the unfamiliar currency.

"Glad you got some Norwegian money. I'm new in town and haven't changed my money yet."

"Well, good luck when you try. With our diplomatic connections, we're able to get small amounts of kroner, but money is one of the big problems in Norway right now. They've got to stabilize the currency to get their economy back on track. If our embassies can't get kroner, we'll have to resort to the black market."

"Black market's big here?"

"Right now, yes, because there's little available to eat or buy, but it'll fade as soon as the supplies coming in lessen the demand. Good thing too," she said finishing the last of her rye coffee. "It's expensive to buy anything on the black market."

"I bet. Let's see more of Oslo."

A left turn out of the café and a few empty stores down took Phyllis and Jay right back to the war. They stopped abruptly with dropped jaws when remembrance of wartime horrors stood in front of them.

The crass writing in thick white letters was slopped on

the front of a store window. Phyllis didn't need to know Norwegian to understand what the words meant.

"Jode. Stengt." She took a steady breath. "I know Jode means *Jew* and I bet the next word means *closed*."

Jay dug out her dictionary, skimmed a few pages and nodded. "You're right." Shaken, she let the small book fall from her hand onto the dirty sidewalk. Her pale face reddened with anger. "Just when you think it's over, the hateful past sends you a reminder."

Phyllis leaned over to pick up the dictionary and hand it back to Jay. "We'll never be free of this war and all the horrors that were committed. Never. We probably haven't learned a tenth of what happened." She clenched her teeth so tightly that her jaw hurt. A calming breath slowed her rapidly beating pulse, but what she'd seen would never leave her memory. Of that, she was certain.

The store had once sold toys. A plastic horse and a small tea set with cups, saucers and a teapot painted in bright pink and blue sat in the dusty window. Phyllis looked past the display to broken toys scattered on the floor with shelves torn from the walls. An overturned desk sat in a corner with papers, headless dolls and ripped stuffed toys tossed about as remnants of another battle. The winners of the fight had caused absolute destruction of this tiny piece of Norway and had gone off to fight other battles. Tears pooled in Phyllis' eyes when she turned to see the moisture collecting in Jay's. Seeking under-standing, Phyllis and Jay stood frozen even as tears slid down their faces. Finally, Phyllis wiped her eyes and reached out to hug her friend. They stayed that way until the noise of the street reached their ears shaking them out of their painful reverie.

"I can't even imagine. Can you?" asked Jay.

Phyllis shook her head. "Let's...concentrate on what we're in Oslo to do."

"And what's that?"

"To help put the country back together."

Small smiles eventually claimed their faces.

"I can do that," said Jay. "Let's go."

Another block down, they came to a city park. Instead of the usual grassy areas with trees and bushes, a small pond perhaps and children's play equipment, the entire park was covered with various plots of land with people working the land, growing gardens. It was a busy place with people hoeing, pulling weeds and harvesting. They walked over to the nearest garden for a closer look. An older man and woman were digging in the dirt. They continued their harvest and smiled benignly when Phyllis and Jay walked up, hands raised in hello.

"Potatoes." Phyllis watched the man with tattered pants and rope for a belt pull the hardy vegetable from the ground. His confident smile showed a broken tooth in front when he proudly held the potato up for his wife to see.

She had crouched down, working on another row and tugged free two heads of cabbage. They said something in rapid-fire Norwegian to one another before showing the vegetables like trophies to the women watching them. Jay sighed and laid her hand on Phyllis' arm as they moved away.

"My boss at the embassy told me to leave my money at home."

"Why's that?" asked Phyllis.

They walked down the many rows of gardens watching Norwegians doggedly pull, tug and cut the food from the ground. Potatoes, cabbage and carrots filled the baskets that lay scattered everywhere. People had the proud looks of mothers and fathers with newborn babies.

"Because," Jay sighed again, "he knew I'd want to give all my money away to everyone I meet."

The corners of Phyllis' mouth curved. "So you're a big softie."

"I am."

"Just think about all the good work you're doing at the embassy."

Just past the park, Phyllis and Jay came upon a building with an open front and Norwegian flags planted on either side. A small crowd of children was assembled, laughing and chattering noisily. Women in white paper hats lined up behind a counter to hand out bread and sausage to anyone who walked up. The children waved Norwegian flags and munched happily as they clustered around the sides of the building.

"What's happening here? I mean, I can see they're eating, but where did all this food come from?" Phyllis tapped the shoulder of one little boy. He was five or six years old wearing a slick rain hat. His rosy cheeks were stuffed with the bread he was eating and his eyes were bright with excitement.

"Ja? Hva vil du?"

She pointed to the bread. "Do you speak English?"

"Engelsk?" he asked.

"Yes."

"No." He shook his head and went back to eating his bread.

A little girl with blonde braids slipped alongside Phyllis and took her hand.

"I speak Engelsk. Du want food?" She held up a bun for Phyllis to take. Her angelic face nearly took Phyllis' breath away.

"No. Where did you get bread and sausage?"

She pointed to the building and the ladies. "They give us."

"But where..." The little girl dashed away to run up the street with another girl. Phyllis chuckled at the sight of twin braids flapping as she went. "Guess that's all I'm getting from her."

"May I help you?" One of the women distributing the food came around the corner. She wore an apron and looked as thin as all the other women Phyllis had seen so far in Oslo. With a limited diet for five years, no Norwegian looked fat or even sturdy. "I speak English."

"Great!" Phyllis swept a hand toward the crowd of children. "Where did all this food come from?"

The woman ran her hands down her apron and straightened her hat. She nodded at Phyllis and Jay before replying. "The bread and sausage were confiscated from German military stores. We hand them free to anyone who wants them. The children come day and night."

"No bread or sausage when the Germans were here?" asked Jay.

"We were lucky to have anything to eat. The first years of the occupation, grain, coffee and sugar were rationed. After that, we had nothing but the fish the Germans didn't want and whatever we could raise ourselves."

"Yes," added Phyllis. "We went by a park with gardens."

"Farmers did a little better than us in the cities, but not much. There was too much..." she seemed to be searching for the right word. "Spying."

"Spying?" asked Jay.

She nodded, glanced back at the other women. "Germans spying on us, traitors spying for the Germans." She blew out a shaky breath. "You didn't know who to trust." The woman thrust out her hand to Phyllis. "You're American, yes?"

"Yes, I am."

"Thank you for the supplies you are sending us."

She turned to Jay. "You're English?"

"Aye, mate." Jay's smiling eyes widened with surprise when the woman enveloped her in a fierce hug. Stepping back, she wiped away tears. They smiled broadly at one another.

"The English are our saviors. We can never thank you enough."

"It was our pleasure, ma'am."

With that, the woman returned to her job handing out bread and sausage to more children who had collected for their treats. And with heads held high, they continued their labor of love as Phyllis and Jay walked by smiling and nodding their approval. A tip of the head from Jay to the woman they had spoken to and they were gone from the pleasant scene.

THREE

"Is that a fjord?"

"Yep."

"What exactly is a fjord?"

Phyllis opened Jay's dictionary, skimmed through and began reading aloud. "It's a deep, narrow lake drain with steep land on three sides. The opening toward the sea is called the mouth of the fjord and is often shallow."

Jay and Phyllis looked at the sight before them. Tall, snow-covered peaks surrounded the body of water with trails zigzagging through the trees to homes built in the mountains. Vivid blue seawater deepened in color farther away in the distance. Standing on a pier, Phyllis pointed to the beach below.

"Look! They're swimming."

Jay arched an eyebrow playfully. "Want to do it?"

Phyllis laughed and they headed down to the beach. Once at the water's edge, she stuck in a hand.

"You'd think it would be cold this close to the Arctic Circle."

"It's July," said Jay. She stuck in a hand as well to test the water temperature. "Warm…"

Glancing around the beach area, Phyllis spotted what she was looking for.

"There it is."

"What?"

"A guy renting bathing suits."

A tiny, wooden hut not far from the pier caught Jay's eye. As they walked towards it, many Norwegians in various kinds of clothing smiled and said hello. Some wore bathing suits, some were in shorts and long pants. A few women wore long, white skirts.

"Friendly people."

The man working in the hut wore a colorful sweater, shorts and a bright red knit cap. When the women walked up to him, a big smile creased his weathered face.

"Goddag, damer. Trenger en badedrakt?" When his request met with blank looks from Phyllis and Jay, he tried pointing at the row of bathing suits behind him. "Badedrakt?"

That, they understood.

"Two, please." Phyllis held up two fingers. The man discreetly checked out their figures, took two suits off the shelf and handed them over.

"How much?" asked Jay. When the man shook his head, she reached into her purse for the Norwegian dictionary. "Hvor mye?"

The man looked confused, probably due to her wretched Norwegian pronunciation, but pointed to a sign on the side of the hut.

"He wants five kroner per suit," Phyllis asked her. "How much is that?"

"About ten cents."

"Pay up, friend. I'll pay you back."

Jay shrugged, fished out her wallet. "Going on the town with you is getting expensive. I thought you Yanks had money."

"Some do and apparently, some don't. I promise to get cash tomorrow."

"I'm not worried." Jay smiled. "I know where you live."

They changed in a small restroom behind the hut and hurried down to the water. Stowing their clothes on a chair recently vacated, Phyllis and Jay ran into the water and turned to one another to laugh before diving in. Phyllis was surprised and pleased at how warm it was. She swam underwater until she had to surface for a breath of air. What was it about water that seemed to protect and cleanse? Phyllis floated on her back for several minutes drinking in the impossibly blue sky overhead dotted with fluffy white clouds. It was a beautiful day and all seemed right with the world. Turning her head to the right and then the left, the mountains seemed larger from her new vantage point and she knew they'd been there for millions of years. They would stand for millions more.

The beauty of the area softened her sadness of what Norwegians had endured during the war. The cleansing water washed away thoughts of ruined stores and stolen goods, destroyed homes and stolen lives. But the water couldn't entirely wash away her thoughts about the children.

The children of Norway had perhaps lost the most: their hopes and dreams for the future, their abilities to laugh and play, to be children. Without that necessary developmental step, what would become of them?

Jay swam up behind and splashed water on her.

"Hey!"

"Well, you're thinking too hard and this is our day off. Think tomorrow."

Phyllis chuckled, paddled to a shallow spot where she could stand. "You're right. Tomorrow is soon enough for deep thinking."

"But I know what has put that serious look on your face."

"What?"

Jay's eyes swept the fjord and over to the beach covered with exuberant people talking and laughing. It should have been a typical scene in a typical beach town or port city. Her wet hair dripped from curly auburn strands onto her glistening cheeks and neck. "The beauty we see contrasts sharply with the terror we know was here for five years. It would be unbelievable if we didn't know it happened."

"I know what you mean. The reports I read of bombings,

people shipped off to slave labor camps and other terrors make this moment incredibly poignant." Phyllis nodded toward the people swimming nearby. "I bet everyone here has a story to tell and is counting their blessings the Germans have gone."

Jay took a deep breath. "Come on. Enough philosophizing for one day. We need to get back."

After changing clothes and returning the bathing suits, the women hiked to the pier to catch a trolley back to Army Headquarters. Riding along in the rusted old vehicle with Norwegians going home after work, Phyllis looked thoughtfully around her. She was beginning to like Oslo and Norway very much, but when she turned to speak to Jay, something caught her eye.

Jay was babbling and pointing from her side of the trolley. "Can you believe it's still daylight? Blimey, it must be seven at night at least. Why, I could..."

"Jay." Phyllis tugged on her arm. "Look at that."

"What?" She glanced where Phyllis was looking. Her eyes narrowed just as her lips flattened to a tight line. "What is that?"

The bed of a large truck parked by the side of the street was filled with eight frightened women with shaved heads. Two women had black swastikas drawn on their foreheads and a paper sign with writing in Norwegian fluttered on a window.

"What the hell is that?" Jay and Phyllis stood immediately to get a better look out the window. "Why are their heads shaved?"

A woman next to them touched Jay's sleeve. "Samarbeidspartner." Another woman nodded in agreement.

"What?" asked Phyllis.

The woman was quiet a moment. "Quisling."

Jay thought that over. "They think these women collaborated with the Germans, like Vidkun Quisling. He was a Norwegian official who tried to take over the government when the king was deposed."

Phyllis' confused look became angry. She lowered her

voice. "Yesterday when I arrived, policemen were herding young girls into a building. The driver called them Quisling girls."

"Sure," Jay whispered back. "I've heard of them. It was the Norwegian version of the League of German Girls, so-called youthful Hitler lovers. So?"

Eyes as chilly as her words met Jay's stare.

"Please tell me what a little Norwegian girl could have done to collaborate with Germans." She angled her head toward the women on the truck as the bus rolled past. "And please explain to me what shaving a woman's head is supposed to prove? What are they doing to men who collaborated? Are they shaving their heads too? Parking them out in trucks to be gawked and yelled at? This feels like stoning a woman for something she did in some barbaric third world country."

Jay spoke directly into Phyllis' ear. "This isn't your country or mine. We didn't live through five years of German occupation like they did. It's no telling how we would react had we been through similar circumstances."

"I understand what you're saying, Jay, but there's an unfair quality here, a dark wind blowing through this country. I'm not going to pretend to ignore certain things I see."

"Even if you understand why people are upset with collaborators?"

"Even then."

Jay tugged her away toward the front of the bus. "Let's go. This is our stop."

As they walked towards Army Headquarters, Phyllis ventured a last lingering look at the women on the truck. Something wasn't right; something felt off and she was determined to find out what it was. It could mean sticking her nose in where it didn't belong. Sometimes, she thought, a person just had to do that.

FOUR

Lt. Col. Ronald Lawrence, Military Attaché.

Phyllis stared at the name painted on the frosted glass of the door. Standing on the second floor of the American Embassy in Oslo, Phyllis experienced a twinge of déjà vu. The name took her back to London where she'd been assigned as secretary to an officer. It took her breath away remembering that Lt. Col. Lawrence, Ronnie they called him, had been arrested for espionage and suffered needlessly until Phyllis and her friend Lorraine had found the proof of his innocence. Her pulse fluttered as names and places flashed through her mind: Dick Simpson, Wise Willie, Canning Town, Seven Addison Bridge Place and the dreaded Malcolm. It was enough to make her shudder and back away from the door when it creaked opened in front of her.

"Phyllis! It *is* you! I thought I heard a noise in the hallway. Come in. Come in! I'm glad you've finally arrived." Lawrence's momentary surprise softened to smiling eyes with a knowing look. He thrust out his hand.

"Sir. How are you?"

His energetic handshake left her in no doubt that he was glad to see her. He pushed open the door and swept a hand toward his office.

"Please come in. Let's get reacquainted."

Once she was seated in a chair by his desk, the tall man walked briskly around to address her. His smart brown jacket crinkled as he sat. His tie was expertly knotted and contrasted with his light brown shirt and pants. Straight military posture gave away his dedication to duty and service. Everything about Lt. Col. Ronald Lawrence screamed upstanding Army officer. But his intense look caused her to glance down at what she was wearing. Was her gray rayon dress too...dressy for the office? Maybe she should have worn a skirt her first day on the job or maybe...

"You're a sight for sore eyes, Miss Bowden."

"Colonel, we saw each other only two weeks ago in London."

"Yes, yes." He leaned forward in his chair. "How's the family in Washington? I heard your dad was doing better."

She nodded happily. "My sister was always sending me doomsday letters, but he's actually feeling pretty good."

"Cancer, is it?"

"Yes, but it's in remission. Since the war ended, he seems like a new man."

"I hope his treatments continue to go well."

"Thank you, sir."

"I know it's not my business to ask, but how is your young man, Joe Schneider? I believe he's an MI5 chap."

She smiled. "And you would know that because you met him when he spoke to you about what Lorraine and I...our activities..."

"Yes, he told me some and Dickie told me the rest. It's something I'll never be able to thank you enough for doing, Phyllis. What you and your blonde friend did for me is beyond duty, beyond loyalty, beyond any thanks I can ever bestow upon you."

"Colonel, I..." Phyllis blushed. "That's too much praise. I did what needed to be done and luckily it turned out well." She met his intense stare with one of her own. "The whole scenario could have turned out very badly indeed."

"Indeed it could have, but it didn't." His eyes twinkled.

"So how about I have Joe come for a visit very soon, if you want to see him." He snapped his fingers. "Red tape no more. How about sometime in the upcoming weeks?"

"You'd do that for us?"

"Absolutely." Ronnie sat back in his chair with folded hands on the desk. "I may have to stop praising you, but I can certainly throw in a perk or two for a job well done. How would that be?"

"Wonderful, sir."

His smile remained, although he grew serious. "Let's talk about the job now, shall we?"

"Yes, sir." Phyllis pulled out a notebook and pencil. "What will I be doing as your secretary?"

"The usual—letters, intelligence reports, supplies—but I need help setting up this office, Phyllis. It's a mess, which you couldn't possibly have noticed yet, and I need you to straighten up the system. For heaven's sake, the stationary is in German."

"German?"

"Sure. They were here for five years. Everything of value is in German. The telephone operators all speak German." He sighed audibly. "It'll take months to straighten things out just administratively."

"Filing?"

"Filing is the least of it. I want you running the office of Military Attaché, working our communication lines with Washington, handling queries from Norwegians who come to the embassy for help...as well as...something else."

She looked up from jotting in her notebook. "And what's that?"

Lawrence stood, straightened his jacket and walked to the window. The view from his second floor office looked over parts of Oslo, on out to the Oslo Fjord. She could see the breathtaking scenery from where she sat. After staring out the window for a moment, he walked over to close the door. Once he had returned to lean against the desk, his eyes and voice became somber.

"You've proven your abilities one hundred percent, Miss

Bowden. I want to take you a little further into the organization."

"Sir, I've already had tradecraft training for my job."

"I know but this will be more intensive because I intend to send you out on assignment occasionally."

"Out of Norway?"

"No, but I need eyes and ears in the city and perhaps out in the countryside."

"Um..." She put her pencil down.

"No need to get worried, Phyllis. It wouldn't be anything you didn't do in London—parties at the embassy, state department, Army and Norwegian officials, some travel."

"Parties?"

"And meeting certain officials occasionally. I'll need you to glean different kinds of information than you gathered for us in London. I can tell you more as the time comes. You know," he offered, "as the need arises."

"All right, if that's what you need."

"You still look worried, Phyllis. What is it?"

"Sir, I don't want to carry a gun and I would prefer not to be involved in anything dangerous."

He laughed. "This from the woman who wrestled a killer for his revolver in the middle of a V2 bomb explosion."

"And got shot for my efforts."

"All the more reason for more training."

She tried not to roll her eyes. "I was doing what needed to be done, sir."

"Phyllis." He leaned over to touch her hand. "Not only did you save your friend's life, you saved mine."

Her cheeks warmed with his praise.

"You've been in military intelligence ever since you stepped off the transport plane in England, Miss Bowden. I'm just asking that you do the occasional assignment for me."

When she still looked unconvinced, he continued. "General Donovan will thank you personally."

"I've met him already, sir."

Lawrence watched her a minute before his eyes

widened. "Sure, I remember. Didn't he fish you out of the Potomac River when the boat you were in broke down? That was way back before you transferred to England, wasn't it?"

"It was."

"It's good to have friends in high places."

They smiled knowingly at one another.

"Do you have any questions about Norway that I can answer?" He walked around the desk to sit down.

"Yes, I do. I went around Oslo yesterday, just to see the city, and wondered about some things I saw."

"Such as?"

"I saw terrified women in a truck with shaved heads and swastikas painted on their foreheads. What's that about?"

He shook his head wearily. Glints of silver in his dark hair seemed more pronounced. "The Norwegians are a fiercely proud people. The resistance here was stronger than I've ever seen in an occupied country. We're still learning of the heroic deeds done by ordinary citizens and even children to push back at the Germans." He glanced over. "You know who Vidkun Quisling is?"

"Yes."

"Well, his name has become synonymous with traitor. Anyone who collaborated with the Germans in any way would be labeled a *quisling.*"

"The women I saw? What did they do?"

"It could be anything from merely cleaning a German officer's house all the way up the scale to sleeping with a German. What's happening now, Phyllis, is a national purge."

"A purge?"

"Purge, witch-hunt, they mean the same in this context. Anyone who had anything to do with the Germans is being purged from society. Right now the well-to-do Norwegians who socialized with Quisling are hiding in their homes hoping to be spared. But they won't be." He paused. "Maids, window-washers, barbers and even clerks who did the slightest thing to help the Germans are being jailed or loaded on trucks to take to slave labor mines."

Phyllis jaw dropped. "You're kidding."

He shook his head. "I wish I were. It's going to get worse before it gets better, so...watch your step."

"Why? I'm American."

"You'll be dealing with all sorts of problems that the Norwegians are having. President Truman has asked that we cooperate fully with the Norwegian government to help get the country going again. We'll need to be tactful in what we say and how we act."

Phyllis glanced out the window. Bright streaks of sunlight reflected on the floor and walls.

"I haven't gotten used to a new president yet, Colonel. I'm still grieving for President Roosevelt."

"I know how you feel. Donovan's tearing out his hair because Truman is making noises about dissolving the organization."

Her eyes widened with surprise. "Really? Dissolving the Office of Strategic Services? How would that affect us?"

"No idea. We'll all find out together, I fear."

Something else occurred to her.

"You mentioned children, sir."

"Yes, the schoolchildren antagonized the Germans something fierce. They'd sing the Norwegian national anthem when they weren't supposed to, and wore national clothing like red caps or paper clips on their jackets."

"Paper clips?"

Lawrence shrugged. "It has to do with sticking together. When you saw a paper clip, you knew that person was with you in resistance. Teachers and the clergy are especially sainted since so many of them refused to follow Quisling's orders on Nazi propaganda, and ended up in labor camps or concentration camps."

She was quiet a moment. The swirling blades of a fan made the only noise in the room. Lawrence brushed a fleck of lint from the sleeve of his jacket.

"Anything else you want to know?"

"When I arrived, I saw a group of young girls going into a building being escorted by Norwegian police. My driver said they were Quisling girls and he wouldn't care if they were shot."

He nodded knowingly. "The children were required to be in these Nazi organizations from age eight and older, boys in one and girls in another. It's similar to the Hitler Youth in Germany, a step-by-step indoctrination into becoming a Nazi."

"These were little girls under ten years old, Colonel."

A look of sympathy swept his face before disappearing. "I know it, but they've been tainted with the Quisling brush and the purge is blind right now. Anti-German feeling is overwhelming and pervasive." He pressed his lips tightly together. "You know we can't get involved in that kind of internal country politics, right?"

"They were just children."

"Children on the wrong side doesn't cut any mustard with Norwegians. Stand apart from this, Phyllis. I've got plenty for you to do without you getting into trouble by trying to 'do the right thing'." His fingers dipped to put the phrase in air quotes.

"The right thing for us..."

"Is not necessarily the right thing for a Norwegian."

"...Huh. I'll have to think about that, sir."

Lt. Col. Lawrence stood and Phyllis did likewise.

"That's all for now, Miss Bowden. Your office is right out the door. Get acquainted with your equipment and deal with whatever walks in the door."

"Is there a supply closet close?"

"Yes, and Dickie said you've had a few problems getting stuck in supply closets. Anything you care to tell me?"

"I...ah...I've had a slight fear of closed places, sir. But... I'm fine now."

His eyes narrowed. "Okay. Thanks for the information. I'll keep that in mind."

"Thank you, sir."

Settled at her new desk viewing the electric typewriter, phone and Dictaphone, Phyllis thought about what Ronnie had said. What's right for one person may not be right for someone else. Sure, but when it came to children? Why wouldn't everyone be on the same page? Especially in light of how Scandinavian countries feel about their children. She'd read reports that the well being of children was of the utmost importance in their culture.

Phyllis chewed on her pencil eraser gazing distractedly at the papers piled on her desk. She should get to work, but thoughts circled in her mind.

Children are impressionable and want to please. Whoever got to them first would make the impression. Does that make them bad? Does that make them bad forever? She supposed it would depend on the children's actions.

Agitated, she shook her head to shake loose the unwanted thoughts and picked up a piece of stationary to write a letter home. Her eyes read the phrase at top of the paper.

"Der Reichskommissar Fur Die Besetzten Norwegischen Gebiete." She looked around for a language dictionary and skimmed through to find the words needed for a translation.

"The Chief for the Occupied Country of Norway."

Oh boy. Wouldn't her family back in Washington and her friend Lorraine in London be surprised to receive a letter on German stationary? A few letters for souvenirs and then she would throw out the rest. Maybe she'd send Joe one too.

Time to get this office in shape.

FIVE

The noise in the mess hall bounced off the walls. All the American diplomats and military working in Oslo ate meals at the officers' mess in Army Headquarters. German buses picked up employees with the War Department, American and British Embassies, State Department and other military and government staff each day to deliver them to the mess hall. With several days under her belt now, Phyllis noticed the swastikas had been scraped off the plates and she smiled at the Army's efficiency.

"What are you smiling about?" Jay reached up to smooth her hair made frizzy from the morning rain. Phyllis watched her try to control her upswept hairdo.

"You know, I had a roommate in London with red hair and she never had the problems you have."

"Did her bloody hair dryer ever conk out leaving her knackered?"

"Crikey," said Phyllis. "Would you please speak English?"

"I have this big old clunker of a hair dryer that, of course, doesn't work well here."

"So how do you dry your hair?"

"I do exercises and stand in front of the fan in my living room."

Phyllis laughed. "Mine works a bit better...when I have electricity, which is only sometimes."

"True. So tell me what you're so happy about today."

Phyllis stabbed a fork into her spaghetti and twirled it neatly before popping it into her mouth. As soon as her lips closed around the fork, a happy sigh escaped.

"You're enjoying your food too much, missy." Jay pointed a finger at her. "You'll be gaining weight next."

"No chance. I run from morning to night in this job."

"What's up?" Jay cut a bite from her sliced ham before dipping it in mustard. "This mess has the best food."

"To answer your question," began Phyllis. "I was smiling at Army efficiency, but then it hit me why it's so efficient."

"And why is that?"

"People like me are working their butts off, to be frank. There isn't a lazy person in sight. Everyone has a job and by God, they're doing it to the very best of their ability." Phyllis twirled more noodles. "I've worked in the Pentagon and the embassy in London, but the Army operation here has them all beat."

"Who says Americans can't get things done?" Jay said with a smirk.

"No one I know."

"Which brings me to my preferred topic today."

Phyllis glanced over at her. Jay's peaches and cream English complexion had two patches of pink contrasting with her hair color. Jay was such a take-charge kind of gal...was she embarrassed about something?

"Preferred topic?"

"A friend of mine has a problem, Phyllis. I was wondering if you could help."

"Sure. What's up?"

She watched Jay turn her head slightly and beckon to a slim blonde woman, very young, who began walking over to their table.

"Please bear with me here," Jay muttered quickly. "She's Norwegian. I didn't know who else to ask."

Curious now, Phyllis smiled at the pretty woman joining them.

"Phyllis Bowden, this is Astrid Hansen. She works in the British Embassy with me as a clerk."

Phyllis held out her hand. "Nice to meet you, Astrid. Would you like to join us?"

"Yes, thank you, but just for a moment." Her sunny hair was swept back with two small combs leaving short curls to play on her neck. It was an attractive hairstyle making her look older than she probably was.

"Pardon me for asking, Astrid, but you don't look old enough to work at the embassy."

Astrid blushed deeply. "That's kind of you to say, miss."

"Please call me Phyllis."

In the pause that followed Phyllis glanced at Jay who was looking at Astrid. When no one spoke, Phyllis cleared her throat.

"Now that we're all here, tell me what's on your mind. I'm betting this wasn't a random encounter."

Jay nodded and then with much effort, Astrid began to speak. "I'm from Trondheim."

"Trondheim? Up north?"

"Yes, Miss Phyllis. My family has been there for generations."

When she paused and nervously played with the hem of her blouse, Jay leaned forward. "Phyllis is my friend, Astrid. She may not be the one who can help you, but she's a good place to start. Please continue."

Even more curious, Phyllis straightened in her seat, gave her full attention to the young woman with wary eyes flitting around the room. Finally, she focused on Phyllis.

Astrid bit her lip. "When the Nazis came a few years ago, they tore down our churches, took away our food and issued ration cards." She swallowed so hard Phyllis could see her throat muscles contract.

"Do you need some water?" She pushed her glass forward. Astrid grabbed it and took a quick gulp. Still clutching the glass, she began again.

"Our ration cards were stamped with the letter J." She watched Phyllis carefully. "Do you understand?"

Phyllis' eyes swept to Jay and back. "That means you're Jewish."

"Yes, miss."

"I'm hesitant to ask this, but since you opened the door... did your family members survive the war?"

"Several of my extended family, cousins, aunts and uncles, left for Sweden when we heard the Germans were coming. My family waited for my brothers to return from the university here..."

"In Oslo?"

"Yes, but as soon as they got back, the Nazis took them and we haven't seen them since."

"The rest of your family was all right?" Phyllis steeled herself for the worst. She wasn't disappointed.

"No. My father is a rabbi and he and my mother were detained before being deported on the Donau."

"The Donau?" Phyllis' eyes slid to Jay.

"It was a German cargo ship used as transport between Germany and Norway," replied Jay. She glanced at Astrid before continuing. "It was called the 'slave ship' because so many Norwegian Jews transported on it were sent to..."

"Auschwitz," finished Astrid. Her gaze was on the table where tears began to dot the tablecloth. Phyllis' eyes filled up in response.

"I'm so sorry, Astrid. Do you know what has become of them?"

"No. There's been no word." She looked up then, eyes filled with resolution as well as tears. "That's why I asked Jay to see if she could help me. She's had no luck, but thinks that you, as an American, might have different resources."

"To do what exactly?"

"Find out what happened to my parents. Find out what happened to my brothers. There's not a day that goes by, an hour, a minute that I'm not thinking of them and wondering." She swallowed again. "I *have* to know. Whether it's good news or bad, I have to know."

Phyllis processed her request watching and admiring the courage of the young woman. She wasn't sure if she would be able to stand upright if her entire family had disappeared without a trace.

"May I ask you a question?"

"Certainly," replied Astrid.

"Are you the remaining member of your family?"

"I have a sister four years younger."

"You obviously weren't picked up by the Germans, so how did you escape?"

Her blush returned deeper than before. Her eyes flitted to Jay who nodded.

"Is it a secret?"

"No, miss, but it could be dangerous for me if anyone found out."

Phyllis' eyes narrowed. "I promise I won't tell a soul."

Astrid's bitten lip began to bleed. She blotted it with a napkin. "A...German soldier was lodged with us."

"He lived with you?"

"That's what the Germans did all over Norway. There was no housing, so any Norwegian with a house had to put them up." She paused, glanced around the room. "First I must declare myself a true Norwegian and never did anything that was against my country."

"It's okay, Astrid," encouraged Jay. "Go on."

Astrid lowered her voice. "The soldier who stayed with us was not much older than me. Sometimes when my parents were gone, we would talk. I know," her jaw jutted out defensively, "we were supposed to ignore the soldiers and not give them any attention, but I was lonely too. The Nazis had closed the schools and churches and we couldn't gather with friends, if any were even left."

Phyllis nodded. "It's okay. Please continue."

"So we talked some. I know a little German from my grandparents. Anyway, he was...lonely, missed his home. He wasn't as mean as many of the other German soldiers in town. In fact, he was actually Austrian and had been a baker

in Vienna. I thought maybe he didn't like being a soldier very much."

"He was conscripted to fight in the German army."

"So he said." She spoke to the folded hands in her lap. "One day he told me that he...liked me and wanted to help our family. When I asked him how he could do that, he whispered that my parents were probably being detained as we spoke and soldiers would be coming for me and my sister next."

Phyllis blinked. "What did you do?"

"He told us to take what food and clothing we could and pretend to be going to the forest to cut wood. He told us to... hide. There were others hiding in the forest he knew, but his commanding officer wasn't interested in finding them. So he told me to go. He even helped my sister and I pack a few things. For some reason, he was very nice to us."

"So you and your sister escaped."

"Yes, Miss Phyllis, but I am no quisling." She looked Phyllis in the eye. "All we ever did was talk a few times. Like I said, he was homesick and said I had a nice family."

"Even though you were Jewish."

"One time he said he knew many nice Jewish families in Austria, but kept his feelings to himself."

"That young man doesn't sound like a typical German soldier."

Astrid shrugged. "I don't know. All I know is that he looked the other way when my sister and I fled the house and didn't return. No one came looking for us in the forest."

"How did you survive?"

"We met other villagers hiding out and lived with them until the war's end. Eventually, townsfolk came to find us and we went back into town. That's when the British had raided," she paused to smile at Jay, "and the Russians had come in from the north."

"That must have been very scary for you and your sister."

"It was but we had each other and prayed every day to find our brothers and parents once again."

She sat back exhausted. A shaky hand picked up the

glass and drank down the water. When she looked at Phyllis, the tears had dried and her face was set with determination. At that moment, so was Phyllis. She nodded once.

"I can't promise anything, but I'll see what I can do. Remember when all is said and done, I'm just a secretary."

Astrid smiled and rose. "Thank you, Miss Phyllis." She turned to Jay. "I'll see you back at the office."

When she'd gone, Phyllis pushed back her plate of spaghetti.

"Lost your appetite?"

"I'll say."

Phyllis' brows drew together over narrowed eyes. "Why the ambush, Jay? Did you think I'd say no?"

"I'm sorry about that."

"No, you're not."

"Let me finish. I am sorry to have sprung Astrid on you like that, but we both know you're more than a secretary to the Military Attaché at the American Embassy here."

"Whatever are you talking about?"

"Please." Jay rolled her eyes. "I'm not dumb. I have trade-craft training too."

"Are you..."

"...We say nothing aloud and there's nothing overt, but I can recognize one of my own when I see her."

Phyllis leaned back in her chair, her gaze fixed on Jay's intent stare. "Was our meeting again some kind of set-up?"

"No." She shook her head. "No, it wasn't and no one has put me up to this, but I'd like to help Astrid. There are many people in her situation, having had loved ones up and disappear and hers isn't the last request you'll get while you're in Norway." She lowered her voice. "You have good resources, Phyllis, and can make discreet inquiries without raising eyebrows. All I'm asking for is a little assistance to help my clerk."

"I don't know."

"You saw the effort it took for her to tell you her story. She's devastated and is trying so hard to make a life for herself and her little sister."

SIX

A wave of happy feelings flooded through her as she greedily grabbed the envelope. *Joe!* Her eyes hungrily read the address written in familiar handwriting. She looked back at Lawrence who didn't try to hide his grin.

"Go on back to your office. Our business can wait because I know you want to read that letter."

"Thank you, sir."

Phyllis rushed back to her office, closed the adjoining door and sat at her desk clutching the envelope to her chest like it was a sack of treasure.

Joe. She tried and failed to slow her quickened breathing by taking a few calming breaths. They had only been separated for a few weeks, but it felt so much longer than that. Jittery fingers didn't wait to find the letter opener and they ripped into the letter scattering bits of envelope on the floor. Her smile grew with each word.

Dearest Phyllis,

I miss you more than words can say. After seeing you off at the airport, I felt all the air has been sucked out of London and I'm waiting for my heart to begin beating again. Sorry to be mushy, as you Yanks say, but it's heartfelt and honest.

Lorraine and all your friends at Seven Addison Bridge Place say hello and that they miss you too, even the nosy Mrs. Stewart.

I hurried to get this letter to you because, thanks to your boss, I will be coming to visit you next week.

Phyllis had to stop reading. A fat tear rolled out of one eye to land directly on the letter. She had to wait for the paper to dry before she could continue.

Don't cry, sweetie, I'll be seeing you soon. Lt. Col. Lawrence will notify you of the transport plane bringing me in. Can't wait to see you.

Love, Joe

She glanced around the room. How did he know she was crying? But that was the Joe Schneider she knew. Since they first met, he'd always been sensitive to her feelings, her moods. The man had an uncanny ability to ferret out what she was holding back, to see her as she really was. And she loved him for it. She had never met a man like Joe Schneider. Besides being loyal, handsome and brave, he'd literally saved her life that scary night in Canning Town. Both she and Lorraine would have been goners, had Joe not shown up when he did.

Smiling shyly, she pressed her lips to the letter with a sigh. Phyllis knew she was being ridiculously romantic and perhaps idealistic, but it had been a long war and these feelings were worth fighting for. They were worth everything.

And he was coming soon! She tucked the letter in her purse and buzzed Ronnie.

"Yes, Phyllis? Finished reading your letter?"

"Yes, sir. Are you ready to begin?"

"Any time you are. Come in."

She grabbed her steno pad and walked briskly back into Lt. Col. Lawrence's office. He put down his pen and returned her smile.

"Joe say anything you want to share?"

"Yes sir. You know that he's coming to Oslo?"

His grin deepened. "I invited him."

Her jaw dropped. "You *invited* him? You mentioned that earlier, but somehow I thought you were joking."

"Phyllis." He motioned her to a chair. "Please sit down." When she was comfortable, he began again. "I told you I was going to invite him for a visit. I guess you didn't believe me." He paused. "I know you don't realize the scope of what you did for me in London, but I do."

"Sir, I didn't do that much."

He held out a hand to stop her.

"I would be in Leavenworth had it not been for you and your friend Lorraine's efforts. My wife and daughters will be arriving in a few weeks to join me and to thank you in person."

Phyllis blushed deeply. "Sir, that's really not necessary."

"I think it is and I won't dwell on it, but know this: if I can do a favor or two for you, just ask. Understand?"

"Yes, sir. Thank you, Colonel." She stopped, thought a moment. "Actually, there is something."

"What is it?"

"Could you tell me how to find Jewish Norwegians who were deported to Germany?"

He frowned, toyed with his pen. "Why do you want to know that?"

"A young woman approached me and asked for my help. Is there a way I can find anything out?"

"What's the story?"

"The woman is from Trondheim. Her older brothers were university students and her father was a rabbi. Apparently, the Nazis took the brothers as well as the parents. She said the parents were deported on the Donau, but she's no idea what happened to the brothers."

Ronnie nodded solemnly. "That's not good, Phyllis. You know the story of that cargo ship, don't you?"

"Yes, but wouldn't there be a record somewhere of who was on the ship and where it went?"

His eyes were wary. "It went to Auschwitz."

Phyllis sucked in a breath. Lawrence didn't seem to be breathing either. The implications of what he said sat in the middle of the room like an elephant.

"Her name?"

"Astrid Hansen."

"And the other names?"

"I'll get them for you."

"I'll see what I can find out, but Phyllis...at the end of the day, I'm merely a Military Attaché."

They smiled broadly at that comment.

"Thank you, Colonel."

"I'll make a few calls, if the damn phone operating system starts working again," he blushed. "Sorry, Phyllis."

"That's okay, sir. I know what a mess it is having calls go through a German military exchange."

"Which is a tangled mess currently."

"I know, sir. I'm working on it."

He watched intently, something on his mind. "Be careful you don't get too personally involved, Phyllis. It's easy to do and we're more limited right now than I'd like. Do what you can, but keep your feelings in check."

"All right."

"Anyway..." He brightened. "I'll let you know what day Joe is coming and I'll have someone pick him up and bring him to the embassy."

"Wonderful, sir."

Lawrence smoothed his tie, picked up his pen. "Now then I have two letters to dictate to you. How are you coming with the new filing system and the Washington communications network?"

They worked together on several projects for the better part of an hour. When Phyllis rose to continue in her office, he stopped her.

"Oh, one more thing, Miss Bowden."

She turned back to the tall officer who had risen from his desk. He'd worked hard all day, but still resembled the unfazed, unwrinkled military man that he was. Ronnie reached for a slip of paper from his desk.

"Sir?"

"I understand you're still billeted at Army Headquarters."

"I am."

"Take this."

"What is it?"

"It's the address of an apartment that has become available."

Her eyes widened skeptically. "An apartment? In Oslo?"

"Yes. One of my couriers recently found it and I've checked it out for you. A couple of German officers abandoned it when they fled the country. It's a mess inside and you need to meet with the lady whose name is on the paper. She's your new landlady."

She couldn't believe her good luck. First Joe and now a place to live. "An apartment! How wonderful! Thank you, sir. Any news on my luggage?"

A frown consumed his face. "You still haven't gotten your luggage?"

"No. It's taken longer than it should have."

"I'll say. Let me compose a letter to the Transportation Officer back at the UK base and maybe we can track your bags down."

"Thank you, sir."

Ignoring Jay's request at the end of the day for a bracer at a local café, Phyllis took a trolley to the address on her scrap of paper. An apartment. And it wasn't just any apartment!

SEVEN

The address was in downtown Oslo. For Ronnie to have found an apartment for her in this area of town was nothing short of a miracle! Walking along the crowded sidewalk, Phyllis fought the urge to hurry as she passed stores and cafes in her quest to find the building where her new apartment was waiting for her.

She stopped in front of a recently opened restaurant with a new red and white striped canopy. It was as bright and cheery as the people eating within. Phyllis glanced at the paper in her hand once more and checked the number of the building. A match! She noted there were four stories above the restaurant with a top floor that must have a tremendous view. Phyllis straightened her hat before smoothing the front of her dress. She was glad she'd worn her favorite flowered jersey today because she would be meeting her new land-lady. If the woman were anything like her former landlady, Mrs. Stewart in London, she'd need to look her best. Wearing low heels had been a smart choice too since it was a bit of a hike from the trolley stop to this part of town.

The building had been a beauty in its day. Ornate cornices and statuary graced the sides with large curved windows, many with strips of tape holding them together. Although paint peeled everywhere like the structure was shedding its skin, eloquence still shown through the shabby appearance. Small round dents punctuated the stonework. Bullet holes? The large wooden door was carved with abstract designs and the stained glass above had been shattered. But the glass knob beckoned with Old World elegance. Phyllis took a deep breath and turned the knob easily in her gloved hand.

The moment she stepped inside, Phyllis felt she had been transported back in time. The lobby entrance was a large room with an arched doorway to the right and a stone fireplace to her left. Straight ahead was a unique staircase of marble stretching to the floors above. The curved railing looked to be decorated with carved animals running through a forest. Like the exterior, the interior seemed like an art deco beauty. She stepped lightly onto the threadbare carpet, torn in places with more tape trying in vain to hold it together. Before her eyes had adjusted to the dimmer light, an older woman in a long white dress and scarf tied at the waist strode up to her. Clear eyes in a deeply lined face took in Phyllis with a subtle sweep of her head.

"May I help du?"

"Yes...I'm Phyllis Bowden. Lt. Col. Ronald Lawrence..."

"Ja, ja. Jeg vet hvem du er." She shook her head, smiled slightly. "Excuse me, you're American." The woman cleared her throat. "I...know who...you are," she finished proudly.

"I was sent here by..."

"Ja." Her hands waved about. "Mr. Lawrence...call me. Come, come!" Hands continued to wave wildly toward the staircase. "I have leilighet waiting for du." She laughed. "I mean...apartment. Come, please!"

Phyllis hesitantly placed a foot on the worn staircase. Although marble, the steps showed their age and in the impressions made by heavy foot traffic in the decades the building had been standing. She hurried to catch up with her speedy new landlady when suddenly the woman stopped and turned around. Phyllis nearly bumped into her.

"I forget," she said placing one hand on her chest. "Mrs. Lind."

"Lind?" asked Phyllis.

"Ja. Lind." She stuck out her other hand. "Miss Bowden."

"Phyllis."

Mrs. Lind shook her head. "Miss Bowden."

To which Phyllis smiled and nodded. "Sure."

She beamed and continued her route. Four flights later and both Mrs. Lind and Phyllis were breathing harder with slower steps. The older woman finally stopped at the last landing placing hands at her hips to catch her breath.

"Up," she said between breaths.

"Up, indeed," huffed Phyllis. "No elevator?"

THE WOMAN TILTED her head with a pinched face. "El-e-vator?"

"Oh, ah..." Phyllis mimed going up in the air with both hands.

Mrs. Lind's face broke into a smile. "Ah! *Heis!*" She shook her head. "No, she's broke." Then she pointed to a door in the middle of a long, carpeted hallway.

"That's the apartment?"

"Ja. Come."

She tagged along after the woman whose steps quickened the closer she got to the door. Taking an old black skeleton key from her skirt pocket, Mrs. Lind opened the squeaky wooden door with a flourish and stepped back.

"Look. Iz nice."

Is nice was right, thought Phyllis as she gazed around the apartment. She'd had no expectations but if she had, this place would have stomped them in the dust. It was a penthouse apartment with an incomparable view of the city. The furniture was all jumbled around and many possessions were tossed about in disarray. Obviously, Mrs. Lind had not thought to clean or even empty the apartment before renting it out, but it didn't matter. Having a place of her own was worth the price of admission.

The large living room opened to a kitchen and dining space. Phyllis wandered down the hallways to view a bathroom and two bedrooms, one with a prominent sitting area. Coming back to the living room, she strolled out on the patio to breathe in the fresh air blowing in from Oslo Fjord. Her new view encompassed rooftops and street scenes with water in the distance and snow-covered mountains hugging it all. If she lived to be one hundred, she didn't think she would ever again live in such a fine place as this.

Mrs. Lind smiled at Phyllis.

"You like?"

"I like. When can I move in?"

"Now." She handed Phyllis the old key. "Now iz good. I'm down...if you...need me."

"Oh, what is the rent?"

Mrs. Lind smoothed her long skirt. "Fourteen American dollars."

"A month?"

"Iz good price."

"It really is." Phyllis took the money from her purse and handed it over. Mrs. Lind tucked it in her skirt pocket. When she patted the pocket and smiled, Phyllis stretched out her hand. "Thank you, Mrs. Lind. Thank you so much."

"Vaer sa god, kjaere en." She shook her head. "You are welcome, my dear."

When she left, Phyllis took her time going through the apartment. She hadn't brought much with her on the flight over from London and her footlockers and steamer trunk had not arrived. Good thing it was summer because all her fall and winter clothing was in that trunk. She made a few notes on what she would need for toiletries and food, locked the door and took the trolley back to the base. The newly opened PX had most of what she would need, so she gathered her bags and rode back to her new apartment.

Her feet felt lighter as she walked down the street to her new building. Climbing back up four flights of stairs didn't take as long as the first time because she was going to her new home. The skeleton key was cumbersome at first, but she got the hang of it and opened the door with as much flair as Mrs. Lind had.

She was home!

Details she had overlooked before in her excitement to have a place to live suddenly loomed large. Phyllis turned over a stuffed chair to find a German pistol underneath. She picked up the weapon carefully making sure the safety was on. The metal was cold but still had a lingering smell of gunpowder. Handling guns was part of her training although she rarely had to fire them in her course of work. She knew this gun was a luger and set it aside, wondering what she'd do with it.

An array of clothing was strewn throughout the apartment. She found a metal helmet in one corner of the room sitting on the floor looking out onto the patio. Picking it up was like reaching out for a dead snake. Phyllis knew the helmet wouldn't bite her, but it was scary just the same.

An olive colored cloth belt with a good quality steel buckle lay curled on the sofa. In the master bedroom, a pair of German jackboots was in the closet and a few SS tee shirts lay on the floor, but what sent a shiver through her was the red wool Nazi armband with its menacing swastika peeking out from under the bed. She picked it up as carefully as she had the luger half expecting some German officer to burst into the room and pluck it from her clutches. Fighting the urge to spit, Phyllis took the German possessions back to the living room where she had a nice pile growing. They were now relics, war souvenirs with all the power sucked out of them. Their mere presence still filled her with dread as it did all the people of Norway and Europe. What should she do with it all?

In the kitchen, the small, pale green refrigerator was relatively new with bread, cheese and wine waiting to be consumed. Assuming the fleeing Germans had left the food, she dumped it all into a waste bin and placed inside the few groceries she'd bought. She smiled at the tiny container of coffee she'd managed to buy at the Army PX and put it in a cupboard as a treasured treat. Indeed it was. Although coffee was still rare in Norway, Ronnie had mentioned that the Norwegian government was working on a trade agreement with Brazil to supply the coffee it so desperately needed. Norway would have to barter fish, but Brazil didn't seem to mind.

It didn't take long to unpack her suitcase and the few bags she brought. After righting the furniture, giving the floor and counter a good wash, and changing the bed sheets, she was beginning to feel more at home. A picture of her family had a place of honor on the fireplace hearth along with a picture of her beloved Joe.

Her thoughts turned to him as she poured a glass of wine and sat out on her patio watching the day become night. As dusk fell softly before her, Phyllis wondered where her relationship with Joe Schneider was going. In the aftermath of war and in a foreign country, love shouldn't seem so important. Yet in the faces she had met in Oslo and London, it was all that really mattered. Being loved, being surrounded by loved ones, having those who mattered most with you was what they had fought for and what they had won.

It was what many people had won...what many others had lost. Her thoughts darkened when an image of Astrid Hansen floated in her mind. Astrid had lost nearly everyone dear to her. What would it take to put sweet Astrid together again? To make her feel secure and loved?

Phyllis shook her head. It would take a miracle and Astrid was just one out of so many that had already come to the American Embassy for help finding their lost loved ones. She wasn't sure she had what it would take in her bag of tricks.

But when her head finally hit the pillow that night, the only thing on her mind was Joe. She was going to enjoy every minute of the time they had together because everything was so fleeting in wartime. Permanence wasn't a word used in times of upheaval and she wasn't going to take her time with Joe for granted. Who knows how long they would actually have together. She would soon learn how very right she was.

EIGHT

Phyllis was untangling her crossed typewriter keys after a burst of typing that left a jumbled mess on the page. She painstakingly plucked each key free of the others and had just sat back relieved when her office door flew open.

"May I help..." The rest of her words fell on the floor as she turned to see a beaming Joe Schneider walk up to her desk. He leaned his handsome face closer as one finger softly touched her jaw to close her open mouth.

"Afternoon, sweetheart."

His deep voice resonated from the top of her head throughout her body causing an involuntary shiver of surprise. Phyllis leaped out of her chair and into the strong arms of the man she loved. They wrapped themselves in a tight embrace and hung on for dear life. Footsteps in the hallway softened, the fan in her office quieted, and voices in the embassy died out altogether when Phyllis and Joe kissed for the first time in a long time. Warm breaths intermingled with desperately clashing lips jockeying for the most expressive position. His full lips, so familiar, captured hers with feeling and love. When she pulled away to touch his face, he shook his head.

"In a minute," he whispered as he captured her lips

again. It was some time before either was ready to leave the silky cocoon of intimacy.

With a ragged breath, Joe rested his forehead against hers. "Nice to see you again, Miss Bowden."

"Can it be that you missed me?"

"Lt. Col. Lawrence posted an MP outside the door to give us some time to ourselves without interruption."

She kissed his jaw. "He's a nice man."

"He's a grateful man. You saved his career."

"So he keeps telling me."

Joe pecked her mouth. "The last thing I want to do when I finally have you in my arms again is talk about your boss."

Phyllis laughed, stroked his sweet face, the face she knew so well. Joe was handsome in the mode of a classic movie star, Gregory Peck maybe. She nuzzled the light stubble on his jaw from the day's travel before his dark eyes pinned her in place like a butterfly with clipped wings. She ran her hands lightly over his smooth cheeks up into his dark hair. His subtle aftershave infiltrated her senses and filled her with his overwhelming scent, the scent of Joe Schneider, not to be mistaken with any other man in Norway or on the planet, for that matter. Phyllis leaned closer to breathe him in, to soak up his essence, to be marked as the one and only man for her.

"Lawrence said to take the rest of the day off. Could I take you to dinner?"

Still surprised to have him so close, Phyllis continued to gaze at him with the loving adoration of a cheerleader and her football steady.

"Phyllis? Honey?"

"Mm?"

"You with me?"

She blinked and smiled. "I can't believe you're here. Ronnie didn't mention when you were coming, just that you were."

"I do believe he wanted you to have a nice surprise."

"He sure was successful."

He kissed her again. "Come on. Grab your coat and hat. Let's get out of here."

The clunky trolley took them to Arne's little café across the street from Phyllis' new apartment in downtown Oslo. Phyllis and Joe watched one another with playful eyes that didn't notice the inquisitive stares of fellow riders. Oslo was bustling with people. Phyllis tucked her arm in Joe's and proudly showed him part of her newly adopted city. Once inside the café, Joe noted the austerity of the place with a practiced eye. Phyllis shook her head and pointed to an item on the still unreadable menu when Arne took their order. They were both pleasantly surprised when the shy proprietor brought in meat cakes, cod and cabbage stew.

"Tusen takk, Arne."

"Vaersagod, Miss Phyllis. Takk for sist!" He frowned, bit his lip. "Thank du," he said tentatively.

She smiled. "You're welcome. Where's Lars?"

Arne brightened immediately. "Lars? Iz home."

"Tell him hello."

The man nodded with bright eyes. "Hel-lo."

"God save King Haakon." Phyllis held up two fingers and Arne copied her.

"Gud redde Kongen Haakon."

With that, Arne hurried back to the kitchen for the bread. After he'd left, Phyllis turned to Joe. "He's teaching me Norwegian and I'm teaching him English."

"Are you going to learn how to say God save the King in every language?"

"Nope. There aren't many monarchies left in Europe."

"World War I fixed that."

"I'll say."

The café had eventually filled with people by the time Phyllis and Joe said goodbye to the busy proprietor. Business in downtown Oslo was picking up faster than she thought it would and it was a good sign of economic growth. But the economy was the last thing on Phyllis' mind when she brought Joe up to her fourth floor apartment in the old, ornate building. After stowing his duffle bag, Joe joined her on the patio for a glass of wine.

"This is some view."

Joe's gaze took in the rooftops and side streets of the city, but lingered on the body of water beyond with surrounding snowy mountains. Fishing boats made their way to the docks in the fjord and he watched fishermen bringing in the day's catch. Happy voices floated up to them through the moist air.

"I take that back. It's not just some view, it's majestic." Joe turned to see Phyllis watching him. He smiled at her. "So?"

"I like the view very much, but it's not the scenery that's so great. It's the good-looking young man with deep dimples who has captivated me this evening."

"I have deep dimples?" he joked. Joe set his glass on a small table and sat down beside her. "Tell me more."

Phyllis smoothed his thick hair, ruffled in the evening breeze. "You know you're a handsome man, Joe Schneider."

"So you only love me for my looks?"

"No, I love you because you're you, but I still don't know much of your background. You were filling me in when I had to leave London. Please fill in a few more blanks for me."

"Sure, sweetie. Anything you want to know." He clasped her hand, pressed his lips to it. "You know I'm from Manchester. Do you know where that is?"

"It's north of London."

"Over two hundred kilometers actually, a good three hours by train." He kissed her palm. "I've told you a bit about my childhood."

"You mentioned your father was a police officer."

"Aye, my dad was a copper for sure." Joe shook his head. "He was a gruff old duff who had bugger."

Phyllis bit back a smirk. "Wait a minute, limey. You're retreating into slang and I'm not able to follow."

He laughed and tugged her closer. "I meant that my parents had grown up poor and had nothing."

"Until your dad became a policeman."

"He was a first-rate bobby and I wanted to be just like him."

"You were a cop before joining MI5?"

Joe nodded. "Actually I was recruited for MI5 in a procedure I can't talk about. Well," he grinned, "I could tell you, but then I'd have to kill you and I don't want to do that."

She placed a solid kiss on his smiling mouth. "I don't want that either, so maybe we should skip that part and hit the highlights."

His hand slid around her neck to keep her lips close to his. "Maybe we could even skip the highlights for now. Your bed looks very comfy, as you Americans say."

"But Joe, I'm interested in..."

Joe placed soft kisses on her cheek, nose and the base of her throat. When a contented sigh escaped, he kissed her waiting lips. "I will tell you all, Miss Nosy Parker, but not tonight. I'm dying for you, sweet girl. Please take me to bed."

The loving look on his face pushed her to a quick decision. The scenery, the history lesson and anything else could wait until they had drunk their fill of one another. She knew it would take a while and smiled. Phyllis stood and took his hand.

"It's this way. I know we've been here before, but I'm a little nervous, Joe."

"Hey." He lifted her chin so her eyes met his. "Want me to sleep on the couch?"

"I just said I was nervous. That doesn't mean I don't want to sleep with you."

He laughed and tugged her closer. "So we'll be sleeping?"

"Eventually."

With smiling faces, they zigzagged down the hallway in a tangle of arms and legs like crazy dancers tripping on the dance steps. Once in the bedroom and clothes began falling to the floor, Phyllis gently pushed Joe on the bed and arched an eyebrow at him before turning off the light.

Silky sounds of skin sliding on skin filled the darkness as the lovers rediscovered the intimacy only they shared.

Morning would be the sweeter for it.

NINE

By midmorning, Phyllis and Joe had dressed, had breakfast and were on a walk around downtown Oslo. She was eager to show him the new businesses that had sprung up, practically overnight it seemed, and how war-devastated Oslo was making a Herculean effort to pull itself out of the black hole which the Germans had dug.

"All these shops were closed when I got here." Phyllis pointed. "Several of them were Jewish and had writing on the windows. Jay and I were appalled."

"What's Jay's last name? Maybe I know her."

"You probably do. She's in British diplomacy and you seem to know everyone in London." Phyllis pushed curly hair behind her ear as they walked along. "Her name is Jay Lawlor."

"Sure, I've met her at embassy parties. Seems like a good sort. She's probably in military intelligence too." Joe shot a quick look in Phyllis' direction.

"I gathered that. It's not hard to tell us intelligence types, is it?"

Joe chuckled, threaded his fingers in hers. "It is for the uninitiated. You mentioned Lawrence is sending you for more training?"

"I shouldn't have told you that." Phyllis blushed. "You

caught me at a weak moment."

He laughed. "I believe it was between rounds one and two." Joe kissed her cheek. "Never underestimate the power of sex."

She lightly punched his arm. "You're a bad influence, Joe Schneider. What's your middle name, by the way?"

"I'm Joseph Michael Schneider, thirty-two years of age, born and bred in the UK. My parents, Michael and Mary Schneider of Manchester, England, are alive and well and very happy the war is over."

"Siblings?"

"Only child, I'm afraid."

"So that means your parents spoiled you rotten."

"Hardly. How about you?"

"How about me?"

"Family?"

"You mean you don't know?"

Joe blushed this time. "Okay, so I did a teensy background check on you."

Phyllis stopped abruptly, folded her arms across her chest. A couple walking behind veered around them and shot them curious looks as they walked by.

"What?" Joe looked into her cross face. "You know what I do for a profession. It's my job to check people out."

"So I'm just 'people' to you?" Her toe impatiently tapped on the sidewalk.

A nearby shopkeeper came out to sweep in front of his store. Joe took Phyllis' arm to move her away.

"Be mad at me if you must, sweetie, but do it quietly." He leaned forward to kiss her, but she turned her head away. "And you're not just 'people' to me, you know that."

Her toe began tapping again. Suddenly, the tapping stopped. A knowing look filled her face.

"You're working, aren't you?" When he didn't respond, she tried again. "Joe, are you active?"

Again he took her elbow to move them farther down the sidewalk. "Phyllis, I..."

Tears pooled quickly. "I thought you came here to see

me, but you're working. Tell me I'm wrong."

They rounded a corner and Joe hurried them toward her apartment building. When they entered the lobby, Joe tried to pull her into his arms. She pushed him away and turned her back to him. When he moved behind her as close as she would allow, he spoke softly in her ear.

"Phyllis? Please listen to me." She stiffened. "Are you listening?"

"Yes."

"Could you turn around to face me?"

"Why?"

"Because I need to say this to your pretty face, not your back."

She snorted. "My back isn't pretty?"

Joe bit back a smile. "Of course it is, honey."

Slowly Phyllis turned around. A hand reached out to caress his face before she could stop it. Joe grabbed her hand and kissed it lightly.

"Well?"

"I'm not working, Phyllis," he said finally.

She waited. "That's not the whole story."

His eyebrows curved. "You know me too well."

"All evidence to the contrary."

"...All right. The truth is that I'm not working now, but I will be when I leave here. I have a job in Bucharest."

"Romania? Why?"

He shook his head. "The only thing I can say is I have a couple of things to check out. The Communists have moved in and my sources could dry up if I don't act quickly."

Her jaw dropped. "You're going to infiltrate the Communists in Bucharest?"

"You know I can't say any more. I probably said too much, but I wanted you to know that I'm here now for you. Only for you, sweetheart." He kissed her scowling mouth. "Please believe me and let's enjoy the time we have together."

Exactly what she had been telling herself before Joe got here.

She softened and moved into his arms. "Sorry. I should know better, but now I'll be worried."

His arms tightened around her. "Which is why I didn't want to say anything."

They stayed close together until Phyllis heard, "Miss Bowden? A word please?" from a clear Norwegian voice. She broke away from Joe to look across the lobby.

"Mrs. Lind? Yes, I..."

"Alone please."

Joe and Phyllis exchanged *what-now* glances.

"This is Mr. Schneider," she began. Mrs. Lind waved her hand impatiently.

"Yes, yes."

"I'll wait upstairs, Phyllis," said Joe.

She nodded. "I'll be up in a minute." She handed him the key and watched him mount the stairs. When Joe was out of sight, Phyllis walked briskly toward her irritated landlady.

"Yes, Mrs. Lind?"

Mrs. Lind stiffened regally like a peacock about to strut. She smoothed her long skirt before returning to her ironing board posture. Her chin jutted out and her eyes spoke the question.

"Who iz that man?"

"He's Joe Schneider from England and he..."

"He's staying with du?"

"Yes, I..."

She shook her head so hard her frizzy gray hair flew about her face. "No. This iz decent place."

"But Mrs. Lind, he and I are..."

"Engasjert?"

"Pardon me?"

"Engasjert." The older woman's hand flew up in the air as she searched for the word. "Ekteskap. Um...bryllup." At Phyllis' blank look, she began pacing.

"Wait a minute." Phyllis dug a small Norwegian dictionary out of her purse. Mrs. Lind rushed back to grab it out her hands. She quickly skimmed a few pages and excitedly pointed to something.

"Engasjert! Here. See?"

Confused, Phyllis followed Mrs. Lind's finger to a Norwegian word and its English translation. Her eyes widened with understanding.

"Oh! Engaged. You think we are engaged?"

"Ja! You and the man are...engaged!"

Phyllis backed up a step. With the look on Mrs. Lind's face, she understood the situation at once: if she wanted Joe to stay with her, they had to be engaged to be married. Phyllis bit back a groan. Glancing down at the gold chain and locket around her neck, she made up her mind.

"Yes! We are engaged." She fingered the locket. "Mr. Schneider gave me this for an engagement present."

Mrs. Lind's face puckered like she had bitten into a lemon as she glared at the necklace. "He give du this?"

Phyllis swallowed and nodded, hoping her white lie would go down as easily. "Yes. Isn't it pretty?"

"Iz funny gift for engasjert."

She shrugged, glanced at the locket. "It just happened yesterday, so we've yet to buy a ring."

That seemed to mollify the stiff Norwegian woman—for the moment.

"All right?"

The old woman's face slowly smoothed and a small smile crept out. "Iz all right." She reached out to hug Phyllis. "Gratulerer, Miss Bowden." She stepped back. "Congratulations."

"Thank you." Phyllis smiled. "Tusen takk."

Phyllis climbed the four flights up to her apartment. Joe was waiting for her at the doorway.

"Am I bunking at Army Headquarters tonight?"

Phyllis sighed heavily, pushed past him to pour a glass of wine in the kitchen.

"That bad? Is she kicking me out of the country?"

After swallowing a huge gulp, Phyllis looked him in the eye. "No, but congratulations are in order."

He chuckled. "Congratulations?"

"Yes."

"For what?" Phyllis downed the rest of her wine. Joe took the glass out of her hand and set it on the counter. "Tell me."

She blew out a breath. "We're engaged to be married."

Joe's reaction wasn't exactly what she expected.

After a stunned silence, an exuberant smile stretched across Joe Schneider's happy face. He looked positively lit up. His shoulders moved back and he seemed taller somehow. With sparkling brown eyes and a twitch of his lips, Joe took a step closer.

"I should buy you a ring in that case."

"Joe, don't be ridiculous. I told her a little white lie so you could stay here with me. That's all."

He moved closer still. His warm breath teased her lips. "Does it have to be a lie?" he murmured.

She blinked wide eyes. Phyllis placed her hands on his chest. "What are you saying?"

He gazed at her adoringly. "I'm saying something I wished I could have said in London, but it wasn't the right time. You had to go. I understand that and I wanted this opportunity in Oslo for you as much as you did, but now..."

"...Now what?"

"I'm asking you to marry me, Phyllis Bowden. Will you be my wife?"

Phyllis was dumbfounded as he dropped to one knee and took her hand.

"I have money saved and a flat in London. I know my job involves travel, but I truly believe we can work out the job problems to concentrate on being together. So what do you say, sweetheart?"

When Phyllis continued to stare at him, he gently kissed her hand.

"I...I'm speechless, Joe."

His happiness wavered, a look of confusion swept his face. "That's all you can say?"

"I wasn't serious with Mrs. Lind and I certainly didn't say that to goad you into really proposing."

"I know that. Phyllis..." Joe rose, took her hand to walk her into the living room. Once they were settled on the couch staring at one another, he continued. "I've known you were the one for me since we first met. Aren't I the one for you?"

Her resolve melted like an iceberg on a sweltering day. She'd known he was the one for some time now, but there was always a war between them. Now the war was over. Phyllis' shy grin brought out Joe's. They grinned playfully at one another.

"That's what I thought, sweetie. You love me."

"I certainly do love you, Joe. I love you more than I can say, but..."

"No buts, Phyllis. We can figure this out."

She laughed. "You're always saying that."

"Because it's always true." He looked down at their joined hands. "I'll repeat myself." Joe's gaze locked with hers. "Phyllis Bowden, will you marry me as soon as I get back from the Bucharest assignment? I promise to love you for the rest of our lives no matter where we live or what we do for our careers. I want to be with you. Forever."

Tears pricked her eyes and slowly slid down her warmed face. "Yes, Joe Schneider. I will marry you whenever it's convenient for us both because that's exactly what I want too. Mrs. Lind apparently read the signs better than we did."

In his arms, they sealed their love with a kiss and a promise for the future.

Joe smiled, breaking their lips apart.

"You've made me the happiest man in the universe, sweetie."

"I know how you feel."

"Maybe," he winked, "we should ask Mrs. Lind where to buy you a proper ring."

"I can't imagine Norway has luxuries like that right now. We might have to try Sweden."

"Or maybe you can fly back to London sometime soon to pick one out."

Later that night in bed, Phyllis and Joe whispered words of devotion and babbled about plans for their future until the wee hours of the morning.

Another sweet morning.

TEN

Joe sat utterly still, but his eyes took in every nook and cranny of the scene around him. The dingy café was in a poor section of Bucharest. Few people strolled up the street and even the skinny waiter with the grease-stained vest and boozy breath made it plain he'd rather be elsewhere. Service was bad and Joe's undrinkable coffee had cooled as quickly as it had come.

Most of the city was in tatters after Allied bombing due to Romania's association with Germany during the war. Only at the bitter end had the king of Romania managed a coup to take back the country and join the Allies to oust the Germans. But it cost the king dearly, one of the reasons Joe was sent to Bucharest, the other being discovered at the camp outside of Oslo.

Joe squeezed his eyes shut. Maybe he couldn't see yet another war-torn city, but the smells were the same. His nose caught the aroma of some kind of vague, unappetizing food, as well as gasoline, dust and grime. All the cities he had been in during and after the war needed a good scrubbing with gallons of disinfectant.

He laid his fedora on the table. Shaking his head to rid his mind of unwelcome thoughts, Joe drifted to yesterday when he said goodbye to Phyllis at the train station. His smile was automatic. During the sweet visit, though only four days, they'd decided to marry. They had seen much of Oslo and her life there seemed productive. Discussing what a future without war might have in store for them, they couldn't decide where they'd live.

A life without war was hard for him to imagine. Maybe the guns had stopped, but a new coldness had descended between the various countries of the Allied Powers. Stalin, head of the Communist party in Russia, wanted to grab as much territory as he could and United States and England were having trouble putting the brakes on his aggressive ambitions. Joe's work with MI5 had intensified instead of lessening.

In his mind, Joe envisioned pretty Phyllis Bowden, all five feet, five inches of her, with curly brown hair and twinkling brown eyes. He could hear her infectious laugh, her subtle jesting and loving pillow talk. What he'd give to be back in Oslo with her again, but just as she reached out for him, Joe became aware of new scent—body odor—and her image faded.

He opened his eyes reluctantly to see a bulky body plopped heavily in the seat across from him. A fat man with dark features and darker intentions stared back. His contact. Having to deal with scum like this, his job was rapidly losing its appeal.

The man's smile peeled back his transparent skin as if a cadaver were smirking at him. "Mr. Green?" His work name.

"Constantin?"

"Da." Constantin's squinty eyes peered into the gloomy café. "Coffee okay?"

"Not particularly, but drink at your own risk."

The cadaver smirk flashed again. "You Brits have strange sense of...how you say...humor."

"That's how we say it. Now let's get this over with. You can introduce me to the head of the Communist party here in Bucharest?"

"Da. Sure. Anytime you say." He glanced back into the café.

"How about now? That's what I'm here for." Joe's patience was evaporating in light of Constantin's less-than-forthcoming information.

"What's the rush? Let's eat." He waved to someone, but the skinny waiter had disappeared. In fact, Joe couldn't observe anyone in the café at all, or on the street. Time to go.

Joe rose quickly, knocking over his chair. He didn't bother to right it as he backed away from Constantin. When he saw the gun, Joe knew he'd been had. A flash of light was the only warning before the pain exploded in his chest. He caught another whiff of gunpowder when something bit into his shoulder and that's all he remembered before the world went dark.

ELEVEN

Lt. Col. Lawrence sat at his desk, pen in hand. His attention wandered to the cloudless sky outside his second floor office at the American Embassy and he just couldn't figure out where to start.

Phyllis had made her request several days ago, but for the life of him, he didn't know who to call for information.

Ronnie stood suddenly, walked to the window and looked unseeing through the glass. For a man used to being in charge and having the answers, Phyllis' request had caught him unaware. Heaven knows it wasn't going to be the last time he would be asked to find a lost loved one, but Astrid Hansen's name had been weighing heavily on his mind. It was time to do something.

He took off his jacket, draped it carefully over a chair and sat back down at his desk. After pushing aside pertinent embassy business and other important military paperwork, he reached for the clunky black telephone. He automatically barked at the German operator who came on the line and took a breath to calm his tone. Knowing the Germans would eventually leave Norway didn't mean dealing with them on a day-to-day basis would be easy. The embassy had been working to take over the telephone exchange from the Germans, but it hadn't been accomplished yet.

"Put in a call to Major James Stevens, War Department in Washington, D.C., please." He added *please* because he should.

The German operator on the other end was efficient if nothing else because Lawrence was speaking to Stevens in a brief two minutes' wait.

"Lt. Col. Lawrence!" A cheery voice came over the line. "How goes it in Norway? Eating any lutefisk?"

Ronnie laughed. "There's none to be had right now, Jim, but hopefully soon. We're working hard to help the country get up to speed."

"Boy, that'll take some time."

"True enough."

"So how can I help you? I assume you called for a reason unless you just want to hear how my son is doing at Georgetown."

He chuckled again. Ron had known Jim Stevens from the early days of his Army career and they'd done favors for one another from time to time.

"No, but I hope he's doing well."

"He is, thanks."

"I've got a problem, Jim, and I'm not sure where to start to solve it."

"You?" Jim laughed heartily. "Mister I'm-always-in-charge-and-you-damn-well-better-know-it?"

"Ha. Funny. Listen, this is serious. I have people coming to the embassy here in Oslo looking for relatives that the Germans exported to God-knows-where. How do I start finding them?"

Jim whistled. "We've been slammed here too with requests from Americans to find their European relatives. It's a mess for sure."

"Where should I start?"

There was a pause on the line.

"Jim? You still there?"

"Okay. I'll give you the official line that Washington wants us to use, but it's only because President Truman hates General Donovan so much and is dissolving the agency."

"I heard that. What's going to happen to the OSS?"

"No one knows, so here's who to call. First, there's a captain in the War Department who is spearheading the effort and I would certainly give him a try."

Lawrence reached for a pad and pencil. "What's the name?"

"Captain Reuben Ayers. You got the War Department number? Just call the main number and ask for Ayers. Tell him I referred you."

Ronnie scratched the name on his pad. "Thanks and the second name?"

Jim lowered his voice. "This didn't come from me. We clear on that, Ron?"

"Crystal clear. An elf brought me the information in my sleep."

"An Army elf..."

Ronnie laughed. "Absolutely."

"Name of William Casey should get you more information. Lt. Casey, one of General Donovan's top aides. Just mention what you need and see if he'll help. I know Donovan has resources that Truman won't ever have. An international superspy beats a Washington politician any day and twice on Sunday."

Smiling, Ronnie put down his pencil. "Thanks, Jim. I owe you one."

"You coming back to Washington?"

"One of these days, but I probably have three years here before I'm moved."

"Glad to have you back after that messy business in London."

"Thanks again. Bye, Jim."

"See you, Ron."

The call to Captain Ayers netted exactly zero information. Ayers wasn't in and a disinterested secretary dutifully took Lawrence's request and information in a monotone voice. The call to Lt. Casey was more interesting. The man was actually in his office and answered the phone himself. Refreshing in the world of bureaucracy where Ronnie lived.

After introducing himself and explaining what he needed, Casey got right down to business.

"Lt. Col. Lawrence, I don't think I need to tell you how hard it will be to get the kind of information you need."

"Yes, sir. I'm fully aware."

"Why, the Germans just surrendered in May and it's only August of the same year! I know Norway is crawling with Germans you can't get rid of and we're still fighting that damn war in the Pacific!"

"Yes, sir, I know that too, but isn't there any way to find out about these people?"

Casey was silent for a moment. When he spoke again, he seemed to have made up his mind.

"The big problem is that Truman is dissolving the OSS. You know that, correct?"

"I'd heard the Office of Strategic Services would be no more and probably soon."

"Soon enough, but here's what I've got for you right now. When the concentration camps and labor camps were captured, the British, Americans and Soviets all took certain regions to liberate. Some camp officials kept records of Jews and other prisoners used for slave labor, but the military force going in seized those records. You can count on the British to help you if they can, but not the Soviets. They have minds of their own." He paused. "Do you know where this Astrid Hansen's parents went?"

"You mean which camp?"

"Right."

"They were shipped on the SS Donau, straight to Auschwitz."

Ronnie could almost hear Casey shaking his head. "The retreating Germans burned all the records from Auschwitz. The best we can do to learn if anyone survived is if the individual became a prisoner at another camp. The Germans did that sometimes: sent prisoners for labor from Auschwitz to a nearby camp to work in a factory or some kind of construction work."

"Her father was a rabbi, age fifty-five. The mother was about the same age, a housewife."

Casey clicked his tongue. "Doesn't sound good for the parents. What about the brothers?"

"They were seized coming home from the university and taken somewhere. Astrid thinks maybe to a labor camp. She just doesn't know which one."

"That could be more promising. I'll call some of our contacts in Poland, Czechoslovakia and Hungary, countries that had more slave labor camps, but there are other countries that were occupied during that time. There could be camps we don't know about yet."

Ronnie tapped the pencil on his desk. "I understand and will appreciate any information you can get for me." He thought a moment. "Lt. Casey?"

"Yes?"

"While you're at it, would it possible for me to get names of any Norwegian individuals you come across who died in the camps? I have people knocking on the doors of the American Embassy every day begging for information about their lost relatives. I know it's a bad time for me to ask for this favor, but there's never going to be a good time."

"You're right about that and I'll do what I can. I'll get my staff working on this immediately and try to get back to you next week."

Lawrence smiled and stood. "Thank you very much, Lt. Casey. I'm in your debt."

"Not at all, Colonel. I'm happy to help. My agency is folding and it's a last hurrah for me." He laughed. "Who says government agencies can't help one another?"

"Indeed. I'll be awaiting your call."

After he hung up, Ronnie stretched his arms out wide. He'd yell "Yippee!" if it were an approved Army expression, but since it was not, he buzzed Phyllis to let her know.

"That's wonderful news, sir! I know Astrid will be happy someone is working on it."

"No, Phyllis. Don't inform Miss Hansen just yet."

"But sir. She has a right to know."

"It could amount to nothing. The men I called might hit huge brick walls and come up short."

"It would still help her to know someone is looking for her family."

He shook his head. "I'll let you tell her at the appropriate time. Now sit down, I have a new job for you."

Lt. Col. Lawrence came around to lean against the side of the desk. Phyllis took out her pad and pencil, prepared to take notes.

"First, how's it going with the telephone exchange? I hate hearing German voices on the other end of the line."

"Working on it, sir. We're training Norwegian women to take their places, but they aren't ready to work yet."

"Okay. The new filing system?"

"I've been working with various staffers on it, but some of them are so new, they don't know the old system. I'm having to train them on what we have just so I can switch them to the new one."

"I can hear your frustration, Miss Bowden. How about the communications network with Washington?"

"We're more interested here in Norway than the people I've spoken with in Washington, D.C., sir. They're more concerned about the war in the Pacific than what's happening in Oslo."

"Understand, but I hope you'll keep on it." He focused on her expression.

"Your day is pretty busy, isn't it?"

She shrugged. "Well, I've barely been here a month and it doesn't seem like I've gotten much of anything accomplished, to be honest. The letters on my desk are piling up and the office isn't running as smoothly as I'd like. We need more staff, sir."

"All right. I'll take the matter up with Personnel. In the meantime, I want you to attend the embassy party tomorrow night. It's too bad Joe had to leave so soon; he could have gone with you."

Phyllis smiled. "He left two days ago."

"Did you have a good visit?"

"We really did."

"...I understand congratulations are in order."

"Excuse me, sir?"

Ronnie couldn't hold back his grin. "Your landlady, Mrs. Lind, called to tell me the news and that she was very happy for you. She hopes you and Joe stay in Norway and have lots of babies."

She sat back in her chair stunned. "Well, I...ah...she..."

"I know you're trying to say that snoopy old woman should mind her own business, but that's not life in Norway. Good news circulates fast here."

"I...haven't adjusted to being engaged, Colonel."

He laughed. "Take all the time you need. You'll need it to figure out the logistics of marrying a British citizen who's an MI5 agent. Just getting him through immigration at the Washington Airport might be interesting." Ronnie laughed again, his eyes twinkling.

"Yes, sir," she groaned. "Hadn't thought of that."

"Anyway, Miss Bowden, back to work. I need you to attend that party for specific reasons. No guns needed, nothing more dangerous than wearing a nice cocktail dress and having a glass of champagne will be required."

Her eyes narrowed. "You want me just to show up and look nice?"

"Look nice, listen attentively, and ferret out what's going on in the Norwegian government. There will be many officials, military personnel and diplomats in attendance, besides some bigwig business people trying to set up shop here. Let me know what people talk about. Lots of secrets spill out when the champagne is poured."

Phyllis smiled, put down her pencil. "That doesn't sound very hazardous. I can do that."

"Good." The tall officer rounded the desk to sit down. "Now go get busy. You have lots to do. I'll call about getting someone in here to help you."

"Thank you, sir. Much obliged."

She had her hand on the doorknob when he called out. "And Miss Bowden?" Phyllis looked back.

"Sir?"

"Get that communications network up and running with Washington, and I'll make sure you're on the next military transport for a weekend in London to see your betrothed and good friend Lorraine."

Her smile stretched from ear to ear as she saluted him.

"I'll do it."

But back in her office, Phyllis lamented ever taking any task to completion. She'd written a list of things Lt. Col. Lawrence had asked her to do and had not yet, in the weeks she'd been here, been able to finish one. Plus he had a new job or two every day to add to her ever-growing list. Staying later at work didn't seem to make much difference and she hoped he could find someone to give her a hand. She needed another one before she fell behind so far she couldn't get out.

So it was with a heavy heart and one that was missing Joe very much that she made her appearance at the embassy party the next night.

TWELVE

Normally, the large room on the first floor of the American Embassy was used as a cafeteria, but not this evening.

Tonight small round tables with white cloths and floral arrangements were pushed to the periphery of the room leaving a huge center space for the group of people within to socialize. A long table with chafing dishes and plates of finger foods waited to one side while several waiters in short white jackets circled with drink trays.

Army officers in their dress uniforms of deep blue with polished gold buttons, shoulder boards and decorations mingled with men in black tie and slick dinner jackets. Women in long, shiny gowns of taffeta and crepe, strapless or backless, slithered silkily in black, pink or blue. Phyllis glanced down at her princess ball gown in bright pink with its drop sleeves, tight bodice and full skirt and knew she'd landed on another planet. Generally, she wore print or floral dresses of rayon, the poor man's silk, or cotton to work. Her friend, Lorraine, in London had told her she had to take the ball gown with her to Oslo because she might have need of one. It was ridiculous really. She'd only brought two suitcases and the silly dress had taken up way too much space.

Still Phyllis was happy she'd let Lorraine talk her into packing the frothy dress. Here she was wearing it within a month of landing in Norway. She'd never needed one in the London embassy, but with the war over, everyone wanted to wear fancy dress clothes and step out on the town.

But she felt like a spy in her pretty gown moving from group to group dropping in to catch a conversation before moving on to the next. She listened to several enthusiastic members of the Norwegian Labor Party discussing Norway's budding economy. Her eyes glazed over with meticulous details of social programs and new trade deals. Stifling a yawn, she moved to a British diplomat discussing the war with Japan with a colleague from the American Embassy. She lasted long enough to insert an opinion before her feet got itchy.

A group of Army officials nodding their heads at a tall Norwegian man in a black tie caught her eye. The impeccably dressed officers in their crisp Army uniforms listened with rapt attention to the man with a commanding presence. He smiled warmly when Phyllis joined their circle.

"And who are you, lovely lady?" If any other man had said that to Phyllis, she would have stalked off in the opposite direction, but from this man it seemed sincere.

She extended her hand. "Phyllis Bowden, American Embassy."

"John Edelland at your service." He softly pressed his lips to her hand. The officer closest to Phyllis arched an eyebrow at the cavalier gesture. When Edelland took a step towards her, all the officers muttered fast farewells and melted into the throng of people, since his intention to speak with Phyllis alone was obvious. She watched them disappear in dismay.

"Um...Mr. Edelland..."

"Call me John, please." He steered her toward a circling waiter in a silky white jacket. John plucked two glasses off the silver tray. "Champagne, Phyllis?"

"Oh, ah, thank you, Mr., um...John." She took a quick sip casting a glance around the packed room before meeting the Norwegian's soft blue eyes. His expression caught her like a fish to a colorful fly.

"What do you do at the embassy?"

"I'm a secretary."

His eyes twinkled. "To anyone I would know?"

"Probably not." She took another sip. The golden liquid slid too smoothly down her suddenly parched throat. "And what do you do, John?"

"I'm merely a businessman, but may I say how lovely you look this evening, Phyllis."

"Thank you." He seemed pretty sure of himself. "How do you know that I don't look like this all the time?"

John chuckled, curving the corners of his pleasant mouth. "I assume you don't wear silk and ruffles to the office. If you do, it's my mistake."

She shrugged. "Okay, you got me there. With the end of the war, everyone is getting out their finest clothes again."

"That's a beautiful dress. Is it from Paris?"

Phyllis nearly choked on her drink. "Hardly, but enough about me. What kind of business are you in?"

"The boring kind. I'd rather talk about you."

She tried not to roll her eyes. "Please, Mr. Edelland... John, I'm not that interesting, but I bet you are. What do you do?" She looked over his fancy clothes. "I have a feeling you're not poor like so many of the Norwegians I meet every day."

He laughed out loud. "That's what I like about you Americans: your honesty."

"Well?" she persisted.

"To answer your persistent question..." He took of a sip of his champagne. "I was fortunate to have moved my investments to Switzerland when war with Germany seemed imminent."

"How did you know that?"

A shy smile appeared. "I have contacts within the government. In fact," he added, "my family is friendly with King Haakon and Crown Prince Olav." Impressive. "Perhaps you would like to meet the royal family sometime."

He took her elbow to escort her to the banquet table. "The Holmenkolldag Ski Festival will be held for the first time since the German occupation. Would you care to go with me?"

"It's still summer, John."

"The first snow will be here before you know it and I'd hate for you to miss the event. The tickets are on sale already."

"I'll consider it."

"Phyllis, let me take you to dinner." Glancing at the food-laden table, he pursed his lips in distaste. "I'm sure the embassy worked hard for tonight, but this food is not up to standard. Let's go to a place I know that has just opened. It's delightful."

She reached out a hand to block him. "John, before this goes wherever it's going, I have to tell you that I'm engaged to be married."

He automatically looked at her left hand. "I don't see a ring."

"That's because it just happened this week."

John straightened to search the room. His questioning eyes came back to her. "Is your fiancé here tonight?"

"No, he's in...London."

"Is he in diplomacy as well?"

Phyllis considered his question. "In a manner of speaking."

He kissed her hand. "Let me offer my congratulations to you both. Perhaps he would like to join us at Holmenkolldag for the festival."

"Perhaps."

She expected John to take off for greener pastures when she'd told him of her engagement, but this Norwegian flicked off the news like a crumb on his black silk jacket.

"How about that dinner? We're both hungry, I'm sure, and this food will simply not do."

Laughing, Phyllis finally nodded. "Just let me freshen up first."

"Certainly. I'll escort you to the ladies' powder room and wait for you."

"Oh, you don't need to do that."

"I insist." His blue eyes twinkled with mischief. "A gentleman always sees to the lady's needs before his own."

"Is that in the Norwegian book of etiquette?"

A smile lit his face. "Americans have the most delightful sense of humor. And American women are the prettiest in the world."

"That takes in a lot of territory."

They'd reached the restroom. "Freshen up. I'll alert my driver that we're leaving and meet you here."

She looked up into the open face of a very attractive Norwegian. He obviously didn't care that she was engaged to Joe and Ronnie had told her to find out what was going on in Norway. A rich businessman might have a few pearls to spill.

She grinned. "I'll be right back."

The ladies' room wasn't big enough to hold a mop and a broom, much less a few women in need of its services. Luckily, she was alone. At first, after combing her hair and freshening her lipstick, it crossed her mind she wasn't being loyal to Joe. But then she wasn't flirting back; she was acting directly on orders from her boss. Why did it feel like a date then?

Okay...maybe it had datelike elements because John Edelland was tall, blonde and handsome, like some sort of Nordic god with an angular face on which she could carve an ice sculpture. He smelled good and looked like a million bucks in his silk suit. There's something about a well-dressed man.

She stared in the mirror. It was nice to speak to a Norwegian who didn't have a problem for her to solve. Day after long day, she dealt with tears and grief from people who had nowhere else to turn but the American Embassy in Oslo. Her burden was heavy and her duty was constant. John didn't seem to need anything from her—he just wanted to take her to dinner.

As she stared, moisture collected in her eyes. The walls of the tiny room began closing in. Beads of sweat dotted her forehead and her hands felt icy and clammy. Rubbing them together neither warmed them nor lessened the anxiety that had come over so suddenly she couldn't catch her breath. Phyllis staggered a step to lean against the cool tile of a wall. Her full skirt swished and got in her way. While she concentrated on breathing, the door opened slightly and a deep Norwegian voice spoke softly.

"Phyllis? You still in here?"

She closed her eyes. *Go away.*

"Phyllis?" The heavy door swung open and the towering man with a worried expression hurried to her. In two steps, he filled the space, adding to her claustrophobia. "Are you ill?"

She swallowed hard. "I have a...slight fear of small places." She opened her eyes. "Perhaps things are progressing a little too fast for this slow American."

John smiled, put his hands on his hips. "Maybe you just need to eat something."

She took a deep breath before nodding. "Maybe so."

"Come on." John took her arm. "My car is waiting."

"Thank you."

Many pairs of eyes tracked them as Phyllis and John Edelland left the embassy party. Though obvious now, she knew tongues would be wagging before the lights dimmed for the evening. Since she couldn't control what others would be thinking or saying, Phyllis decided to enjoy dinner with a nice man instead and try to learn what he was about. She'd write Joe all about it, so there would be no secrets. Besides, dinner wasn't a big deal, was it?

THIRTEEN

He came to on a floor somewhere. When his blurry eyes finally focused, dim light from a window revealed a dirty prison cell with stripes from bars reflecting on the floor. The cell was bare except for an old bed in one corner with uneven metal legs and a filthy mattress.

When he moved slightly, everything seemed to hurt at the same time. Taking in a deep breath was a bad idea; the smell of urine permeated the cell and his chest was on fire. Why couldn't he move his arms? Oh, they were tied with rope. Shivering, it finally dawned on him that he'd been stripped to his underwear.

This wasn't good.

A matron in a black dress sat outside the cell reading a paper. Squinting, Joe could read a few Romanian words. He really needed to go back to foreign language school for a brush-up. When the woman noticed he was watching her, she walked to a door, slid open a small window and spoke rapid-fire Romanian to someone outside. Joe knew the drill and shifted to prepare his response.

All too soon he heard heavy footsteps come into the cell and someone dragged a chair close to him.

"Cine esti?" A boot kicked his leg. "Ah? Cine esti?"

Joe opened his eyes. A rough-looking man with shaggy

dark hair, a wiry mustache and penetrating eyes looked back at him. Not anyone he knew.

"Cine esti?" the man repeated. Joe's tentative grasp on the Romanian language came up with the loose translation of 'Who are you?'

When Joe shook his head, the boot struck again. A new place on his body ached along with the other places.

"Engleza? Da?" When Joe didn't respond, the man continued. "Ce faci aici? De unde sunteti? Anglia?"

"I'm English," he muttered not wanting a strike from the boot again.

"Da. I...know. What tu...um, want?"

"I want to meet with Nicolae Dinescu."

The man's dark eyes narrowed. Joe knew he was on thin ice. If he had to guess, he'd apparently fallen into the clutches of the Romanian Communists and these people were known to be ruthless. He knew too that nothing good would come of this conversation.

"I'm with the Allied Forces—so are you. Let me speak to Dinescu."

The penetrating eyes flashed pure hatred. He rolled Joe over on his back smearing blood from his chest on the filthy floor. With an upraised fist, Joe heard the shout, "No!" just as the fist connected with his face and Joe's world went dark again.

FOURTEEN

Lorraine Watkins waited impatiently in the big lobby at Victoria Station in London. A crowd of people coming off the train from Copenhagen rushed by in their haste to meet loved ones. Lorraine pushed past stragglers to buy a newspaper at Smith's, a bookstall that had been in Victoria Station for a decade. The headline was enough to make her pale: *US Drops Bomb on Hiroshima*. Scanning the article, Lorraine read that the number of civilian casualties wasn't known at this time.

Dropping on a bench to read further, Lorraine buried her nose in the Daily News and read aloud.

"*The most terrible weapon in history, an atomic bomb with more explosive power than 20,000 tons of TNT, was dropped on Japan last night, it was disclosed today as President Truman hurled a new ultimatum at the Japanese warning them to surrender or be wiped out.*

"*In revealing the most closely guarded secret of World War II, the President announced in a dramatic statement issued through the White House: 'Sixteen hours ago (7 p.m. Sunday, New York time) an American airplane dropped one bomb on Hiroshima, an important Japanese army base. The bomb had more power than 2,000 times the blast power of the British Grand Slam, the largest bomb ever yet used in the history of warfare. It is a harnessing of the basic power of the universe. The force from which the sun draws its power has been loosed against those who brought war to the Far East.'"*

Unbelievable. She sat back stunned.

As an American citizen working in London, Lorraine was grateful for U.S. intervention in the war with Germany and she could appreciate Truman wanting to end the war with Japan as quickly as possible, but at what cost? She tried not to delve too deeply into the political decision since it was way over her pay grade at the American Embassy, but war sure had a high price tag. The collateral damage alone was enough to make a sane person question his or her beliefs.

"Hey, Lorraine! That you, honey? What are you doing here?"

Henry McKinnon, her boyfriend from the State Department, cast an appreciative eye her way. Dear Henry. He wasn't a very complicated man, so she always knew where she stood with him. It was refreshing in the tumultuous times in which she found herself, away from home in the midst of a world war. Shifting her hat on a twist of sunny hair, Lorraine rose to buss his cheek.

"Hi Henry. I'm just waiting to pick up one of my room-mates. You know Norma."

"Sure."

"She was off to Copenhagen for the weekend."

"Lucky girl." He pecked her lips. Glancing at the newspaper headline, a frown quickly consumed his face. "So you read the news of the day."

She blew out a breath. "I don't know whether it's good news or not. It's horrendous."

He shrugged, smoothed a wrinkle in the lapel of his business suit. "Horrendous or not, it's bound to make the Japs surrender and for that, we must be grateful. This war has gone on long enough."

"I hear that." She wanted to change the topic. "Will you be going back to the States soon?"

"No chance. After a war, the diplomats have much to mop up." He grinned. "Hoping to get rid of me?"

She laughed. "Not yet." They smiled at one another. She watched as he glanced at the incoming train. "You picking someone up, darlin'?"

"Say that again." Henry raised an eyebrow over twinkling eyes. "Your southern accent drips like honey to the bees."

"Whenever did you get so poetic?"

"It's in my bones. My daddy was a tire salesman."

"Henry, sweetie, that makes no sense." Lorraine's eyes roamed his face looking for a telltale sign of insanity.

"Have you heard from your best friend this week?"

She smiled, patted his cheek. "I have. Phyllis is enjoying Oslo, although Ronnie is working her like a slave."

He stood on tiptoe to look over the crowd.

"Who are you looking for?"

"Joe."

"Joe? Joe Schneider?"

"Yes, he was supposed to be on that Copenhagen train."

"It's come and gone. Joe didn't get off. Are you sure he was coming in today?"

"Yep." Henry raked his fingers through sandy-colored hair making him look more unhinged. "We prearranged the time and date of his return before he left for Oslo to see Phyllis."

"Henry, that was weeks ago. Phyllis wrote me that his visit was a short four days. And..." Lorraine beamed. "They got engaged!"

"Wow! How wonderful!" Henry picked Lorraine up and swung her around, nearly knocking over a little old lady with an umbrella. She scowled, tried to poke Henry with the pointy end of the umbrella and mumbled to herself as she hurried away.

"Sorry!" He called after her. She just quickened her steps.

He set Lorraine down and righted her tilting hat. "Maybe we should get engaged too. What do you think?"

Lorraine blinked wide eyes at him, suddenly speechless.

Henry tried to kiss her, but she moved away.

"Henry!"

"What, honey?" He lifted his eyebrows in jest and flashed those baby blues.

"You can't just throw marriage at me in a rebound gesture from Phyllis' news."

"A rebound gesture? What the heck is that?"

She folded her arms across her chest, glaring at him. "We will discuss our future at another time, preferably at a nice restaurant with wine and flowers."

Henry laughed out loud. "Always trying to call the shots, aren't you? Well, honey, you've met your match."

She harrumphed. "That remains to be seen, but can you focus for one minute? Please?"

"What?"

"Joe. The timeline for Joe coming back to London isn't right. Something's wrong."

"Enlighten me."

"Joe went to see Phyllis two weeks ago."

"So?"

"He should have been back by now."

Henry's shoulders moved up and down. "He's a secretive type. Maybe he had business elsewhere. Maybe he went to see another friend along the way. Who knows?"

Who indeed knows? Lorraine considered the timeline from when Joe left London to when he left Oslo. It didn't match.

Henry smiled. "You've got that I-have-to-check-some-thing-out-so-don't –mess-with-me look on your face again."

"When have you seen that look on my face?" But she had to return his smile. It was no good trying to be mad at Henry; he was just too cute and she liked him more than she'd admit. Maybe love was even seeping into the mix.

He leaned down to kiss her. "I know your curiosity is piqued, but I've got to get back to the office. Joe has apparently stood me up or missed his train, so I'll wait to hear from him. What say I pick you up for dinner at that little Greek place by Harrod's tonight? Then we can discuss timelines and engagements to your heart's content."

She poked him in the stomach. "You're too cocky, Henry McKinnon."

He kissed her again. "That I am. Look who my girlfriend is...Lorraine Watkins. The entire male population of London is jealous of me."

"I take in more territory than that."

He laughed and left leaving Lorraine frowning, not for the last time that day.

Where was Joe?

She tried to call Phyllis in Oslo from a phone booth at the train station, but there were too many people waiting in line to use the phone. Calling from her row house at home would be difficult, since nosy landlady Mrs. Stewart listened in to all their calls. She'd know Lorraine was worried and bug her incessantly about Phyllis and Joe. The only thing left for her to do was to go home and write a letter. Her roommate, Norma, came walking toward her through the hustle and bustle of the Victoria train station. Considering Joe's plight would have to wait.

FIFTEEN

John Edelland insisted. Ordinarily Phyllis would have flicked off Edelland's request with a shrug, but she was overworked and overwhelmed on a couple of levels.

The Office of the Military Attaché in Oslo was humming. She was juggling so many projects that her head swam with all the details involved. Phyllis would wake up nights despairing that the women being trained for the military telephone exchange would ever be ready. Or she'd be second-guessing her decision to push that secretary in Washington to get their communications line set up. Was that the best call? Would the Washington gal get her nose out of joint and put Phyllis' request at the end of a long line?

The days were long, but the nights were longer without Joe. She hadn't heard from him since he left Oslo. That wasn't surprising because she knew he'd gone on assignment in Bucharest, so she didn't expect to hear from him soon. But he left a few weeks ago. With worry creeping into her bones, Phyllis would lie awake at night counting ceiling tiles instead of sleeping. Even Lt. Col. Lawrence had remarked that she needed to get more rest. When John Edelland called and insisted she go for a ride in the country with him, she figured his company would beat her own. Work and worry had become her constant companions and she needed to break the routine.

"What a beautiful car, John."

He smiled and patted the steering wheel as he glanced around the interior. "King Haakon was driven in a similar one in the parade given in his honor upon his return to Norway after the war."

Egelland had picked Phyllis up at her apartment in the sleekest, shiniest car she'd ever seen. The black convertible would comfortably seat four people and had to be new. She was nosy about where he got it, but not pushy enough to ask. His business ventures were more prominent than he'd let on.

"If you were trying to impress me, you're making a good start."

Grinning, he turned on the radio. "There's a new radio station in Oslo. We're thrilled to receive information from the world on a city radio station once again."

"All that stopped with the occupation?"

"Yes, the Germans didn't even allow us to own radios."

"Although some in the resistance had them." She was willing to bet the farm that he had owned one or several. "Were you here during the occupation, John? You don't seem too affected by five years of oppression."

He glanced at her with the wind blowing his light-colored hair. She tightened her scarf trying to keep her curly hair contained. "I wasn't here for the last four years, that's true. My family had international connections and we bought off a few German officials to leave as soon as we could."

"You're from Oslo?"

He nodded again, fiddled with the radio volume. "I told you my family has connections with the King of Norway. We also have friends and relatives in England; it wasn't hard for us to get out."

"That was good for you."

"It was good for many people, Phyllis. My family was able to get many Norwegians out about the same time.

People who would have lost everything when the Germans came."

"Many still did."

"True, but not all and now we are able to fulfill some of the promises we made when we left."

"We?"

"My company: Ostfold Enterprises."

"What sort of promises?"

Turning off the road, he pulled into a parking lot by the train station. When he shut off the engine, John turned to her. "You've an inquisitive nature."

She laughed. "It's okay. You can call me nosy."

"Come on." He got out of the car and went around to open her door. Getting out, Phyllis glanced around.

"Just where are we going?"

"I'm mixing business with pleasure. There's a train to Moss today in..." he checked his watch, "exactly ten minutes and we're going to be on it."

"Oh, but..."

"Don't worry. It's only fifty-four kilometers to Moss, a quaint little village along the Oslo Fjord, about an hour and half travel time, so we'll be there in time for luncheon. I know a nice restaurant by the water with a breathtaking view of the falls."

How could she refuse? Ronnie had half pushed her out the door after work yesterday whispering in her ear to find out what the mysterious John Edelland did for a living. He was a major player in the rebuilding of Norway and Lawrence was eager to know how. Phyllis couldn't believe how disinterested she was.

But here she was now—on a train to Moss midmorning on a glorious Saturday in Oslo. This time last year she was meeting Joe Schneider for the first time. Joe...

"How do you like the private railway car I ordered for today?"

"This is yours?"

John nodded, swept the room with pleased eyes. "It is. I ordered it to be here to take us on its maiden voyage."

"It's...indescribable, John. Incredibly luxurious." That was an understatement. She was having a hard time taking in the elegance of the carpeted interior with its velvet armchairs of purple and gold. Plush matching curtains hung from golden rods above every sparkling window. Embossed paper covered the walls all the way up to a series of crystal chandeliers hanging precariously overhead in a row like diamonds in a necklace.

"I'm glad you like it. You're the first to travel in it."

Phyllis shook her head. She knew her rose-colored silk dress with matching jacket was nowhere close to being in the same league with John's usual crowd. Tucking a swing of flyaway hair behind an ear, she turned to watch the Norwegian landscape pass by. Pastoral views of farmland, streams and snow-capped mountains sped along like scenes from a movie. It was almost a sense of culture shock transitioning from the luxurious private railway car to rural Norway in the windows.

She looked over at him, seated in another armchair across from her. John Egelland was a man of substance, position. He'd unbuttoned his grey wool jacket and was smoking a pipe. A snowy white handkerchief peeked out from a chest pocket and his blue tie was tightly knotted over a crisp white shirt. John looked like a model off a men's fashion magazine.

What was he doing with her?

Her anxiety grew with each passing kilometer.

"You seem nervous, Phyllis. Are you all right? May I get you a beverage?"

He motioned to a porter waiting by the door. The lean Norwegian straightened his cap and red vest as he hurried over.

"Sir?"

"Would you get Miss Bowden something to drink?" John turned to her. "What would you like?"

"Coffee, please."

The porter brought coffee in silver cups on a gleaming silver tray. After he offered her small cubes of sugar with a dab of cream, Phyllis took a sip. A healthy sigh left her lips the moment she put the cup down.

John smiled, sipped his own coffee. "Good?"

"It's heavenly! Where did you get rich, honest-to-good-ness coffee? The Oslo restaurants are still making do with rye coffee."

He scrunched his nose with distaste. "That tastes horrible."

"Could you explain how you have coffee on your private railway car then?"

John set down his polished cup, turning the handle away from him. He picked up his pipe and packed down the tobacco inside.

"And how in the world do you have tobacco when the parts of Norway I've seen so far do not?"

He shook his head slightly, tilted his head. "So many questions."

"That's what Americans do—we ask questions."

John shifted in his seat, met her gaze straight on. "I have many businesses, Phyllis, and I work in the foreign invest-ment market. To answer the question I see in your eyes, but you are too polite to ask—no, I don't do anything illegal, but my family did prosper in the war. Again, not through illegal means."

Wow, what were they? Gunrunners? She started to inter-rupt when he held up a hand.

"One of my businesses is arranging exports from Brazil for coffee." He pointed to his cup. "Thus we're able to enjoy the wonderful beverage on board today." He smoothed his tie. "I also dabble in railroads and shipping, so you see, my nosy American friend, I'm a man of many interests."

"John, listen." Phyllis glanced out her window at the passing landscape. The rural farm scene had changed to a small fishing village complete with fishermen bringing in their catch and people enjoying a day at the beach. They looked happy and after the oppressive occupation, that small fact was so important. Her protest nearly slid down her throat with the pleasant scene before her. She swallowed and tried again.

"I have to ask what you're doing with me. I'm of little consequence in the big scheme of things, especially in this part of the world. I have little money, no political influence and I'm engaged to another man." She shrugged. "There must be someone else in Norway more aligned with your interests, more in your social sphere. Single even."

He smiled slightly. "Americans are so concerned about appearances. I can do whatever I want, Phyllis. Why wouldn't I be attracted to a beautiful, interesting woman? And remember I met you at the American Embassy, so you *are* in my sphere of influence."

"Oh..." she huffed.

"You underestimate yourself, I believe."

"And my fiancé?"

"A mere...bump in the road perhaps."

A bump in the road? Joe wasn't a bump—he was the whole road.

The train chugged to a stop alongside a canal. Rain began to splatter the windows with a cool breeze permeating the railway car. Stepping down from the train to the platform, Phyllis could smell the sea air, fresh fish from the boats. She closed her eyes and took a deep breath. Sea smells swept away aromas of stinky city air, making her feel refreshed. Worry from work faded, along with frown lines about why Joe hadn't written.

Enjoy yourself, she thought. Just relax and have a good day. One day at a time.

She opened her eyes when the porter passed her an umbrella.

SIXTEEN

They dined at a tiny café right on the water. She'd never tasted fish prepared this way, but the Norwegian haddock was perfectly cooked in a rich onion sauce and served with mashed potatoes. The fish was fork tender with the creamy potatoes lending a unique flavor and a rich aroma stoking her hunger. Phyllis ate like she was starving. Catching a glance from John, she slowed her intake.

"I gather you like the fish?"

"It's incredible! I've had haddock before but never like this."

John smiled. "Norwegian food is best when it's fresh, fried lightly with various spices."

"I've heard of another famous Norwegian fish called lute-fisk. What exactly is it?"

"Well," he began, "it's a dried cod soaked in a lye solution for several days, rinsed, then boiled or baked and served with butter, salt and pepper."

Her nose scrunched as her lips flattened. "Soaked in lye? Sounds...tasty."

John laughed. "It's also said that half the people in Norway love it and the other half hates it."

"Where did it come from?"

"The history of the lutefisk dates back to the Vikings.

The story goes that some plundering Vikings had burned down a fishing village, including wooden racks with drying cod. When the villagers returned, they poured water on the racks to put out the fire and ashes buried the fish. After a rain, the villagers were surprised to see that the dried fish looked like fresh fish. They rinsed the fish to remove the lye, boiled it and proclaimed it, 'Not bad!'"

"Oh, ha. Did you make that up on the spot for this curious American?"

"No. It's supposed to be a true story and lutefisk is used in celebrations to this very day." When Phyllis' eyes narrowed, he added, "Or would be if Norwegians had any cod."

"The Germans confiscated all their good fish, didn't they?"

"Yes."

But he shook off his frown. "I used to come to Moss as a boy. My parents had a summer house and I've spent many enjoyable days here." He motioned to a waiter. "Come. I see you've finished. I have to mix in the business portion of our trip now." He paused to look at the bill.

Phyllis gathered her jacket and hat. "Where are we going?"

"I have a paper mill that I need to check. It was destroyed by Allied bombing, but was partially rebuilt by Germans near the end of the war. I had a team complete the renovation recently and I want to see the progress. Paper is an important industry here. There is an urgent need for commodities and Norwegian paper products are among the best in the world."

The rain had stopped but leaving the restaurant put another hitch in Phyllis' step. Several children, haggard with pale faces and ragged clothing, clustered by the entrance. John noted her reaction before digging in his pockets for loose change. After distributing the money to the forlorn children, John went back into the restaurant. As they walked away, a man came out to speak to the children.

Phyllis looked back at the tiny crowd. "What did you do?"

"I arranged for the manager to feed them."

She blinked surprised eyes. "What...what a generous thing to do, John."

He grinned wrinkling his smiling eyes. "Thank you, Phyllis."

"Would you be up to helping out with any other small task?"

He tucked his arm through hers as they walked along the street toward the paper mill. The day had turned warm with the sun shining brightly overhead, although fog was beginning to creep down the snowy mountains towards the village. The place was picturesque with wooden houses along the water painted in red, blue, yellow and orange colors.

"What did you have in mind?"

"My boss has turned a clothing distribution project over to me and I'm already up to my eyeballs in projects."

"What can I do to help?"

"Once I get into it, I'm sure I'll need help with logistics. You know," she angled her head toward him. "Where to distribute and to whom."

"That sounds like a wonderful thing to do for the people of Norway. They haven't had new clothing for five years."

"And America has had clothing drives to help. My boss told me nearly a million pounds of clothing was heading our way."

He stopped suddenly, surprised look on his face. "It's all coming to you in Oslo?"

"No." She shook her head. "I'd be drowning in work if that were the case. No, it's going all over Norway, but Oslo will get its fair share."

"Just let me know how I may assist you."

She smiled broadly as they turned a corner heading for a long building that encompassed the whole block. Built on the water, the two-story building with rows of chopped timber stacked to one side was plain on the outside, but bustling with activity on the inside. John led her into a large, noisy room with wood stacked everywhere while an anxious man in a sturdy brown suit hurried to keep up with him.

"Miss Bowden, this is Mr. Torberg."

"How do you do, Mr. Torberg?"

"Jeg har det bra," he said with a reddened face. "Kan jeg vise deg rundt?" He shook his head slightly and looked at John.

"He's fine and asked if he could show us around."

Phyllis nodded and John turned back to the man.

"We have a train to catch in an hour."

When Torberg looked confused, Edelland leaned closer and spoke a few soft words to him. Torberg straightened immediately, ushering them further inside the plant. John kept a running commentary as they walked.

"That long machine you see runs paper fibers and water in one continuous sheet on an endlessly moving conveyor belt. After the water is removed, the paper is wound around these drums. See over there?" He proudly pointed to large rolls of paper some six feet thick, maybe thicker. "The paper making process is long and intensive, but Norway spruce makes some of the finest paper anywhere."

As they progressed through the paper mill, Phyllis saw paper being made in every step of the process. It was a quick run through history as Norwegian paper made the not-so-big step from its origin by the Chinese. John talked animatedly for an hour with his hands pointing and waving every step along the way. Phyllis' head was spinning by the time they finished the tour. Mr. Torberg hadn't said much, but blushed with pride every time John looked his way.

"Thank you so much, Mr. Torberg, for the tour." Phyllis glanced at Edelland. "And you, John. I'm impressed you know so much about the process of making paper."

He grinned. "It's in my genetic makeup. My grandfather ran a plant like this not far from here and I was happy to be able to bring this mill back into production."

"I assume you're hiring locally."

"Absolutely. I've had Torberg hire as many men and women as he can."

"Women?"

"Sure. Women are better at making the finer products like writing tablets and stationary."

Phyllis smiled as they walked back to the train station. John appeared to be a good guy, on the level. The mere fact that he was hiring people left and right gave her the impression that he was one of the factors going into Norway's budding economy. It wouldn't take long to get the country back on track financially if there were other businessmen like John Edelland. She was still feeling enthusiastic until they rounded a corner in the village to head to the station and came upon a small group of excited people. Perhaps more of a mob. Phyllis stopped in her tracks to watch what was going on.

Angry men and women wielding sticks and throwing rocks were chasing some other people down the street. The people being chased looked frightened and Phyllis took a step in their direction. John's arm shot out to block her access any farther.

"Leave it be, Phyllis."

"But John! Don't you see how scared those people are? What's happening here? Surely nothing good will come of it."

He turned her around to face him, away from the sight of the angry mob.

"This is what a purge looks like."

"A purge? I've heard a little, but what's it about?"

He shook his head dispiritedly. "It's not something I'm proud of right now...what my country is going through, but I can understand it." John took ahold of Phyllis' elbow and steered her carefully around the hostile sight. With all the shouting and screaming, Phyllis couldn't hear anything he might have said until they reached the train. John all but pushed her onto the train platform and then up into the railway car.

Breathless, Phyllis plopped into a plush armchair, tugging off her hat.

"Why did you propel me along like that?"

"Because mobs can turn fast."

"I'm an American."

"Which might have helped you and might not have. Mobs are not clear-thinking people."

She watched him unbutton his coat and take out the pipe to light it. When he leaned back into the cushioned chair more in control, he met her gaze, but he waited to speak until the train began to pull away from the station.

"You have questions, I'm sure."

"You bet I do. It's all right with you if Norwegian people are chasing fellow countrymen through the streets with sticks and rocks?" Her face warmed. "It's all right with you if Norway gets rid of the German oppressors just to begin oppressing their own people?"

"Phyllis," he began. John laid down his pipe and leaned forward. "You don't understand what is happening now."

"Apparently not. Explain it to me, please."

"Certainly, but with embarrassment, not with pride."

Phyllis slid back in her chair, stared out the window as the train moved farther down the tracks. Muted shouts lessened to dim noises before she relaxed somewhat.

"I know this upsets you."

"I'm not upset."

"Well, you're doing a good imitation. Anyway," John's look was intense. "Norway fought two wars for five years: an active one with the Germans and a covert one with the Germans."

She looked at him. "Does this have to do with collaborators?"

"Exactly. You know about Vidkun Quisling?"

"Yes."

"People of means who socialized with him were called quislings, meaning traitors. The men and women being chased tonight were those whom some considered traitors; those who helped the Germans in some way."

She chewed her lip. "What will happen to them?"

He shrugged. "I'm not sure. They could go to jail for a while and then be run out of the country. Some quislings in the cities have been rounded up and sent to labor camps."

"I've heard that some so-called traitors were merely barbers or housecleaners for the Germans."

John shrugged again. "Collaboration comes in many forms."

"So you approve of this behavior?"

"No, but I have no control over it either. Phyllis..." John reached for one of her icy hands, rubbed it between his. "I do what I can, like with the children at the restaurant. Like hiring as many local people as possible for the paper mill. I do the same in my other businesses. It's all I can do."

Her intense gaze hardened. "I understand but I'm worried for the children of Norway. From what I've seen so far, their childhoods have been robbed one way or the other. If their parents were loyal to Norway, they were starved, turned out of their schools and churches. If they were quislings, their parents are shipped off to labor camps. What happens to the children, John? Are they really at fault because of their parents?"

"I'm afraid so."

"Then Norway is damning part of its population for no fault of their own."

John had no answer to that. He leaned back in his chair and tapped down the tobacco in his pipe. After striking a match and taking a puff, he watched the Norwegian landscape change from fishing village to pastoral landscapes. Phyllis watched too until they were back in Oslo once more. Leaving the railway car, John touched Phyllis' arm.

"We're doing the best we can, Phyllis."

She nodded. "I hope your best is good enough."

SEVENTEEN

His eyes reluctantly opened to cracks in a dirty ceiling. His hands were free and felt the lumpy mattress below him. Fragments of light splintered in the room and with the way his head was spinning, Joe couldn't tell if it was day or night.

Not that it mattered.

His circumstances hadn't improved much.

He had no idea how long he'd spent in the filthy cell. Maybe an hour, maybe a week or so. It was impossible to tell except he was so thirsty he was ready to drink his own urine.

Moving slightly, everything seemed to hurt at the same time. Gauze crisscrossed a wound in his chest and a stout bandage was wrapped around his right shoulder. Turning his head, Joe noticed the same matron sitting just outside. When the woman noticed he was awake, she walked to the door and spoke to someone outside. Joe closed his eyes and waited for the inevitable. But it would be a waste of their time; he had told them nothing and would continue to say nothing until the end. He knew it might come to that.

Soft footsteps shuffled into the cell. A heavy chair scraped along the floor.

"Agent Schneider? Are you awake?"

He opened his eyes. An intelligent looking man with worn metal glasses and a calm demeanor looked back at him.

"Yes."

"I'm sorry Constantin shot you. He is a most unfortunate creature, but we have patched you up. After all, our countries were on the same side in this terrible war with Germany." The man's squeaky voice sounded strange with his thick Russian accent. "And please dispense with the usual denials. We know you are Joseph Schneider, agent for MI5 out of London."

"Then why am I here?"

"Your government chose to send you on this fruitless mission. Is too bad, really. Your talents are wasted."

"That right?"

"Absolutely. Why don't you work for us, Mr. Schneider? We would make it worth your while...as you Brits say."

"Who are you?"

The man smoothed his scant mustache with a nicotine-stained finger. "Who I am is of no matter. Who you are is more important."

"What do you want?"

"We plan to keep you for a while, Mr. Schneider. It wouldn't look good to send you back to England with the wounds you have sustained. My country wouldn't want an international incident, now would it? So you will stay with us a little while longer until you are feeling better." The man glanced around the cell. "If you were a bit nicer, I could put you in better surroundings."

Joe turned his head away.

"We need to know what the British and Americans are up to now that the war with Germany has concluded." He shook his head and tsk-tsked. "This is the thanks my country gets for helping rid the world of that awful Hitler. To the victors belong the spoils. What business is it of your government if we wish to help Poland or Romania get back on their feet? Yes? I ask you?"

"My name is Joseph Michael Schneider, serial number 483029. I have nothing further to add."

"Great Britain should thank Russia for helping defeat

those dreadful Nazis. You must know we aren't going into any country that doesn't want us and with full knowledge of the other Allied Powers. You wanted our help at any price, remember?" The man cocked his head at Joe. "So now you're snooping around about that girl and hoping to meet with comrade Nicolae Dinescu? Why? What do you want with him? He's truly committed to the Communist cause, you know."

"I don't have anything to tell you."

"Perhaps your pretty young girlfriend does then."

Joe turned to look at the man. "What are you talking about?"

"We know about Miss Bowden, Mr. Schneider. Perhaps you spoke with her about your mission here in Bucharest. Perhaps she knows the girl."

He shook his head. "I don't know who you mean."

"One of our agents may meet her in Oslo to see what she knows."

Joe's mouth dropped open as he met the man's hard stare. "She knows nothing about what I do."

Shrugging, the man rose from his chair. "Perhaps not, but we intend to find out or..." He pointed to Joe. "You could save us the trouble and tell us what we want to know. That way our agent in Oslo will have no need to bother Miss Bowden."

Joe knew he was really between a rock and a hard spot now. His silence bounced off the walls of the dingy room.

"As you wish, Mr. Schneider." He began to walk out of the room.

"I have nothing to tell you," Joe repeated.

The man shrugged again without slowing. "I guess you will have to stay until you do then. Enjoy the music."

When the cell door clanked shut, Joe's ears were suddenly bombarded with sound from a speaker close to the ceiling. It was loud enough to make him wince and put his hands over his ears. But the booming of the big band music that he would ordinarily enjoy made him acutely aware of the message being sent—"Tell us something or your American girlfriend will be in our crosshairs."

Joe understood the subliminal message loud and clear.

EIGHTEEN

September came and with it, mixed news. The good news was the Japanese formally surrendered on the deck of the USS Missouri in Tokyo Bay on a cloudy September morning, thus ending the War in the Pacific between Allied and Axis powers. A collective sigh was felt worldwide when the Japanese foreign minister signed on behalf of the Japanese government. With Supreme Commander Douglas MacArthur signing on behalf of the United Nations and Admiral Chester Nimitz signing for the United States, the much-anticipated twenty minute ceremony ended with the sun bursting through low-hanging clouds.

The most devastating war in human history was over.

The good news was the best news the world had had since the Germans surrendered just this past year, 1945, in July.

The bad news hit closer to home.

Phyllis had gone skiing with John Edelland in the mountains around Oslo. Winter storms had hit early this year making fall the wettest on record. *Morketiden,* the dark time, perfectly summed up the first half of winter lasting roughly from mid September to early January and, as the name suggested, was the darkest time of the year. Snowfall generally tended to be washed away with frequent rainstorms, but this year was a bit different.

The rains had transformed with the dropping temperatures producing a series of snowstorms, one after another. After the third, John had telephoned Phyllis to entice her out on the slopes. Although she had never skied before, Ronnie insisted she give it a try and, because she was with John Edelland, ease more sensitive information from his smiling mouth. An Oslo spy she was to be.

John had a ski chalet where they could get ready before skiing and relax afterward. The rustic wooden house wasn't large, but comfortable with a front door divided into two doors, keeping out the snow yet allowing for fresh air. With a pot-bellied stove inside for heat, the chalet boasted a mountain interior of sturdy chairs, a dining table seating six and a hefty couch John remarked had taken three men to install. Phyllis sat on the front steps adjusting her skis under John's precise direction. Her rosy cheeks and wintry breath from the chilly air made her feel giddy and caused John to laugh. He'd been telling her about another family business as they drove up to the chalet. Just when he was getting to an interesting part about the shipping business, they had arrived and John became more excited about skiing. Maybe she could bring him back around to the subject on the way home.

For a novice, Phyllis felt the skiing that day was perfect. The sky was clear with few clouds and a sun that warmed the frigid climate enough to produce a powdery snow that felt heavenly beneath her skis. Under the proud Norwegian flag and a pampering escort, Phyllis felt protected and sheltered from harm ever being flung her way in their mountain retreat. They made several good runs down the slopes in the afternoon until the sun left its cozy spot overhead and began its gradual descent towards the horizon.

It was then that she met him.

Phyllis knew he was the real deal when she observed the tall man with an angular, clean-shaved face and an obvious regal attitude. Crown Prince Olav skied toward her and John with brisk strides covering the ground between them in a heartbeat. Up close, he was handsome with a princely posture and beaming countenance. His snow clothes fit snugly over a muscular physique.

Prince Olav whipped off a glove and stuck out his hand to John. "Edelland! Hvordan har du hatt det?"

"Jeg har det bra, takk skal du ha, din hoyhet," John replied, pumping the man's hand vigorously. "Og du?"

"Fint, fint, takk." The prince's eyes swung towards Phyllis. John nodded and smiled.

"Your Royal Highness, please meet Miss Phyllis Bowden of the American Embassy in Oslo. Phyllis, may I present Crown Prince Olav of Norway."

The smiling prince didn't miss a beat as he brought Phyllis' hand to his lips. "How do you do, Miss Bowden?"

She smiled. "Nice to meet you, Your Royal Highness."

"The pleasure is mine, madam. It's always nice to meet a friend of John's and such a lovely one at that."

Phyllis couldn't help blushing. He was a charming man. "Thank you, sir."

"Are you enjoying the fine day?"

"Indeed we are. John has been teaching me how to ski."

Prince Olav looked back at John. "I'm sure he has been an absolute gentleman and devout instructor."

"He has, thank you."

Olav smiled benevolently from one to the other. Then his eyes lit up. "Say! I'm having a little party at my chalet this evening, just a few intimate friends. Could you both come? Please, I would love for you to be my guests."

Phyllis' eyes widened with surprise, but John recovered for them both nicely. "It would be an honor, sir."

The prince slapped John on the back and laughed. "Wonderful! You know where it is, John, so I'll see you around eight." He glanced back at Phyllis. "Please don't worry about fancy dress. We're in the mountains, my dear, and a good wool Norwegian sweater is the best up here."

"Thank you, sir. That I have with me."

"Superb. I'll see you later then." With that, Prince Olav skied away as quickly as he'd come. He was gone so quickly down the slope that Phyllis shook her head wondering if he'd actually been with them.

"That was King Haakon's son, wasn't it, John? The king of Norway's son? And he invited us to a party tonight?"

John shook the snow from his boot. "He did indeed. He's a wonderful man and entertains a wide circle of friends. It'll be fun."

"So you do know the royal family."

John looked annoyed. "Did you doubt me? I'm a man of my word, Phyllis."

They skied back to John's chalet to rest up and have a light supper before going to the party. John must have been a successful businessman because he was able to have a telephone installed at his chalet. Since they would be spending the night instead of going back to Oslo, Phyllis called Lawrence to let him know of the change in plans.

"Now, Phyllis," Ronnie teased, "Remember you're an engaged woman."

"Funny, Colonel. I remember very well, but wouldn't it be a breach of etiquette to turn down an invitation from the Crown Prince of Norway?"

"Yes, it would," he chuckled. "Have a good time."

"Thank you, sir."

"Before you go, I received a letter from Lorraine for you. I just wanted to let you know. I'll put it on your desk."

"Oh! A letter from Lorraine? Finally! I've been waiting forever to hear from her." Phyllis caught her breath. "Lt. Col. Lawrence? Would you do me a favor?"

"Sure. What do you need?"

"Read the letter to me?"

"Oh...um...Not sure I should do that. Won't it be...personal?"

"I just can't wait another moment to hear from her and now I won't be back until tomorrow. Please, sir?"

"Okay," he sighed. "Remember you asked me. Just a moment." Phyllis heard him set down the phone and paper ripping in the background. He came back to the phone. "I'm ready. You?"

She squirmed in her chair with the phone receiver glued to her ear. "Yes."

"All right, here goes. She writes:

'Dear Phyllis,

It's been forever since we've spoken and I miss you so much. All the gals here at the row house miss you too, as does Mrs. Stewart, who wouldn't claim such a position if forced.'"

Phyllis chuckled.

"'Mick and everyone at Angel's is dying for news of you and I can't keep them properly entertained this way. I will have to ask Ronnie for a visit and soon. With the war in the Pacific ending, it looks like I may be transferred back to the States sooner than I thought. With that in mind, I can't wait to see you.

I hesitate to write the next few words, not because they're strange, but because of the path of worry I may send you down. Anyway...I went to pick up Norma at the train station yesterday and bumped into Henry. He mentioned he was to pick up Joe, but Joe never got off the train. It didn't bother Henry much that Joe didn't appear, but I have to say it bothers me. I thought he had been to see you weeks ago, so why was he coming home now? He's a bit of a mystery that one, but still, he should have been back in London by this time.

I don't mean to alarm you, just wondering what is up. Congratulations again on the engagement and I can't wait to have an engagement party for you here. Or in Oslo. Perhaps you could have two! Wouldn't that be grand?

Thinking of you. Take care.

Your best friend, Lorraine'"

Phyllis heard Ronnie stuffing the letter back into the envelope. He came back on the line. "How's that?"

She twisted the phone line between her fingers. "Sir?"

"Yes, Miss Bowden."

"When was her letter written?"

"Let me check." A pause. "It was written four days ago and arrived by military transport today. Why?"

"Because Joe's not back in London yet."

"I caught that, but perhaps he had other business after leaving Oslo."

"He did, but it was supposed to have been of short duration." She twisted the phone cord tighter. "Sir? Could you do me a favor?"

"Of course."

"Could you...would you...I mean," she stammered.

"Do you want me to find out why he's not home yet?"

She breathed a sigh of relief. "Yes, sir. I realize his...um... situation, but surely he should be back by now."

"Leave it to me. I'll make a few discreet inquiries."

"Thank you, sir. I'll worry if I don't know something."

He laughed. "Just have fun with the Crown Prince this evening and I'll see you back sometime tomorrow."

"Thank you again, Colonel. I'll see you then."

She set the phone back in its cradle and leaned back staring out the window. Joe wasn't back from his Bucharest assignment. Not that she would know when the assignment was completed, but still...there was a heaviness to Lorraine's words that soaked Phyllis with an uneasy feeling she couldn't shake. The light supper lost its flavor before touching her lips and the bad news settled over her like a dense Norwegian fog.

She noticed their clothing first. Every person at the party was wearing a colorful Norwegian wool sweater. Long or short, many sweaters had unique designs of reindeer and snowflakes in bright red, Navy blue or cream. Some featured a knitted rose pattern in the shape of an octagon and were traditional going back a few centuries. Even though Prince Olav's friends were contemporaries of his, she noted colorful, traditional headbands worn by a few women. John had told her with a grin that the headbands generally indicated the women were unmarried, but were worn more for fashion now. Men smoked pipes and were good-looking, some blondish, others dark-haired, but all exuded confidence and were well fed.

John had joined a group immediately upon arrival, but

Phyllis preferred to skirt the periphery observing the assembly before making a commitment. The Prince's guests spoke different languages in addition to Norwegian making it harder for her to converse. After greeting the Prince and thanking him for the invitation, she joined a small English-speaking group with two men and one woman. Their animated discussion enticed Phyllis.

"The government simply must exert market control over fisheries and agriculture," exclaimed one man. "That's an important step to getting Norway up-to-date." His bright red pullover sweater had a small hole by one sleeve. Maybe moths had gotten to it. The woman's pinched expression emphasized her skeptical attitude.

"No, that's not the way to control overproduction, Magnus. You sound just like a member of the Labor party."

Magnus puffed on his pipe with skeptical eyes. "You think you know better than I, Yliana?"

The blonde Yliana gave him a pouty look. "With currency depreciation..."

"With currency depreciation," he interrupted, "the government has to regulate the manufacturing output, exports and import substitution if the market is going to grow."

"Yes," put in the second man, "ship owners are trans-forming their ships to diesel engines and tramp to line freights. Now that the war is over, everything seems to be happening at once. Regulation must come from the govern-ment to impose order over chaos."

Phyllis cleared her throat and the three people turned to her. Yliana's pinched face broke into a broad smile.

"You must be the American Prince Olav spoke about." She extended her hand to Phyllis. "Don't mind my overzealous companions. The economy is all anyone can talk about, it seems. I'm Yliana Abernus. This is my husband, Magnus, and his brother, Peder."

Phyllis smiled. "Phyllis Bowden. It must be wonderful to be back in charge of one's own destiny." She looked from

Magnus to Peder. "I take it you're with the Norwegian government."

"No, no," said Magnus quickly. "We're Swedes, mere bystanders to Norway, but good friends with the Prince. We went to university together."

Peder nodded his head. "So nice to make your acquaintance. Are you enjoying your time in Norway?"

"I am, although I'm working as hard as I play."

"What do you do?" asked Yliana. Her hand rested on her husband's arm, proof of ownership, Phyllis suspected.

"I'm with the American Embassy."

Three sets of eyebrows raised simultaneously. Who knew that would be a provocative statement?

"Indeed?" Magnus took a step closer. "How does the Military Attaché feel about the proposed aid we've heard about?"

Phyllis frowned. "Aid? Um..."

"We had heard there were plenty of American politicians who don't agree that money is the best way to help the countries destroyed by Germany."

This wasn't good. She was being asked to give information when she was there to get it. "Well, you know politicians." She smirked to Magnus. "They change their minds so very frequently."

They all laughed. "So true," replied Yliana. "Just like our husbands."

John rescued her. "Phyllis, come meet some people." He took her arm to escort her to another small group, Danes this time. Apparently, Prince Olav's friends were from the Scandinavian countries, all in various businesses and saturated with glowing ideas about Norwegian reform. Before the evening was over, Phyllis had heard ideas about centralized economic planning, fixing the hard currency, how to bolster currency depreciation, and opinions galore on how Norway should use the millions of kroner from the United States through a proposed aid plan being soundly debated.

How had this group of well-heeled Scandinavians known about a U.S. aid plan when she didn't?

As an American, she was treated very kindly and with deference. After all, it was her country that was proposing the funding to rebuild Norway and Western Europe. She understood through various conversations that immediate goals for this funding were to rebuild the war-torn regions, remove trade barriers, and modernize industry all to make Europe prosperous once more and to prevent the spread of Communism. Phyllis made a mental note to ask Lt. Col. Lawrence what the heck everyone here, obviously government insiders, knew that she didn't. They thought she was being discreet when in actuality, she didn't know anything about the proposed aid plan.

She felt foolish. And then her stomach lurched. Efforts were being made to prevent the spread of Communism? So the Allied countries weren't keen on the Soviets spreading their influence in the eastern European countries. How did that translate to Joe's assignment in Romania? She'd heard the country had a strong Communist party and Stalin had made a big push in all the eastern countries. Would that mean Joe would be harshly treated if the Communists learned he was on assignment and possibly trying to infiltrate the party?

Her earlier feeling of unease returned and neither the happy party of Olav's friends or tempting libations could quiet her misgivings. She was relieved when John told her they should go. The party was breaking up. Once back in the chalet, John asked her what was the matter.

"You seem...out of sorts, this evening, Phyllis. Is there something I can get for you?"

"No, thank you, John. I think I'm just tired and need some rest. I'll bid you goodnight."

"Before you go, I have to ask if you're upset by anything that was said at the Prince's party this evening."

"What makes you say that?" She rubbed a spot on her forehead that had begun to throb.

He shrugged, tapped down the tobacco in his pipe. "It's that you..."

"I what?"

"You seemed fine before the party, but towards the end you didn't seem well. You don't look well right now. What's bothering you?" When she shook her head, he tried again. "Are you missing your fiancé?"

She looked up at him sharply. "Why would you say that?"

"It would seem logical if he's not here that you would miss him."

"I do," she admitted. "I do miss him."

He motioned her to a chair. "Please sit. Tell me about him."

After settling in a large cushioned chair by the fireplace, Phyllis spread her hands to feel the fire's heat. "Why do you want to know?"

"I'm curious. Have you been able to see him at all? He's from London, I understand."

"How would you know that?"

"Phyllis," he began slowly, "For one thing, you told me. Besides that, I'm attracted to you and you say you're engaged, but the man isn't here. Being naturally curious, I've asked around about him."

"What did you find out?"

"That he's British and you met in London."

She sighed, settled back in the chair. "He is British and I'm American. That may cause problems."

"How so?"

She shook her head. "I'd rather not say."

"But he has been here recently?"

"Yes, and he's returned to his business in London."

"What business is he in?" John puffed on his pipe. "Perhaps I know him."

"His name is Joe Schneider and he works as a liaison to the American State Department."

"Sounds important." He casually slid his eyes away. "Has he returned to London?"

"Not...that I'm aware," she replied cautiously. John still didn't meet her eyes.

"That's too bad. Perhaps he had business elsewhere that you don't know about."

"Perhaps."

"So you don't know?"

"Know what?"

"What business he had after visiting you in Oslo?"

Her careful gaze became suspicious. "What are you asking me?"

"It's a straightforward question, Phyllis. What kind of State Department business could he have between here and London?"

"I wouldn't have the slightest idea." She stifled a yawn, pretending boredom she didn't feel and rose. "I think I'll head off to bed, John. This conversation has become too taxing and I really must get my rest." When her lips twitched at the end of her little speech, John laughed.

"You Americans are such kidders. I'll never become accustomed to your sense of humor."

"Anyway, thank you for the wonderful day and I'll see you tomorrow."

"Good night, Phyllis."

After she'd gone, John returned to his warm chair by the fire and relit his pipe. Once he'd taken a good puff, John gazed into the crackling fire considering what Phyllis had said. And what she hadn't said. He wondered if there really was an engagement and if so, where the man could be. He was a fool to be somewhere besides by Phyllis' side, allowing a man such as himself to swoop in where he should be. Foolish and stupid.

No matter. Phyllis interested him very much and it would be no problem to slowly sweep away the memory of a man who wasn't around. He puffed on his pipe. Perhaps he needed more information to successfully accomplish this so-called sweeping. More information.

Yes.

John picked up the phone and asked the operator for a specific number. A number he'd used many times in the past to get the information he needed. He'd use it now to learn what he needed to know and to get what he wanted. John Edelland was a man who was used to getting whatever he wanted and this situation was no different.

He cradled the phone like he was born using one. The person on the other line picked up after the first ring, as expected.

Yes, he would get what he wanted.

NINETEEN

The mirror above the sink reflected only the curly fuzz on the top of her head. Her long hair was in disarray and if she stopped to think, she wouldn't be able to remember the last time she'd put a comb through it. Rising on tiptoes, the reflection included a thin, dirty face with sooty markings on her forehead. Frowning, she wet her sleeve and rubbed her forehead until it glistened pink and the dreaded symbol faded away. She breathed a tiny breath of relief.

But rising again to pat down the fuzz, her eyes locked with those in the mirror. Hollow with dark circles, they were the eyes of an older child, one whose recent memories were anything but pleasant. In an instant, she was tied up in the backyard of someone's home, certainly not hers, with an old dog who looked as tired as she felt. After being starved and whipped for several days, she preferred the quiet of the chilly outdoors to the horrors inside. She shared the dog's meal when she could get a few bites from him and shivered relentlessly during the endless nights.

"Devil child!" she'd been called more than once. "Offspring of Satan" was another favorite. She cried when they called her mother a German whore, but tears were hard to come by these days. She felt limp and would become a puddle in the dirt by the dog if she didn't do something.

Late one night, she'd found a broken bottle by the dog bowl and set about cutting the rope that bound her. Running as fast as her little legs would go, she hid in bushes, behind garbage bins and trees until she came to a main street in Oslo. She cut down an alley behind several tall buildings hoping to find a place to sleep for the night. Good smells from a restaurant lured her closer with the promise of something, anything to eat. She waited, hidden in the dark, until someone came out the back door to empty a bin in the trash. When the person had gone back inside, she dug remains from a meal out of the container and shoved it in her mouth. The hole in her stomach lessened a little.

Bright lights and happy voices sucked her in farther. She stuck her nose to the screen door wistfully remembering happier days with her family. Her eyes fell to another door marked "Toalett" and she slipped inside with barely a whisper from the slightly open door. At least the bathroom was clean and warm, and she could eat from the trash bin outside. It would do for now.

She attempted to wash the rest of her face, but too many days outside guaranteed the dirt would only come off with soap. Glancing around the bathroom, she froze when she heard a voice outside the door.

A close voice.

A woman's voice.

She darted into a stall, closed and locked the door behind her. Someone came in just as she tucked her feet up so she wouldn't be detected. Shivering with cold and fright, she wrapped her arms around her small body willing herself to become invisible. It wasn't the first time she had prayed for invisibility, but her prayers never helped.

Phyllis staggered into the bathroom and leaned tentatively against the sink. Her teary eyes stared into the mirror, unseeing. As her cheeks began to glisten, the collar of her blouse dampened. Grabbing the sink for support, Phyllis began to sob uncontrollably, her cries of anguish filling the air. She fell on her knees as if in church with her head falling forward on her chest. Not caring who saw her this way, she wearily opened her eyes and caught motion in her periphery vision. Her eyes slid to the bathroom stall behind her.

She knocked on the door. "Excuse me. Is anyone in here?" Feeling a little embarrassed, she mopped her face and tried again. "Hello?"

When she heard a tiny squeak of breath but no reply, Phyllis leaned down to look into the stall. A small girl huddled tightly with her eyes squeezed shut. The look on her heart-shaped face was abject terror.

"Are you all right? I'm not going to hurt you."

The scared look on the child's face didn't lessen. Phyllis wracked her brain to think of any Norwegian words. She stood up and knocked on the stall again.

"Kom ut, vaer sa snill."

She repeated her request several times in as soft a voice as she could manage until finally the lock clicked and the door opened a fraction. Phyllis offered a hand to the little girl who timidly ventured an inch farther.

Phyllis was appalled at the filth on the girl's ragged clothes and face. "Hello. I'm Phyllis. Who are you...I mean... hvem er du?"

The girl mumbled something and looked away.

"Excuse me? Um...tilgi?"

"Jeg er Lisbet," she said suddenly, her voice rose slightly above a whisper.

"Lisbet. That's pretty. Do you speak any English? Engelsk?"

"Yes, my father taught me."

Phyllis crouched down to be on the same level with Lisbet. Her eyes widened with despair at the little girl's condition. Her hands ached to wash her sad face.

"Why are you hiding in the bathroom?"

"Why were you crying?"

Lisbet's wary eyes roamed Phyllis' face for an explanation.

"Answer my question."

Lisbet shook her head. "No, mine first."

Phyllis wobbled before rising. She walked over to the

sink, found a paper towel and wet it. After washing her face, she glanced back at the little girl who hadn't moved. She crouched down again, looking Lisbet in the eye.

"May I wash your face?" When Lisbet nodded, Phyllis talked while wiping some of the dirt away from Lisbet's cheeks. "I just found out that my fiancé is missing."

"Fiancé?"

Phyllis thought a minute. "The man I love."

"Oh. Where did he go?"

The towel stopped moving.

"He left Oslo and went to Romania. Do you know where that is?"

Lisbet shook her head. Phyllis rose to get a clean towel, rub soap on it and continued washing Lisbet's face and hands.

"It's another country far from here."

"Why is he missing? Does no one know where he is?"

Phyllis' eyes filled again with tears. She patiently rubbed more dirt off Lisbet's hands. "His business may have gotten him...in trouble."

Lisbet took Phyllis' hand and kissed it. "You have good heart. He will come back."

With watery eyes, she pulled Lisbet into her arms and whispered softly. "Thank you, sweet girl." After a brief hug, Phyllis wiped her eyes. "Now then. Tell me why you are hiding in the bathroom."

A loud voice was heard outside the bathroom door. Lisbet stiffened and hurried back into the stall. Phyllis stepped in front just as a Norwegian policeman poked his head in.

"Miss? Beklager! Har du sett henne?" His Norwegian sounded vaguely familiar, but he spoke too rapidly for her to understand.

"I'm sorry. I don't understand Norwegian."

"Ah...Engelsk." His face scrunched in thought. "Have du...seen...girl?"

Phyllis shook her head, hoped she looked innocent. "No."

"Takk." He left slamming the door behind him.

Phyllis turned when Lisbet came out of the stall.

"I have to get you out of here."

"There's a back door," offered the girl.

"Stay right here. I need to get my coat and purse."

Back in a few minutes, Phyllis took off her sweater and put it on Lisbet. She attempted to comb the girl's unruly hair, put on her coat and hat.

"We're going out the back. I told Arne I had business down the block so he won't be concerned about me."

"Arne?"

"Never mind."

With that, Phyllis picked up Lisbet, adjusted her purse and walked calmly out of the bathroom. She took a sharp left to the back door and out into the dark Norwegian night. It wasn't the first time she'd taken a step into the unknown since coming to Norway, but this time she felt a solid purpose.

She wanted to help the little girl. But could she?

TWENTY

Luckily, Mrs. Lind wasn't around when Phyllis smuggled Lisbet up to her apartment. She carried the little girl up four flights of stairs close to her chest like a mother kangaroo cuddling her baby. The first things she did were to run Lisbet a warm bath and then feed her soup she had made yesterday. When the girl was clean and fed, she and Phyllis went into the living room and made themselves comfortable on the couch. She wrapped Lisbet in a blanket and watched her long lashes close sleepily.

"I remember you."

The girl's eyes snapped open. "You do? Where did you see me?"

Phyllis leaned back into the cushion, tapped a finger on her chin. "It was my first night in Oslo and my driver stopped at a stop sign. You were being herded into a building with other little girls by Norwegian policemen."

"Herded?"

"Taken in a group." Phyllis smiled. "You turned and looked right at me."

Lisbet nodded, her damp hair glistened. "I remember a woman in a bus. That was you?"

"Yes."

A smile spread across the girl's pale face. "I was hoping we would meet again."

"Life is strange."

"I don't understand."

Phyllis shook her head, reached over to touch Lisbet's arm. "Never mind. It's not important. Tell me, how old are you?"

"Almost five."

"You're only five years old? What in the world happened to you?"

When Lisbet looked confused, Phyllis tried again. "Where are your parents?"

At the question, Lisbet's face reddened and tears pooled in her eyes. "My mother is gone."

"Where did she go?"

"She...was sent to a labor camp." Lisbet swallowed hard, the muscles in her small neck constricted.

"Is she Norwegian?"

"Yes."

"But why..."

"My father is German. We had a little house outside town where Mama grew vegetables and Papa would come visit when he could. He was very busy."

"Did he visit wearing a uniform?"

She nodded. "It was green with lots of shiny medals. He was nice to us."

Lisbet's father was probably a German officer who had had a love relationship with the girl's mother, a local Norwegian woman. It was a story Phyllis had heard over and over. Lisbet was a lovely little girl with dark blonde hair. She could almost see the blonde mother in her face and body. A sad look crept over Lisbet's face.

"What?"

The girl's lips trembled and she began to weep. "One day our house was bombed and some men took us away. They were very mean. We were put in jail and then my mother was gone."

"But you think she was shipped off to a labor camp?"

"The other children in the jail told me that was what happened."

"What happened to you?"

The little girl looked away, memories clouded her face like butterflies. Snuggling deeper into the warm blanket, she began her story. Words dripped from her mouth sparingly as if they were ripped away. Phyllis couldn't drag her eyes from Lisbet.

"An older girl in jail with me who had been there a few weeks told me no one knew what to do with us."

"Why not?"

She shrugged. "Papa is German. Everyone hates Germans. That's all I understood and no one was very friendly. Even the others with me. We didn't become friendly and I so wanted a friend."

"How long were you in jail?"

"I'm not sure, several days and nights. A policeman came to pick me up one day, me and another girl. We went to live with a family not far from where I'd lived before with my mother."

"A family?"

"Well, a man and woman." Lisbet shuddered, nestled deeper into the blanket.

"Are you all right?"

Her head briskly nodded before looking Phyllis in the eye. "They beat us and called us names." Phyllis' hand flew to her mouth. "The other girl finally ran away and they tied me outside with an old dog."

Phyllis felt light-headed. "How did you live?"

"I ate the dog's food and slept in the dog's house with him at night."

"Did you see the man and woman?"

"Not much. Just when they came out to feed the dog and yell more names at me. Once..." Lisbet's face closed up. Her eyes shut tightly against the memory.

"What happened?" Phyllis didn't want to hear, but knew she had to if she wanted to get the whole picture.

"A few days ago, the man used coal to write something on my forehead."

"What was it?"

Lisbet drew a symbol in the air before quickly returning her fingers to the safety of the blanket.

A swastika. Drawn on the forehead of a little girl whose crime was to be born to a German man and a Norwegian woman during wartime. They'd obviously loved one another since the man visited and made sure they were all right.

Phyllis tucked her feet beneath her on the couch while she struggled to understand. Five years of occupation. She shook her head. It would be impossible to justify a love relationship like this. It was worse than the Capulets and the Montagues from Shakespeare's *Romeo and Juliet*. Recognizing love between a German man and a Norwegian woman would mean a softening towards the German oppressors, something Phyllis knew wouldn't happen for a very long time, if ever. In the minds of most Norwegians, little Lisbet was a quisling, through no fault of her own. It was going to take effort and patience to decide what to do with the girl, but time was not on her side.

Lying on the couch, Lisbet's eyes were closed and she was snoring slightly. Her world upside down and torn from her mother's arms, Lisbet could sleep safely tonight while Phyllis mulled over her options.

There weren't many. Being an outsider, Phyllis should give Lisbet up to the Norwegian authorities. What would they do with her? Adopt her out again to be abused and mistreated? She couldn't keep her here forever. With Joe missing, Phyllis had enough worry on her plate already.

Joe.

She went into the kitchen to pour a glass of wine. Taking it out to the patio, Phyllis watched lights from fishing boats reflect off the water. She heard noises from downtown as people were once again enjoying city life. Tears collected anew as she remembered the happy times with Joe right here in this very spot. Joking, teasing, kissing. He was so easy to be with and so easy to love. Phyllis stared questioningly out into the dark night.

Where was he now? Was he alive? Danger came with their business in military intelligence. She knew that, but it was harder to live with that knowledge when everything was falling apart.

Phyllis heard a small noise in the living room. Lisbet was sitting up, wide-eyed and scared looking around the dimly lit room. Phyllis hurried to her side.

"You're all right, Lisbet. You're here with me."

The little girl's eyes widened. "Miss Phyllis?"

"Yes, you're safe."

Lisbet fell into Phyllis' arms sobbing. "I...thought you...left me."

Phyllis patted the girl's head, held her close. "No. You're fine. Try to sleep. Will you be okay in my guest room?"

Lisbet swallowed and nodded once. Phyllis guided her into the small room and tucked her into bed. When Lisbet closed her eyes, Phyllis sat for a few minutes watching the little girl relax slowly until she finally fell asleep.

What in the world was she going to do with her?

TWENTY-ONE

"I haven't seen you for days, Phyllis, and I've missed you. Why won't you go out to dinner with me this evening?"

"John, this really isn't a good time."

"Would tomorrow be better for you?"

"Possibly. Look, I need to go. I have...laundry to do for this week and...some other things, so thank you and I'll speak with you soon."

John Edelland frowned at the phone as he returned it to its cradle. Why was Phyllis being so standoffish? Hadn't she enjoyed the ski trip and meeting Prince Olav? Just when he thought he was making progress with her, she backed off like he had the plague.

John grabbed the jacket laid neatly on a chair in his office and moved his arms into the sleeves feeling the rich woolen material so soft to his skin. He buttoned a front button before smoothing the jacket and a wrinkle in his matching slacks. The slate gray suit with deep red tie looked good on him and he was happy he'd purchased the clothes on his last trip to Sweden. Another business he had hopes of starting was a decent clothing store in Oslo. There still wasn't much to buy in the way of good clothes for men and John meant to change that.

His eyes darted briefly back to the telephone and his frown returned. He really liked Phyllis, but she was skittish as a fish on the line. Perhaps this man she was supposedly engaged to meant more than he had thought. John returned to his desk, picked up the phone and made another call. This time he was calling for the kind of information that only money can buy and secrecy can define. He was going to find out about Joe Schneider.

"HAVE you spoken to Lt. Col. Lawrence about Lisbet?"

"No. I'm not sure what to do. The Colonel once told me not to get personally involved in Norwegian troubles."

Jay smiled and cut her sandwich in half. "Looks like you blew right by that one."

"Tell me about it."

Phyllis took a bite of salad, chewing thoughtfully. She watched Jay fuss with her cheese sandwich, cutting off the ends, salting it with just a pinch of salt.

Phyllis pointed with her fork.

"You ever going to eat that or do you plan to just play with it?"

"Don't be an arse. The blooming thing is going to bugger me senseless."

Laughing, Phyllis poked Jay's sandwich. "You're saying the most dreadful things about your food, I fear."

Jay rolled her eyes. "The PX just doesn't know how to make a decent grilled cheese sandwich." She glanced around the busy room. Officers and diplomats were in abundance chatting noisily while eating lunch. Sunshine pouring in through the windows lent a bright atmosphere with laughter and conversation resounding off the walls. Gazing in a certain direction, Phyllis looked over to see what had caught her friend's eye.

"Astrid?"

Jay nodded. "I may have the solution to your kid problem."

"How could Astrid help?"

"Astrid's younger sister. She could babysit until you figure this out." Jay tucked some gooey cheese back into her sandwich. "Didn't you have to leave her all alone today?"

"I did but she's been taking care of herself for a while now, even though she's so young. She should be all right. I'll try to sneak out a little early today, maybe take some work home. And I gave Lisbet instructions not to make any noise or she would attract the attention of my nosy landlady."

"Ah, yes, Mrs. Lind. How is the old bat?"

Phyllis smiled, shook her head. "Not nice there, limey. She reminds me of the landlady I had in London. Mrs. Stewart was terribly nosy, but had a good heart and helped us out a time or too. I actually miss her."

"Do you think Mrs. Lind will take her place?"

"The jury's out on that one. I just don't know. Oslo isn't London."

"That's right and it makes all the difference in the world. England wasn't an occupied country." Jay shivered. "Thank God."

"Call Astrid over." Phyllis tucked curly hair behind one ear and angled her head towards the young woman across the room.

"Have you found out anything about her family? That might sweeten the pot."

"No and I won't lie to her. I'll tell her that inquiries have been made and I'm still looking. It's the truth. She can make the decision about whether or not to help me with the information I have, which isn't much."

"Well, you're not looking to bargain."

"Certainly not, but this could be a good solution for me with Lisbet. Temporary, but good."

Jay beckoned to Astrid to join them. While she made her way across the room, Phyllis and Jay exchanged confident looks and crossed fingers. It had to work.

THE PLATE LISBET was washing slipped out of her hands and hit the floor with a loud crash. She froze standing on a step stool that she'd moved over to wash the breakfast dishes at the sink. Her new friend Phyllis had been so nice to her that Lisbet wanted to do something nice in return. Washing dishes had seemed like a good idea, until it wasn't.

Phyllis had warned her to be quiet while she was gone because the downstairs landlady might not like her being there. The woman wandered all over the building, so it was no telling where she was at any given time. Lisbet scampered off the stool, picked up the broken pieces and shoved them quickly into the kitchen trash bin. Drying her hands, she folded the small towel neatly and had placed it on the counter when she heard a knock at the front door.

"Miss Bowden? It's Mrs. Lind. I was sweeping the floor and I heard a noise. Are you all right, min kjaere?"

Frozen with fear, Lisbet's mouth dried up and she couldn't have spoken if forced.

The knock was louder this time.

"Miss Bowden? You home?"

A key was being inserted into the lock on the door and Lisbet finally got her feet moving. She ducked behind the living room couch facing the door with its back to the fire-place. Tucking her small body into a tiny ball, beads of sweat popped out on the little girl's forehead as she prayed again for invisibility.

The wooden door pushed open. "Miss Bowden?" The frail voice was closer now. "Beklager...um, I'm sorry to come in like this." Light footsteps ventured into the room. "Miss Bowden?"

Lisbet heard footsteps walk down the hallway. "Anyone home?" The footsteps grew louder as the old woman wandered back to the living room. "Guess no one iz here. Wonder what the noise was."

Footsteps walked out into the hallway, the door was pulled shut and relocked. Then the sounds became lighter and lighter until they couldn't be heard at all. It was still quite a while before the girl stood and wiped sweat off her chilly face. Her fingers felt like ice. Lisbet ran to her bedroom to dive under the covers where Phyllis found her a few hours later sound asleep and totally invisible. She'd had to search her apartment twice before she found the little girl in her bed.

"You're all right, Lisbet, and I need to tell you something."

TWENTY-TWO

"This isn't a good idea, Phyllis."

"I realize that, Colonel, but what was I supposed to do? She was filthy and shivering with fright and cold in the bathroom at Arne's Café. I couldn't just leave her there."

"You said a Norwegian policeman came to the door looking for her." The frown on Ronnie's face deepened emphasizing wrinkles around his mouth. "That would have been the time to give her to the authorities. Now there could be repercussions."

"Repercussions?"

"Yes, it could be a black mark on this office if we're found to be colluding with quislings."

"She's not a quisling, sir." Phyllis sat straighter in her chair. The bright sunlight coming in the window of Lt. Col. Lawrence's office picked that moment to dim casting shadows about the room. "She's barely five years old."

He shook his head wearily. "I know your heart's in the right place, but her father was a German officer more than likely. That's collaborating with the enemy."

"So the sins of the mother are to be laid on the child."

"It would seem so in our present time and context. I don't know what to do other than give her up to the Norwegian authorities."

"But Colonel, the last time that happened, the authorities gave her to a foster family who beat her and chained her outside in the cold with a dog!"

Ronnie winced. Phyllis rose to begin pacing in front of his desk. "There's got to be something we can do to help Lisbet." She turned to face the tall military officer, who had risen from his chair.

"Please sit down, Phyllis, and calm down. It's not going to help the situation to get all riled up."

"Maybe not, but it will make me feel better."

"I doubt that. Please...sit."

Phyllis smoothed her skirt and sat back down. She avoided his stare by rearranging the thick pleats in her wool skirt. When she ran out of pleats, she glanced up at him. Ronnie was smiling.

"You can't help yourself, can you?"

"What do you mean, sir?"

"You just have to be helping someone."

She shrugged and plucked lint off her mud-brown sweater. A staffer had mentioned the sweater was the same color as her eyes. She wasn't sure if that was meant as a compliment. "I don't know about that."

He waved a hand. "No matter. I'm going to have to give this some thought. How to help the little girl without getting the Office of the Military Attaché, a representative of the United States government, in hot water with Norway."

Phyllis perked up. "You're going to help her?"

Both hands went out in front of him defensively. "Now don't get excited, Miss Bowden. It puts this office in a hell of a hum, but I owe you."

"No you don't, Colonel."

"Well, I feel I do and for that reason I'll give the matter serious thought. See what I can come up with."

The smile on her face stretched from ear to ear. "Thank you, Lt. Col. Lawrence. I knew you had a big heart."

"Don't go getting funny ideas about me, Phyllis." He smiled. "But my wife might agree with you."

"There's just one more thing." When his smile faded, she

hurriedly added, "Oh, it's not a big thing, but something you should know."

"What is it?"

"Do you remember Astrid Hansen?"

He nodded, stroked his chin. "Sure. I've made inquiries about her missing family on her behalf."

"Have you come up with anything?"

"Not definitively. The parents are sure to have perished at Auschwitz, but it's hard to tell since the Germans burned all the records when they fled. The brothers have remained elusive, but my sources are still looking." He angled his head. "What about Astrid? What were you going to say?"

"Oh, yes! Sorry, I got sidetracked. Her sister, Helge, will start babysitting Lisbet for me when I come to work. I can't leave her all alone in my apartment. She's too young."

"Your landlady probably won't approve of having the little girl stay with you."

"That's why I don't plan to tell her."

"Phyllis..."

She shot him a shy look. "I know, sir. I hate being deceptive in any way, shape or form, but I don't see any other options right now. I know she can't stay with me for very long."

"I certainly hope not." He rose, walked around his desk. "Well, you've certainly piled more work on my desk, Miss Bowden, but thank you for informing me." She chuckled when he bit back a grin.

"By the way, I may have located your lost luggage."

She stared at him, mouth open. "Really, sir? Where is it?"

"It's on its way to Oslo. Apparently it didn't make the transport plane that you were on or any subsequent one. But I need to warn you."

"Sir?"

He walked her to the door, opened it for her.

"I'm fairly certainly the trunk was broken into." She stopped, watched him finish his thought. "The lock was pried off and there are items missing. You'll have to go through your inventory and make a report."

"Oh, no! Most of my winter clothes were in that trunk."

Ronnie shrugged. "Sorry about this, Phyllis, but with clothing in such short supply, there are looters everywhere."

"But at an Army base?"

"I don't know what to say. It's unfortunate, but perhaps you can take a weekend trip to Stockholm. Sweden has clothing to buy, even if Norway does not."

"True enough. Well, thank you, Colonel, for your concern."

She stepped into her office.

"Oh, one more thing."

Phyllis turned to watch Lawrence pick up a paper from his desk and walk back to hand it to her.

"What's this?"

"More work for you, I'm afraid, and not very cheery work either." He angled his head toward the paper in her hand. "That's a list of Norwegians who died in concentration camps that we know of so far. I'm sure there will be more to come because information from the Soviets is hard to get, but I want you to start on this list right away."

She dangled the list between two fingers as if it might catch fire at any moment. "What do you want me to do with it, sir?"

"Contact the families of those names."

"Contact how?"

"Find out where the families live, which may be difficult in and of itself, and make a visit to tell them personally. This isn't the kind of information you want to get on a telephone. Besides, the phone service countrywide is inconsistent at best."

Her jaw dropped at the request. "Colonel. This is a full time job by itself." She waved a hand at her cluttered desk and a staffer working in the corner. "We're fully immersed in a myriad of projects and you want *me* to do this? Why, sir, if I may ask?"

Ronnie glanced at the staffer and lowered his voice. "Phyllis, I know this is a huge task that I'm asking you to do, but there's no one else I would trust with it. I'll get you a few more staffers to lighten the load, although I think it would be better if you recruited people you felt could help you the most. Train them, make them sensitive to the task. Don't burden yourself with the whole thing. I know it will make you sick."

She laid a hand on her chair for balance and blew out a breath. "I...I'll do what I can, sir."

"I know you will. You've gotten the communication system up and running with Washington and the military exchange is operating smoothly, plus this office is all spit and polish."

"But, Colonel, I'm working on the clothing distribution currently."

"I know I'm asking you to do a lot, Miss Bowden, but you're the right person for the job, I know it."

When he went back into his office, closing the door behind him, Phyllis staggered to her chair feeling the weight of the world bearing down on her.

Why wouldn't an Army chaplain or a team of them be better prepared for the task Lawrence had just assigned her?

Actually, she brightened, that's exactly what she would do—go see an Army chaplain and enlist his aid. He said she could train a few people to assist her. This was right up a chaplain's alley and he wouldn't need training. He would need briefing on the assignment and a sensitive hand with news delivery. She'd even heard a nice chaplain speak at church one Sunday.

She searched through papers piled on her desk for the list of Norwegians who had come to the embassy looking for their lost relatives in Europe. She knew it would be a never-ending list and the thought gave her pause.

Aha! Phyllis held up a folder with the names of people she and others at the embassy had spoken to since she had arrived. It was the place to start. Now what was that man's name? She scratched her chin as her mind sought the information. Oh, yes. She scanned the Army directory for the name she wanted and picked up her phone to make a call.

Chaplain Mark Stevens. Please be in, please.

TWENTY-THREE

Joe's eyes opened to absolute darkness. The cloth over his face was coarse, burlap maybe, and smelled faintly of gasoline. Being so close to his nose made his eyes water and stomach lurch, but since there was very little to vomit, Joe took steady breaths to control his stomach.

And his fear. He had no idea how long he'd been in that smelly cell with near-starvation rations, but recent whispered consultations between the Romanian with the pointy nose and the wily Soviet had ended with a chloroformed rag over his mouth and nose. It was lights out after that until now.

He was lying down somewhere with a headache and his hands tied behind his back. The rope used was tight, chafing his skin. He knew he'd have rope burns if he could ever get it off.

But he was moving. The chilly steel beneath his thin clothes poked through so he was on some kind of rough surface. Not only was it cold, but it too smelled of gasoline and he had to think he was in a vehicle traveling who knows where. It was good to be out of the cell, but not knowing where he was going produced a different fear, that of the unknown. Trying to control his body was just as hard as trying to control his mind from being too anxious.

Joe squirmed to move away from something poking into

his back. Someone swatted him with a rough hand any time he tried to move, so he laid still. With wind blowing his hair slightly and scraping sounds below, he felt a slight rise in elevation. They were going uphill...somewhere. In his trade-craft training, when the odds were against you, it was a good idea to get a bead on your surroundings before deciding on the best course of action.

He lay quietly with only his pounding heartbeat for company as he listened to the myriad of sounds around him. Rushing wind, murmuring voices, a match being struck. The hum of tires on a bumpy road finally lulled him into a fitful sleep, dreams with terrifying monsters with horns and dreadful screams.

The screams might have been his.

TWENTY-FOUR

Helge Hansen resembled her sister. With wavy blonde hair and icy blue eyes, the young woman greeted Phyllis at the door of her apartment building. The heavy wooden door with bits of stained glass above framed Helge as if she were in an old-fashioned picture. She might have been several years younger than Astrid, but Helge was nearly as tall and looked Phyllis confidently in the eye.

Phyllis smiled, shook her hand. "Thank you so much for coming today, Helge. Oh, sorry!" She shook her head. "May I call you Helge?"

"Yes, ma'am. You certainly may."

"Please call me Phyllis. May I say that you're as lovely as your sister?"

Helge's small smile was there and gone. "You may, but Astrid might disagree with you."

"Well, thanks for coming." She motioned Helge over to the fireplace inside the lobby. "I need to talk to you before going upstairs."

"Is everything all right?"

"Yes, but I will introduce you to my landlady first. Mrs. Lind runs the place and wants to know everything happening in it."

"My sister and I live in a building with the very same

kind of landlady. Perhaps it's an epidemic." Her curved lips caused Phyllis to chuckle.

"I do believe nosiness is basic criteria for all landladies. Anyway, I may say a few things to Mrs. Lind that don't ring true. Please just be silent and I will explain my words to you later, when we're upstairs. I have my reasons. All right?"

"Astrid filled me in on your situation, Phyllis. I believe I know where you're going with this, so you can count on me."

When Phyllis turned, Helge touched her arm. "I also want to thank you for what you are doing for my sister and me."

"Oh, ah..."

"Whatever information you find out about our parents and brothers, however small, will be greatly appreciated."

Phyllis took Helge's hands in hers. "Trust me when I say I could never do enough to help you and as soon as I learn anything definite, I'll let you know."

Helge's smile came out full force. She hugged Phyllis to her briefly.

"Okay, now." Phyllis sucked in a breath. "Show time."

The two women crossed the stately lobby. Welcome fragments of light from the huge front window crossed their path like a beacon. Phyllis' anxiety kicked up little by little the closer they got to Mrs. Lind's door. Smoothing her gray skirt, Phyllis hurriedly tucked in a section of her blouse that had worked loose. After she flashed a brief smile to Helge, she held up her hand to knock on the door. It suddenly swung open revealing a no-nonsense Mrs. Lind whose steely look took in both women with a glance. She pursed her lips like she'd just tasted something bitter. The lack of welcome wasn't expected, yet it wasn't unexpected.

"Miss Bowden. How are du?"

"Fine, Mrs. Lind. And you? How are you today?"

"I'm fine, takk." Despite her cheery red vest over a voluminous white blouse with gold buttons, the older woman took serious stock of the situation before her. Her thin hands automatically reached for the depth of pockets in her long, black skirt. "What can I do for du?"

Phyllis ran nervous fingers through her curly hair, then dropped her hand, willing herself to be calm. It wasn't that important...oh, but it really was.

"You received the rent money I slipped under your door last night?'

"Ja, ja. Tusen takk."

"Good." She cleared her throat. "Well." Her hand moved towards Helge.

"I want you to meet Helge Hansen. She's going to be my assistant for a little while. My footlocker and steamer trunk finally arrived from London."

Mrs. Lind's watery eyes narrowed. "Just now? Why, you've been here a few months."

"Yes, I know." Phyllis' roaming hand began to stray towards her hair again, but she caught it in time. "They were lost in transit and found, but were broken into. I will need to inventory my belongings and make a report on the stolen items. I had the luggage brought here last night when you were out."

The old woman's eyes slid to Helge. "So dis woman..."

"...Will be helping me with that chore. It'll take a few days and I'm overwhelmed with work at the embassy, so I've asked Miss Hansen here to assist me at home. Will that be all right with you?"

"It's just for a few days?"

"Yes, ma'am."

"During the day?"

"That's right."

Phyllis did her utmost to look confident and steady.

Mrs. Lind's gaze never wavered as she scrutinized poor Helge.

"And one more thing."

Her stare strayed back to Phyllis. "Yes?"

"She will have her sister with her, a little girl five years old. She can't leave her alone during the day."

"The girl's mother can't take care of her?"

"No, ma'am. It's impossible."

Phyllis' mouth had dried up with each little white lie

until it was drier than the toast she had for breakfast without jam. It wasn't a total basket of lies—

Helge *did* have a sister. She just wasn't Lisbet. Also, it wasn't a lie that her mother couldn't take care of the little girl. She really couldn't, if she was even still alive.

Finally, Mrs. Lind's mouth formed what Phyllis guessed was a smile. It wasn't a frown, her teeth were partially showing and she wasn't snarling. Good enough.

"Dat should be fine. There'll be no extra noise, correct? I don't want others disturbed."

Both Phyllis and Helge shook their heads.

"No, ma'am," said Helge. "We will be quiet as the fjord in summer."

Mrs. Lind did smile at that. "Flink...er, good. Takk, Miss Hansen, Miss Bowden." She looked at Phyllis. "Anything else?"

"No, Mrs. Lind. That's it. Thank you and have a good day."

She nodded and closed the door behind her. Phyllis' shoulders relaxed as she hurried toward the staircase. "Let's beat a hasty retreat before she changes her mind."

TWENTY-FIVE

Captain Mark Stevens was a graduate of the US Army Chaplain School that had been created in World War I for service overseas. Chaplains were required to have a four-year college degree and three years of seminary education with the military desiring an additional year of pastoral ministry. Stevens had volunteered for active duty after the attack by the Japanese had forced the United States into the war. He was eager to be of service and had been embedded with troops in several battles including the Allied invasion of Normandy. Not only had he been awarded the Distinguished Service Cross for his wartime efforts, but Chaplain Stevens had also been wounded in action twice.

A chaplain's job in war was never-ending. Besides providing religious services, praying with the living, attending the wounded and assisting medical personnel, chaplains sometimes took the additional responsibility of helping to identify and bury the dead, even digging graves. It was not an easy task to serve God and country, but one swore to do to the very best job they could.

Mark Stevens was one of the best, Phyllis learned through recommendations and the Army grapevine. After the wars in Europe and the Pacific had ended, Stevens had asked for a transfer to Oslo to continue his service helping the pastors of the Church of Norway with their incredible chore of tending to the Norwegian people who had suffered greatly during the five-year German occupation. The core of pastors had been decimated when a majority had helped with the resistance and German authorities had shipped many to labor or concentration camps for their patriotic efforts. Some had died, but those surviving were making their way back to the country and into Norwegian service once again.

Stevens had worked with Norwegian pastors since the previous summer and that's where Phyllis found him one afternoon. He and others were rebuilding a church just outside of town with community help.

"Chaplain Stevens?"

She saw several men sawing boards while others nailed them to a newly framed structure. Women and several children swept the building continuously of dirt and burnt debris. A large man on the roof nailing down shingles looked her way.

"Up here!"

Phyllis twisted her head in his direction shielding her eyes from the bright sun. "Could I have a word with you please?" she shouted up to him.

"Be right down." The man put down his hammer and disappeared over the backside of the church. She caught movement again when she watched him climb a few steps down a ladder. He disappeared again before coming round a corner. Walking towards her, he looked sturdy and rugged from working in the outdoors. With his ruddy complexion, messy brown hair and heavy plaid shirt, Stevens could have been a logger or lumberjack. In ten long strides, he had his hand stretched out to her.

"Captain Mark Stevens."

"Phyllis Bowden."

He tilted his head. "You English?"

She shook her head. "American. I work for Lt. Col. Ronald Lawrence, Military Attaché at the American Embassy."

"Whew." He dragged the cap off his head. "That's a mouthful. What do you need with an Army chaplain?"

"Is there some place we can talk privately, Captain?"

He glanced around, pointed off to one side. "There's a picnic table over there. It's out of the wind and sheltered. We can talk there." Stevens looked back at the church and cupped a hand around his mouth to call out. "Lars? I'll be back in a few minutes." When the man nodded, Stevens motioned to her. "This way, miss."

"Thank you. So you're building a church?"

"Yes. Retreating Germans decided to burn it down on their way out of town, like they did with quite a bit of Oslo."

"Didn't the resistance blow up many buildings too?"

He nodded. "Oslo fared better than much of Norway, but it'll take years to put this country together again. Housing is one of the biggest shortages right now."

They reached the picnic table. From her vantage point, Phyllis guessed the small country church had been a beauty before its destruction. Nestled in tall pines against a backdrop of the bluest sky she'd ever seen, a thin layer of snow completed a Rockwellian picture of peace and harmony.

"Sit down, miss."

"Please call me Phyllis." She pointed towards the church. "What kind of trees are those?"

"The taller ones are Norway spruce. The lower are Balsam Fir, but I bet you didn't come here for a lesson in tree identification." He sat down across from her.

"What can I do for you, Phyllis?"

"You're right about that, Captain." But she didn't take her eyes off the tall trees and the unfinished building begging to be finished. The pastoral landscape was incomplete without the small—

"Phyllis?"

She looked at him then, shook her head slightly. "Sorry. I've got something important to ask you and I'm not sure where to begin."

"Maybe I can help," he offered kindly. "You work for Lt. Col. Lawrence? I've heard good things about him."

Phyllis smiled, felt less tense. "He's a wonderful man and good boss."

"Did he send you my way?"

"In a manner of speaking. He gave me an assignment and told me to find people who could help me. I heard you talk at the base church one Sunday and asked around about you. So I kinda sent myself."

Stevens sat straighter, brushed off tiny splinters of wood from his sleeve. "You're dancing around the subject, Phyllis. Tell me why you came to see me."

She tucked a swing of hair behind an ear and looked down at her heavy skirt. She really needed to go to Stockholm and buy new clothes.

Stevens cleared his throat, bringing her back to the subject, but not with any less discomfort.

She turned to him at last, folded her hands on the picnic table. It was chilly to the touch, not helping her to warm to the task.

"All right. Here it is. I need your help. Lt. Col. Lawrence has given me the task of finding and informing families in Norway of relatives lost to them in the war." She watched his quick intake of breath and hurried on. "He recently gave me a list of Norwegians verified to have perished in concentration camps or slave labor camps, and my assistant and I have been working on finding their families. People come in daily begging us for some word about lost relatives who have disappeared. It's been difficult, to say the least."

"I don't doubt that. What could I do to help you? You sought me out for a reason."

He was making her say it. Phyllis wet her lips and plowed into it.

"We've located five families living in Oslo whose relatives are on my list."

"How did they die?"

"Various concentration camps in eastern Europe and Germany."

"That's where. I asked you how."

She locked eyes with him. "The gas chambers."

"Were they mostly in Auschwitz?"

"No. The Germans burned those records when they fled. We have no evidence at this time of who perished in Auschwitz. We only know who survived the camp if they were transferred to a work site nearby. The Soviets seized those records and are making some available to the Allied countries, but only slowly."

He blew out a steady breath, dropped his cap on the table running a shaky hand through his hair. "Wow. You're sitting on dynamite."

"Exactly." She swallowed hard. "What I would like you to do, Captain, is to help me with notification. I have to tell each family personally the terrible news and to be honest, I don't have much experience in this area. It occurred to me that an Army chaplain would and your name came up when I started asking people around the base. You have a stellar reputation."

"Thank you. Would it be appropriate to ask a local pastor I know to come with us? He may or may not know the families, but he's Norwegian, which would be of great comfort, I'm sure. Besides, he knows the language better than I do."

"Thank you. Thank you so much, Captain Stevens," she gushed. Relief oozed out every pore.

"How do you want to proceed?"

She straightened and got down to business.

"I'd like to set up a meeting as soon as it's convenient with you and whoever you want to help to go over the list. We can assign certain families and decide the best way to approach them, what to say, what to do."

"They will probably need counseling to see them through the grieving process."

"Please. Yes, please help me with these kinds of details. I want to do the very best job I can to help out these poor families." She shivered. "I can't imagine having to go through what the Norwegians have these past years. Losing a loved one is as rough as it gets. Perhaps you and your colleague could work up a schedule to bring them in for counseling. I'll find a place on base, if you like."

"Maybe one of the churches in downtown Oslo would work better."

"Whatever you like. My office will strive to cooperate with local authorities to smooth any red tape that may crop up."

Mark Stevens lifted his dark cap, gazing at it thoughtfully. "You know why I like this cap so much?"

"Tell me."

"Guess."

Phyllis smiled. He was a nice man and would be easy to work with. "Because it fits your head?"

Stevens laughed heartily and slapped his knee. He adjusted the cap on his head.

"I think you and I are going to fit together just fine, Miss Phyllis. I'll contact a few people tonight and try to find a working phone to call you tomorrow."

She brought out a small notebook and pencil. "Here's my number at the embassy." After scribbling, she tore out the paper and handed it to him. "I'm there at eight every morning and usually don't leave until six."

He folded the paper to put it in a pocket. "Got it. You'll hear from me."

"Thank you. I feel better already." She rose to leave.

"And Phyllis?"

"Captain?"

His hand moved toward her. "You're doing a good thing for the people of Norway. You can be proud of yourself."

Phyllis blushed, shook his hand and stepped away.

"Aw shucks," she teased. "Now you have me all embarrassed."

They laughed and parted ways. The chaplain went back to working on the church and Phyllis caught a trolley to town. But the good feeling she rode back with sank like a rock when she saw who was waiting for her in the lobby of her apartment building talking to Mrs. Lind like they were old friends.

TWENTY-SIX

John Edelland.

She'd nearly forgotten about him. So much had happened in such a short period of time that she hadn't thought about him much at all. And she had a feeling he wouldn't like that.

The tall, well-dressed Norwegian turned to Phyllis and smiled broadly as she walked to them. When he took her hand in greeting, Mrs. Lind's smile turned into a frown.

"Good evening, Phyllis. How are you?" His large hand dwarfed her small one like a hand caught in an oven mitt.

"Hello, John. I'm fine, and you?"

"Good, good," he chuckled. "Just talking with your nice landlady here. Mrs. Lind has been captivating and so entertaining." Her weathered face blushed just a little and her smile came back.

"Du are kind, Mr. Edelland." Turning to Phyllis, she gave a quick nod. "I'll just be off. Good evening."

"Good evening, Mrs. Lind. Nice to see you." They watched the regal old woman slowly make her way to her apartment. When the door closely snugly behind her, John turned to Phyllis.

"I'd like to take you to dinner tonight. Do you have other plans?"

"Um, well..."

"Because I checked with Arne across the street and he's serving that dish you enjoy so much."

Her eyes narrowed ever so slightly causing little wrinkles between her brows. "What dish?"

"Farikal. You know, mutton stew."

"Yes, of course, but I..."

"And I have information for you."

"What kind of information?"

"About Joe Schneider, your fiancé."

Her eyes widened as she grabbed his arm. "You have news of Joe? Where is he? What's happened?"

John took her hand, led her quietly out of the building and across the street. People hurried by going every which way, rushing to home or work. Lights hanging from the mass of cables overhead had yet to come on for the evening.

"Come with me, Phyllis and I'll tell you everything I've learned. It may be uncomfortable for you so let me order you a cup of coffee."

Once in Arne's café, they settled on a small table towards the back. He helped with her coat and hat. Arne had taken their order and delivered the coffee before John signaled he was ready to talk. Phyllis ignored the coffee and watched him, expectantly biting her lip. His face gave nothing away.

"So you were checking up on me. Why is that?"

John stirred his coffee and brought it to his lips for a tentative sip. "That's better. The Brazil shipment must have been delivered." He turned to her. "I wasn't sure that this fiancé was even real." He shrugged. "I was curious."

She squirmed in her chair. "What do you know, John?"

"My sources tell me that Mr. Schneider was held by Romanian Communists in Bucharest for some time, weeks apparently." Phyllis sucked in a deep breath. "I'm not sure how long they held him. Apparently, the Romanians didn't take kindly to an MI5 agent snooping around for some reason." He locked gazes with her. "Do you know what he was after?"

Her mind blanked. "No. How in the world did you find out about his...status? That's not common knowledge."

"My sources are reliable."

"Who are your sources?"

"I'm afraid that's confidential, but I can tell you this. I have my fingers in many pies, as the American expression goes, and I meet people from different places. Sometimes I do favors for friends. Sometimes they do favors for me."

"So this was a favor someone did for you."

"Possibly. I can't say."

Her eyes narrowed to fine points. "You wouldn't be working for a foreign government, would you?"

"Other than Norway?"

She nodded.

"If I were," he smiled but the smile didn't extend to his eyes. "I wouldn't be talking to you about it."

Phyllis sat back in her chair as Arne delivered the steaming bowls.

"Here du go, Miss Phyllis. Eat hearty!" Arne's gray hair was frizzier than usual, but his smile was bright. When he left, John dug into his food. After a spoonful he obviously enjoyed, he glanced over at Phyllis.

"Not hungry?"

She pushed the bowl away. "You said Joe *was* held by Romanian Communists. He isn't any more?"

He swallowed another spoonful before shaking his head. "I'm sorry that I have no further information for you about Mr. Schneider." She rose, picked up her coat. "Wait a minute. I do have information about the little girl staying with you. Information you need to know."

Phyllis' mouth opened in complete surprise. She plopped back on her chair still holding her coat watching him warily as if he were an icicle about to break off a roof.

"I...I don't know what you mean."

John wiped his mouth with a napkin, signaled Arne.

"Do you need a refill? Oh, dear. You've not touched your coffee. Please stay and finish your dinner, Phyllis."

Arne brought over a small coffeepot to refill John's cup.

He angled his head quizzically at Phyllis' since it was still full. She shook her head at him and he retreated.

"What do you want, John?"

His smile was just shy of a smirk. "We've been good friends, Phyllis, and with our friendship in mind, I thought you should know about this."

"Know about what?"

"The Norwegian authorities are looking for a girl, about five years old, about this tall." He held his hand out a little taller than the table. "Apparently, her father was a German officer who was captured by the British. According to my sources, she has information her father gave her that the British want. The Soviets will want it too." He shrugged, dug his spoon back into the stew. "I thought you might want to know."

Stunned, Phyllis stared at him blankly. "How do you know any of this, John? What are you? Some kind of super spy?"

He laughed, ate another bite. After wiping his mouth, he pointed to her bowl with his spoon. "You really should try a bite. It's very good."

"Well," she bit her lip, avoided his look. "Thank you for the information, but the girl I know is with her sister."

John leveled icy Norwegian eyes on her. "We both know that's not true."

Trying to maintain an even composure, she rose to leave. When he put a hand on her arm, Phyllis looked down at the hand and back at him.

"I have no wish to trouble you, Phyllis. I like you very much, but I fear you're in over your head with both of these situations. You've been elusive, so I did a little checking because I value our friendship. But you need to be careful."

"Why?"

"Serious people are looking for this little girl. I didn't get the full story but this could blow up in your face and in the face of the Office of the Military Attaché. Promise me you'll be careful."

As she began to slip her arms in coat sleeves, John stood

to help her. With his hands on her collar, he looked at her directly. "I can help, Phyllis. Just let me know what you want me to do."

Nodding, she grabbed her hat and purse. "I'll be in touch." She scurried out of the restaurant needing to ask Lisbet more questions. Something didn't add up.

TWENTY-SEVEN

"People are looking for you. Did you know that?"

Phyllis stared at Lisbet's shuttered face willing it to open. She'd bid goodbye to Helge and took the girl's hand to situate them on the living room couch. The furniture's bright floral pattern did little to dispel her frustration. How could she get Lisbet to open up?

"Your father gave you something. Do you know what it is?"

She shook her head.

"Do you have anything at all from your mother's house?"

"It was blown up."

"Did you take anything with you when the men came and took you away?"

"We weren't allowed to take anything."

"You took nothing at all?"

"No, Miss Phyllis."

"Are you wearing the same clothing from your house?"

"No. We were given different clothes in jail."

Phyllis leaned back into the cushion, her mind spinning. Lisbet's small voice was becoming smaller, practically a whisper at the last declaration. Her downcast eyes flicked thick lashes on her pale face. A chill spread through Phyllis as she gently took Lisbet's icy hand.

"Sweetie, I know this must be hard, but I need to know some things about you. How about..." Phyllis waited until the girl opened her eyes. She could read the fear in them. "... Could you tell me about that last day with your mama and papa? Could you please, Lisbet? I'd really like to hear about that day."

Lisbet took hold of Phyllis' other hand. "Why, Miss Phyllis? That was a sad day."

"I know but try to remember what you can."

Lisbet sat up straighter, a determined look on her face. With a tiny nod, she tightened her grasp. "All right, it you want me to."

"I do, sweetie, I really do."

"Okay." But her eyes glazed staring through the room and out into the night. When she ducked her head and seemed to shrivel, Phyllis knew Lisbet was reliving that day.

"Papa had to go, but Mama and I didn't want him to."

"Was your mama crying?"

She nodded, tears filled her eyes. "I was crying too."

"Was your papa sad to go?"

"Yes, he said he would come back for us, but I don't think he will."

"Why not?"

"He's German and everyone hates Germans."

Phyllis softly kissed her hand. "Sweetie, it may be more complicated than that. He may not be able to come back for other reasons."

"What other reasons?"

He could be in prison for life. He could be dead. How could she say any of that?

"I'm sure if he could, he would. Let's leave it at that."

The girl's eyes darkened, probably unwilling to accept Phyllis' explanation.

"So please continue. What happened next?"

"Mama and I said goodbye to Papa and he said goodbye to us. Then he ran out the door." She flinched. "A loud sound happened and Mama said it was a bomb. Glass from the windows blew everywhere and I got cut in the leg. Not long after that, men came and took us away."

"Were they Norwegian policemen?"

"I don't know."

"Were they wearing uniforms?" When Lisbet looked at her blankly, Phyllis added. "With shiny medals like your papa's?"

"No, but they said we had to go with them. We never said anything to the men at all."

Phyllis pulled the little girl onto her lap. Lisbet snuggled in with Phyllis' arms wrapped around her. Sighing heavily with eyes closing, Lisbet whispered almost as an afterthought.

"Papa gave me my doll."

"What doll?"

"I had several dolls I loved and played with everyday. Sonja was my favorite and I slept with her every night."

"You had a favorite doll? What did she look like?"

"Sonja had braids and wore a green skirt with an apron. We used to go everywhere together and I miss her so much." Little Lisbet began to cry. Tears spilled onto Phyllis' arms.

"Don't cry, sweetie. I'll get you a new doll."

"You will?"

"Absolutely. It'll be all right."

Lisbet sniffled, wiped her nose with her sleeve. Sniffling sounds punctuated the quiet. Snow outside began falling like twinkling stars falling from the sky.

"Lisbet?"

"Hmm?"

"When did your papa give you Sonja?"

"Just before he left. We were saying goodbye and he ran into my room. When he came back, he had Sonja with him."

"Did she look any different than usual?"

"No." Lisbet wiggled out of Phyllis' embrace. "Why?"

Phyllis shrugged. "No reason. I just wonder what happened to her."

"I guess I dropped her when we had to leave."

Lisbet hopped to the floor, smoothed her bright green skirt and white blouse.

"Do you like your new clothes?"

A smile spread across the girl's face. "Very much. Where did you get them? Helge told me it was hard to find clothes in Norway."

"Clothing has come in from the United States by the ton." Phyllis rose from the couch and took Lisbet's hand. "Do you know where that is?"

She shook her head, swung Phyllis' hand in hers. "No. Is it far away?"

"Yes, it is." Phyllis smiled. "Hungry? Let's fix dinner."

TWENTY-EIGHT

Phyllis was falling for this little girl, but knew she couldn't keep her. She was in diplomacy and wading into international waters about adoption would be treacherous, especially after the war. But even if she couldn't keep Lisbet with her, Phyllis wanted to make sure she would be safe and that meant getting her out of the country and soon. How to do that was the question on the table.

The intercom buzzed startling her concentration. Phyllis and her assistant were working on gathering more information about the Norwegian families for her meeting after lunch with Chaplain Stevens. He was coming to the American Embassy with his friend, the Norwegian pastor, so they could plan how and when to conduct the family notifications. Her stomach had dripped acid for the past hour as she put finishing touches on what needed to be done.

Phyllis pressed her intercom button.

"Yes, sir?"

"Could you please come in here, Miss Bowden?"

"Right away." She turned to her assistant. "Be back soon, Nancy. Keep working on that last file and we should be ready for my afternoon meeting." Nancy, a petite brunette with red lips and a mass of curly hair, smiled and nodded.

"Got it, Miss Bowden."

She picked up her pad and pencil before entering Ronnie's office. He was seeing someone out another door, shaking the man's hand and smiling broadly. His smile didn't dim when he closed the door and headed back to his desk.

"Phyllis! Haven't had a chance to talk to you much today. How's it going with your new staffer?"

"Very well, sir. Nancy is an experienced researcher and has been instrumental in finding our first families to notify about their deceased relatives."

"Good, good. I thought she'd work out well for you."

"She has, thank you."

She watched Lt. Col. Lawrence as he pawed through various papers on his busy desk. Pressed uniform, smartly knotted tie on a freshly laundered shirt—Lawrence was the epitome of the model military officer. His closely cropped dark hair was combed neatly to one side and his focused face broke into a grin when he suddenly found what he was looking for. He held up a small piece of paper.

"Guess what I have?"

She refrained from rolling her eyes. It wouldn't look professional even though the situation called for it.

"Colonel, I'm not good at guessing games. Why don't you just tell me?"

His face drooped to a pout. She nearly laughed at his hangdog expression.

"All right. Is it killer diller?"

Lawrence's pout upended with a hearty laugh. "Now we're cooking with gas." He held out the paper to her.

"What is it?"

"This, my dear Miss Bowden, is the name and address of a family in Sweden who have volunteered to take Lisbet."

She looked at the name and blinked surprised eyes at him.

"No fooling?"

He shook his head. "No fooling."

"How...why...um..."

"What you're probably trying to say is how did I find this family?"

"Yes, sir."

"Well, it came about like this. I sent my wife over to Stockholm to buy a new coat, like you did a few weekends back, and while she was there, I asked her to stop in at the American Embassy there."

"Why, Colonel?"

"I'd been advised, discreetly of course, that the embassy might know of a few families who would be willing to take in unfortunate Norwegian children."

"So she did a little spying for you, sir."

His shoulders moved up and down. "Not in so many words, but she was on a mission, that's true."

"And?"

"She ended up meeting with the representatives of two families and liked this family in particular." He clasped his hands on his desk. "They've already adopted a girl from Norway and they wanted to take in another little Norwegian girl. My wife actually met the people, went to their lovely home and looked over their credentials. The man is a glass-blower in Stockholm and his wife tends the house and helps him occasionally. She liked them and trust me when I say my wife is picky when it comes to who babysits our daughters. She's like the secret police."

"Nice." Phyllis grinned. "I knew I liked your wife for a reason."

"Thank you."

She didn't move. She stared at the paper in her hands turning it over and over.

"Phyllis?"

"Sir?"

"I know this is going to be hard for you."

"What is?"

He angled his head toward the paper. "Letting Lisbet go. I think she means more to you than you're saying."

Phyllis blew out a breath. "Possibly, but I know this is the best thing for her."

"And for you."

"Why is that, sir?"

"Phyllis." Lawrence rose, walked around his desk. "She needs to stay in Scandinavia. This is her home and maybe her parents will turn up."

Phyllis' eyes filled. She shook her head and rose. "I'll begin planning the trip immediately."

"Wait a minute." Phyllis looked at him, the paper clutched between them. "You'll need a passport and identification papers for Lisbet."

The paper fluttered in her hand. "A passport?"

"Well, yes. Sweden's another country."

"My diplomatic credentials won't get her in?"

"You, yes. Lisbet, no."

"Huh, what can I..."

He was shaking his head. "Let me work on this one, Phyllis. Don't go off on some half-cocked mission with Jay."

She blinked at him. "Whatever are you talking about, Colonel?"

"You know very well what I'm talking about." His lips flattened. "Don't do anything stupid. Let me chew on this for a while."

Phyllis contemplated him and his words. "All right. Is that all? I'm preparing for my meeting with Chaplain Stevens."

"Sure, sure." He waved a hand, walked back to his chair. "Fill me in on the particulars after you've seen Stevens. And Phyllis?"

"Sir?"

"The clothing distribution project?"

"Nancy and I rented a small warehouse downtown and got volunteers to sort and label. The mayor's staff has offered to conduct distribution drives for us since they know the town and surrounding areas better."

"Is that Gerhardsen?"

"Yes. His office staff has been most helpful."

"Very good." He shuffled more papers on his desk. "Carry on."

She called Jay once she was back at her desk to meet for lunch at the PX. Papers and passports would be the topic as she watched Nancy work at her side desk. And it might get sticky.

"I WANT to go out for a walk."

"I'm not sure that's such a good idea, Lisbet."

"But Helge, look outside! It's a beautiful day and we've been stuck inside for a week now. Please?" Lisbet threaded her hands together like she was praying and Helge felt trapped. She knew she shouldn't, but it *was* a lovely day. What would it hurt?

She relented, but not without reservations.

"All right, but you can't run away from me. You have to hold my hand the entire time."

As a precaution, she bundled Lisbet in a heavy coat and hid her curls under a snug cap. After wrapping a colorful scarf around the girl's neck, she checked her work, deciding that Lisbet wasn't recognizable from any other small Norwegian girl going for a walk with her big sister.

They started off from the apartment building, passed Arne's café and headed towards a recently opened toy store just down the block. Lisbet swung Helge's hand skipping down the sidewalk. The sky turned slightly overcast with a light snow falling, but people weren't particularly upset or bothered by the changing weather. They seemed to be enjoying the day, rushing to make the trolley or strolling along contentedly. A man stood on the corner playing a long wooden trumpet about six feet long and attracting quite a crowd. He was dressed in traditional clothes, black jacket and pants with a red and green vest with many buttons. The series of notes he played produced a charming melody. People listening seemed delighted. Helge steered Lisbet over to listen.

"So you see, Lisbet, the instrument is very traditional for farmers, in particular, and was used in the old days to call grazing livestock or to send messages between farms."

A glance above the little girl's head had Helge looking at a man who was staring at Lisbet with more than token interest. There was something that made him stand out from others in the crowd causing the faces of people around him to blur. Goose bumps broke out on Helge's arms. His attention didn't waver as his eyes roamed Lisbet's pert face. He wore a woolen suit with a dark topcoat and his bulbous nose was red from the cold. When his eyes snapped to meet Helge's stare, fear crept down her spine like pricks of a pin.

It was time to leave. Gripping Lisbet's hand a little tighter, she began moving nonchalantly away from the man. They shouldn't have left the apartment, but it was too late now.

"Ah, do we hafta leave?"

"Yes, we do. Don't fight me on this, Lisbet."

Helge pulled a mildly protesting Lisbet deeper into the crowd around the musician loudly playing the wooden instrument. With each note, their steps took them away from the stranger until Helge turned slightly to see where he was. The man was pawing his way through the crowd after them, so Helge picked up Lisbet and ducked into a nearby restaurant. Luckily it was busy today and people were everywhere. Hurrying through the dining area, Helge briefly stopped to talk to a waiter.

"Mister, er det en bakdor?" The young man pointed towards the back.

"Where are we going? Why are we running?" asked Lisbet.

Without bothering to reply, Helge shifted a confused Lisbet and ran out the back door. Seeing the intense look on Helge's face, the little girl no longer asked any questions. The young woman stopped suddenly, checked up and down the alley behind the restaurant before adjusting the scarf around Lisbet's face. Then she didn't stop moving until they were back at the apartment building. Helge pushed Lisbet in the door and glanced back to see if the man had followed them. He was standing up the block looking around as if he didn't see which way they went. She stepped out of sight watching until the man sauntered away. Only then did Helge exhale a deep breath and relax a little. She hurried Lisbet up the stairs to Phyllis' apartment. Four flights up the old marble staircase didn't take much time at all.

"What was that about?" asked Lisbet in a small voice once they were safely inside the apartment.

Helge shook her head and helped the little girl out of her coat. "Not to worry, sotnos. I should have been more careful with you. Miss Phyllis will not be pleased."

Moisture collected in Lisbet's eyes. "I don't want to upset Miss Phyllis. Don't tell her."

"I have to," replied Helge with a heavy heart. "She needs to know that danger is closing in."

"Oh."

Lisbet didn't understand. It was enough to know that she had Helge and Phyllis looking after her. Lisbet lovingly cradled the new doll Phyllis had given her and headed back to her room. The world was confusing for a little girl who didn't know her place in it.

TWENTY-NINE

Joe had been awake for some time when the vehicle abruptly stopped moving. Although the cloth over his head still kept him blind, his senses were on full alert and he was afraid. For the first time, he was terrified actually that this would be the end of the road for him.

A picture of a pretty woman with dark, curly hair flashed in his mind. Phyllis.

Would he ever see her again?

Suddenly, a wave of regret hit him hard. Why hadn't he married her in Oslo? Why hadn't he stayed in Norway? Searching all the training techniques he'd learned in his years with MI5, Joe couldn't come up with one single idea to help get him out of his current dilemma. Not only was he utterly dependent on the goodwill of his captors, he suspected they didn't have any. Neither the Soviets nor the Romanians had shown him the slightest courtesy, even though they had been on the same side in the war. He hadn't told them what they wanted to know, but then he didn't have any information to tell them.

Joe knew they were all searching for the same target—a little girl. Finding her had been his only goal and the mission had gone south faster than he could say "Holy smoke". Feeling lower than he had in years, Joe had to ask himself why was he doing this. The best thing that had happened to him was meeting Phyllis. Wouldn't he rather be happy with her than lying face down in the cold worrying about his survival?

That realization was the hard truth he hadn't been wanting to face. If he survived this ordeal, he was going to leave the service. If Phyllis was still alive, he was going to throw himself at her feet and beg her to marry him. Even if she wanted to stay in Norway, he could handle that. Hell, he'd welcome it after this joyride.

Yeah, weeks in captivity had narrowed his world and honed his survival instincts to a fine point. He knew exactly what was most important in his life and feeling sorry for himself wasn't going to help in the slightest. But right this minute? It was all he had.

Every nerve ending in his body ignited when a door opened and a blast of cold air blew over him.

He smelled smoke and a rough voice close to him said, "Let's get this over with."

THIRTY

"Is this it? Sure it's not the next house down?"

Chaplain Mark Stevens consulted his notebook. Phyllis nodded at him and Erik, the Norwegian pastor who had joined them for this very first notification.

"Yes, I'm certain this is the right house."

Many rows of houses in Oslo looked the same. Bombs or fire had destroyed some while others looked normal. It was a strange reality like a half-completed housing development about which the builder had changed his mind. Pieces of furniture lay strewn about. A dresser here, a vanity with a large oval mirror rested over there. Men and women carried chairs, books, clothes and bedding in various directions, while others swept and cleaned burnt debris the best they could. Smoke no longer enveloped the scene, but a dusty, acrid smell was still pervasive. Not the eye-stinging smoke that had poured out of the houses initially, but the kind that invaded the structure gifting all with a smoky smell that lingered, sometimes forever. Certainly in the mind, if not the nose.

Mark, Phyllis and Erik had stopped in front of a house that was partially blown away. A third of the roofline was gone and tarps hung over the part of the house that was missing. Snow had fallen the night before coating the structure with a layer of pristine white and causing Phyllis to wonder how anyone could bear to stay in the drafty house that was barely standing. Then again, home was home. No matter how it looked or what the problem. The three exchanged looks they read to mean "Steady now" and stepped forward to the front door. Stevens knocked loudly.

It was several minutes before an elderly woman opened the door. Phyllis wondered what kind of favor they were doing for her by paying this kind of visit. Was notifying next of kin that she had lost something else in the war really of benefit? Phyllis swallowed hard, although what she was trying to choke down just wouldn't go. She had a feeling it never would and it was too late to back out now.

"Mrs. Kruken?"

"Ja."

"I'M Chaplain Mark Stevens and I have some information for you about your son, Toril. May we come in?"

She looked blankly at the three strangers on her doorstep. Her brows furrowed deeply with her shoulders visibly tightening. Phyllis could see she didn't understand, but was growing anxious.

Mark looked to Erik who stepped forward with a serious expression and his cap twisting in his hands.

"Mrs. Kruken, god dag. Hyggellg a treffe dem Erik Lagje. Far jeg presentere Chaplain Mark Stevens og Phyllis Bowden. Kan jeg komme inn?"

The woman's eyes darted nervously between the three people watching her, but she nodded once and opened the door wide enough to allow them entrance.

The inside of the house was nearly as bad as the outside. One whole section was covered with anything she had available—tarps, sheets, clothing—and the cold had settled in permanently. Phyllis shivered through her warm Swedish coat. She watched the woman gather her composure for what she had probably figured out by now wasn't going to be a social visit. Her long coat had many patches and the collar had disappeared. The woman's neck was red where she was exposed to the cold temperature and her hands looked icy. Phyllis had the impulse to tear off her gloves and hand them over. She bit her lip instead.

The elderly woman waved them to wooden chairs in a large open area just off the kitchen and limped to another chair. She dragged one foot like it was either broken or sprained. Phyllis could see bruises where her socks should have been. When everyone was seated, she smiled.

"Jeg har ingen kaffe. Beklager." She cast her eyes towards the threadbare carpet and then towards Erik.

"Det er greit," he replied with a thin smile.

"What did she say?" asked Mark.

"She's sorry, but she has no coffee to offer us."

Mark and Phyllis' pained smiles were small and gone.

"Go ahead, Erik. Tell her why we're here."

For the next few minutes, Phyllis watched the myriad of expressions sweep over the thin woman's face. At first, Mrs. Kruken smiled pleasantly at each of them, but her smile began to fade with each new word from the Norwegian pastor. Erik spoke slowly and softly, so she leaned forward to catch his words as they fell from his lips. Like she was reaching for understanding, but not quite attaining it. The fading smile dissolved into tears and sobs as the full weight of his message became crystal clear. Her son, Kristoffer Kruken had died in a labor camp in Germany. Phyllis knew the story: he was a teacher, a dissident that Vidkun Quisling had exported for refusing to follow the Nazi indoctrination program at his school. Quisling couldn't control the education system and after fourteen thousand teachers quit, he sent more than seven hundred to slave labor camps to teach them a lesson. Many died. Some came back with failing health from doing severe manual labor. Kristoffer was one of the unfortunate ones.

So Mark, Erik and Phyllis sat still watching the poor woman's life be turned upside down once again. It apparently wasn't enough to have a destroyed home and no money to fix it. It wasn't enough to be barely surviving after the horrendous five-year German occupation. It wasn't enough to have little food or decent clothing.

No, it wasn't enough.

Her son wouldn't be returning. Phyllis watched in dismay as the light went out of the elderly woman's eyes. She couldn't have felt more miserable and desired to be anywhere else on the planet at that moment. Maybe Ronnie had picked her for a reason for this mission, but she was going to have to ask him just what that reason was. She'd never experienced the kind of loss this woman was facing... and alone. When she murmured something to Eric, he had difficulty maintaining his benevolent composure. He translated to Mark and Phyllis that the woman's husband died in the resistance and her daughter was killed when the house was bombed.

Phyllis couldn't help it; she cried along with the grieving woman until Mark helped her up and out of the house. Erik made arrangements for the woman to come to his church for grief sessions and Mark made a notation in his notebook. Once they were walking down the sidewalk, Phyllis fished out a hanky and blew her nose.

"What did you write in your notebook?"

"I'm going to get some men over here to help with her house."

"I can get this side of town more food too," added Erik. "These people haven't had much help since the Germans left and they're starving."

"My clothing distribution project should come to this side of town too. I'll check with the mayor's office." Phyllis patted her cheeks and gulped. "I'm sorry I wasn't much help in there."

"That's all right," said Erik. "I told her you were from the American Embassy and were the one who found out what happened to her son."

"That's what her hug at the end was about."

"Yes. It's devastating news, but at least she knows."

Phyllis looked at Mark, clutched her hanky tighter. "This

was the first notification on my list. I'm not sure I have the courage to do four more."

"Maybe you don't have to do any more," said Mark gently. He glanced over at a nearby park. "You go on ahead, Erik. I'll talk to you later. Let me talk to Miss Bowden alone for a bit."

"Sure." Erik nodded at Phyllis, then headed towards his church in downtown Oslo. His severe, dark clothes contrasted with the fine sprinkling of snow on the sidewalks and streets. But his scraggly beard and soft expression lent an amiable air and Phyllis was glad Mark had brought him. Not only did he know the language, but he knew the Norwegian people better than did she or Chaplain Stevens. She didn't know how he could do this at all, much less the five times required of her assignment.

"I'm all right now, Captain."

He touched her elbow escorting her to a park bench. "Maybe so, but let's go over here. I think you need a couple of minutes." He dusted snow off the bench.

She sat where he pointed, sucked in a ragged breath. "Maybe you're right. Thank you."

"You're welcome." When he was seated beside her, they remained quiet. Phyllis struggled with her composure while Stevens watched people strolling through the park or digging vainly in the gardens.

"You okay now?"

"I'm fine."

"You're a tough gal from what I've picked up about you, but do you really want to bow out of the rest of your assignment?"

Phyllis pulled her gloves tighter, glad she had some protection against the cold, against the adversity around her. She straightened her shoulders to look Stevens in the eye.

"No."

He cocked an eyebrow. "You sure? You fell apart in there. I can understand empathy, but maybe you're not cut out for this."

Her eyes flashed. "I *know* I'm not cut out for this type of assignment, Captain, but this task fell to me by my superior officer and I refuse to let him down."

"Okay, okay." A small smile crept out. "You're tougher than I thought."

"Lots of people make that mistake."

"I won't again."

Snow began to fall lightly, on their hats, on their laps and on the ground around them. An ancient trolley lumbered along the street like an old warrior remembering what he was trained to do.

"There's more to this than meets the eye."

"What do you mean?"

"What's behind the tears, Miss Bowden?"

"...Nothing much. I'm just tired." She glanced away, watched the rickety trolley stop to unload passengers. "It's been a rough couple of months in Oslo, even though I've gotten away to Sweden to buy clothes a few times."

"That's all that's upsetting you? Just notifying this woman? We've talked it through what happened to these families and their lost relatives. You've never shown this depth of emotion before. I can't help but think something else is eating at you."

She sighed. "You're not going to let up on me, are you? I bet you're one of those chaplains who makes a real nuisance of himself until the person opens up and tells all, whether he or she want to or not."

"Well, save me the trouble and just tell me, so I don't have to whip out my standard lines to break you down."

She smiled, looked over at him. "I bet you're a really nice guy."

"I have been accused of being nice. It's not something I advertise."

It was several minutes before she spoke again. When she did, Phyllis spoke as factually and calmly as possible. No teary eyes or hesitant language.

Joe.

Lisbet.

Heartache after heartache.

Captain Stevens listened intently until Phyllis finally ran out of words and breath. She didn't slump, but her posture sagged with the effort it took to bear her soul. He could hear the tears in her tone, although she tried to deflect them and sound as strong as she could. It was only natural to want the listener to think well of the person speaking and that the situations she was describing were spot-on accurate. Generally, Stevens had to bestow benevolent language to soothe the ragged souls he heard day in, day out, but it wasn't the case with Phyllis Bowden. She was extraordinary in her delivery, not trying to have him feel sorry for her or what had happened since she came to Oslo. He wasn't to think he had to solve any problems for her.

She just laid out the troubles with her fiancé, Joe Schneider, and wondering what to do with little Lisbet. Mark admired her greatly for the way she was able to handle herself under stress. Stress of long duration. It was a commanding performance from a clear-thinking woman. He had watched her fall apart and then she pulled herself together in a matter of minutes. Impressive.

The park bench was growing colder and the falling snow encouraged them to move.

"Let's walk, Miss Bowden."

She smiled and brushed the snow off her coat. "Only if you call me Phyllis."

"Sure and you call me Mark."

"I can do that."

Time passed slowly as they meandered through the park, watching busy Norwegians plucking what was left of their meager gardens. There was virtually nothing left, it had been picked over weeks ago, but desperate times called for desperate measures. Stevens knew food had been coming in from Sweden and Denmark, as well as the United States, but distribution wasn't always timely. Many Norwegians were still hungry.

"I'm truly sorry about your young man—Joe, is it? He sounds like a great chap and I hope you find him soon."

"Thanks, Mark. I hope so too."

"Are you taking the trolley back to the embassy?"

"Yes."

"Let me walk you over there."

"Thanks for coming today. You and Erik made all the difference and I know our other notifications will go smoothly, thanks to you two."

"You're positive you want to sit in on a couple more?"

Her eyes were defiant. "I am."

"Good. Just let me know when you're ready with the next one."

"I will. Let's get this group done quickly because I have a feeling there's more coming soon."

"All right. If there's many more, maybe we should call in another local pastor I know."

"Fine."

Mark and Phyllis watched the clunky trolley chug its way along the street. It would stop every once in a while to let passengers off and collect more. The conductor with his colorful jacket and red cap smiled at one and all, happy to be at work again. When the trolley was puffing its way towards them, Mark turned to Phyllis.

"I'm not sure what the best thing is for you to do with your little Norwegian girl, but I have information that may be relevant. What you do with it is your business, of course."

"What information?"

"You mentioned Lisbet's mother was taken to a labor camp. There's a woman's labor camp just outside of Oslo on Hovedoya Island. I've been there to hold services and pray with them."

"Hovedoya?"

"Yes, you may want to check it out. I don't know if her mother is there, but it could be a place to look, if that's what you want to do."

Phyllis' brows furrowed. "Even if I find her mother, what would I say to her? That I have her child? Wouldn't that just make her more miserable than she probably already is? I can't imagine anyone is going easy on her. Remember she was with a German officer and had a child with him."

"I understand that, but perhaps the mother could give you a message for Lisbet or help you in some way. I don't know what it would accomplish, but I also know the authorities are planning to release most of the women in coming months or deport them. The Norwegian government realizes they have no real reason to hold the women, since they've committed no crime."

"Maybe Lisbet's mother will be coming home."

He shook his head. "I wouldn't count on it. There's such bad feeling about Norwegian women who had anything to do with the Germans. She'd be better off being deported." He shook his head again, wearily this time. "Besides, some of the women I visited weren't in great shape health-wise. I tried to get them more medical aid."

"No allowance for falling in love?"

"Absolutely not. That would normalize the relationship with Germany in a way that would be completely unacceptable."

"So the women are corrupt."

"And immoral." Mark gazed off in the distance watching the trolley closing the distance between them. "Because she had a child with a German officer, maybe they were even married, her life in Norway wouldn't be worth living. That would be the reason to deport a Norwegian." He took a small breath before continuing. His words were heavy.

"Norway is going through another terrible time. Before it was due to the German occupation and war. Now it's because of those who collaborated with the Germans while they were here. Authorities are pointing fingers and blaming many for things perhaps some of us in the rest of the world would overlook. I'm hoping it blows over soon. A purge is never pretty."

The trolley stopped a few yards away amidst clanks and squeaks from worn brakes. Men and women stepped off as others climbed on.

"You think I should visit the prison and see if her mother is there?" Phyllis climbed aboard the trolley clutching the sides of the open doorway.

Mark shrugged, shook his head wearily. "I won't tell you what to do. I'm giving you information. What you do with it is up to you."

She smiled. "You really are a nice man, Captain Stevens. I'll talk to you soon."

THIRTY-ONE

Hovedoya Island was getting closer and closer. The deep blue water sloshed gently against the boat carrying Phyllis closer to her destination. Chilly air smelled faintly of fish and a variety of birds followed closely behind, perhaps hoping for a handout. She never got seasick, but this mission was making her sick at heart.

She hadn't mentioned where she was going today to Lisbet over breakfast. Helge came early, knowing Phyllis' schedule, and had coffee with them bright and early. Helge had been teaching Lisbet how to read and write in English, so Lisbet was eager to get the day started. That worked well for Phyllis, since she'd gotten the day off for what she had to do. The bright smile on the little girl's heart-shaped face made Phyllis uneasy, like a betrayal of the trust Lisbet had placed in her.

Lt. Col. Lawrence hadn't been pleased either. Their conversation came back to her as she looked out over the placid water. She tightened her scarf against the day's cold.

"Why in the world do you want to go to Hovedoya Island, Phyllis? Are you nuts? There's hundreds of women stuck out there supposedly for their protection from the purge." He'd glanced down at the papers on his desk. "Some of the guys picking on these women should ask themselves why they weren't in the resistance. And you know this office has no authority whatsoever for you being out there." When she just stared at him, his eyes narrowed as he figured it out.

"You found Lisbet's mother, didn't you?"

"Sir, I..."

"Miss Bowden, let me make this plain: The Office of the Military Attaché has no jurisdiction over Norwegian laws. In effect, we are guests here."

"Those women haven't broken any laws, Colonel."

"Legally, no, but the authorities are keeping them there partly for their own protection and partly because they have sexually transmitted diseases." He shook his head. "Yes, I realize it sounds lame and probably no more have health issues than in the general population, but fraternization with Germans is a big deal here."

Phyllis had cleared her throat, stood still facing him by his desk. "The answer to your question is no. I have no idea if her mother is there or not, but I have to make the effort."

"Why?"

"I'm planning to take Lisbet to be adopted by a Swedish family. What if the mother is still alive and wants her back?"

"Phyllis." Ronnie's eyes softened and he sighed. "Even if she is, there's no place in Norway that would accept either of them. Going to Sweden is a fresh start for Lisbet. Maybe she can grow up relatively normal somewhere else."

"What about the mother, sir?"

He shook his head. "Remember when I asked you not to get involved in Norway's problems? Well, that, my fine Miss Bowden, is all you've done since your arrival.'

"Not professional of me?"

"...But very human and one of the reasons I give you difficult tasks to accomplish." His eyes shone. "Because I know you have a big heart and can accomplish most anything you set out to do."

"I'm still going to look for her mother."

"Of course you are and I'll cover you if there's any

residual trouble from the Norwegian authorities. Just tread lightly, all right?"

Phyllis' smile was immediate. "Thank you, Colonel. I'll keep you posted."

He sighed heavily, picked up a sheaf of papers. "I know you will. Have a good day."

She'd managed to wheedle a letter of introduction from Lt. Col. Lawrence for the psychologist in charge of the internment camp. When the boat docked, a courier transported her to what she supposed was the head office. They drove through a kind of wilderness area with enormous trees and other growth for some time before arriving at a large brick building standing behind tall barbed wire fencing. Large lights resembling searchlights were posted at the top of poles. She saw what looked like barracks off to the side. Even though the windows were unbarred and cell doors were open with curious women coming out to stare at her, the whole place still looked like a prison. Phyllis stifled her disapproval and reached out with a gloved hand to open the main door. A short man in a dark suit speaking softly to a young woman who was crying looked over as Phyllis walked in the door. He seemed genuinely sincere when he patted the woman on the shoulder ushering her out another door. When it had closed tightly, the man tugged at his jacket, smoothed his thinning hair and marched over to where Phyllis was standing. A wan smile plastered on his face, he held out a hand.

"Adolf Hals. How may I help you?"

She clasped his hand. "Phyllis Bowden. I'm from the Office of the Military Attaché at the American Embassy in Oslo. I have a letter of introduction from the Military Attaché, Lt. Col. Ronald Lawrence."

"Oh, my." His upper lip began to moisten. "So this is an official visit?"

"No, sir." She glanced around the room. Two women, obviously in distress, were speaking to another woman in sturdy shoes and a no-nonsense frock scribbling in a notebook as they spoke. "Is there another place we could talk? Perhaps a bit more private?"

"Certainly. My office is this way." He waved a hand towards another room. She followed him down a dingy hallway with poor lighting and pictures of the king of Norway on every wall. King Haakon looked smart in his military uniform. Once they were seated in a cramped little room with books piled everywhere and looking awkwardly at one another, he began.

"What brings you all the way out to the island today, Miss Bowden? It can't be a social visit because very few want to visit our detainees."

"I'm looking for a woman who may have been sent here. Her name is Janne Garnes. Do you have her here?"

"Janne Garnes. Garnes. I think I remember a name like that."

"You don't know for sure?"

"Miss Bowden, there are eleven hundred women at this facility, so I don't remember every name, but let me find my list." He slipped wire-framed glasses on his nose as he reached for a folder on an old desk that looked ready for the scrap pile. Opening the folder, Hals moved his finger down several rows before stopping. "Aha! Here it is." He glanced back at her. "We *do* have a Janne Garnes living here."

"May I see her?"

Hals closed the folder, took off his glasses. Tossing them on his desk, he looked at her curiously.

"Why?"

"It's personal."

The man smiled slightly, shook his head. "No. No, I'm sorry, but anything that goes on in this camp happens with my full knowledge and permission."

"You're a psychologist, aren't you? Not a warden."

"It's a matter of semantics possibly. Yes, I'm a psychologist and I see the women for psychological problems, but I have warden-like duties, and one of them is knowing why an American would want to talk to a disgraced Norwegian woman."

"Has she committed a crime?"

"Well, legally, no, but..."

"And she could walk out of here if she chose to, correct?"

"Again, legally, yes, but..."

"Legally is good enough for me, Mr. Hals." Phyllis locked eyes with him. "I'm here to see Janne Garnes. I have information about her daughter."

"We don't want Miss Garnes upset by anything you might say to her."

She nearly chuckled. "You don't think being stuck here in this..." Phyllis glanced around the office, "...prison because of her relationship with a German officer and being torn away from her daughter has been upsetting to Miss Garnes? If you think she's okay with all this, then you probably need to rethink your stance, sir. You're definitely mistaken."

Adolf Hals adjusted a button on his suit, picked up his glasses and set them back down. After tapping a finger on the desk a few times, he nodded once.

"Would you mind if one of my matrons sits outside while you speak to Janne?"

"Not at all."

When Phyllis rose, Hals rose with her. "We're only trying to keep these women safe from marauding crowds and people who would wish harm to them. You know that, don't you, Miss Bowden?"

"Yes."

"These have been trying times for Norwegians. I hope you can appreciate that fact."

"I do, but I don't understand why Miss Garnes' child was taken away from her. I understand there are children here at the camp with their mothers."

He shook his head, walked around his desk to escort her from the office. "I have no control over what happened before these women came to me."

Phyllis made no reply as Hals handed her over to the older woman with sturdy shoes. He murmured something in the woman's ear. She nodded.

"Miss Bowden, it was nice to meet you. Please sign out before you leave."

"Thank you, Dr. Hals."

He went back into his office leaving the woman staring at Phyllis like she had food smeared on her face.

"Where are we going?"

"To the barracks next door, miss. Follow me, please."

THIRTY-TWO

Sturdy Shoes walked briskly out the door of the large brick building and headed for several rows of barracks just outside. Hurrying to keep pace, Phyllis noticed a sign reading *Tysker-tosers* on the first building and wondered what it meant. Hals' matronly assistant had gone down the second row of barracks stopping so suddenly at an open door that Phyllis nearly bumped into the back of her.

"Oh, sorry."

The woman stuck her head in and looked around for a minute. Focusing in one direction, she called out, "Garnes! Come here."

Phyllis watched a roomful of women either lounging on their beds or walking around trying to look busy. One woman's head lifted in a group of several women in the center of the room. She looked at the matron and over to Phyllis uncomprehendingly. Encouraged by a friend, she rose, set down the skirt she was sewing and sauntered without conviction towards them. Hushed tones prevailed throughout the room as conversations halted to observe the new scene before them.

Janne Garnes was a tall Norwegian woman with shoulder length dark blonde hair and icy blue eyes. Wary eyes that measured Phyllis the closer she came. Her loose dress and sweater with patched sleeves might not have been the best, but she faced what was coming with courage. Phyllis could read it in her expression that she'd probably seen much worse.

She was lovely. Phyllis saw the woman Lisbet would be when she was an adult. The little girl looked so much like her mother that there was no doubt in her mind of the connection. One only needed eyes to see. Phyllis held her feelings in check as the matron motioned for Janne to grab a coat. They were going to talk outside away from eavesdropping ears. The woman motioned to a table with chairs a few yards away under a small tent. It had begun snowing again, so the tent would give them some protection from the cold. Phyllis sat down with the young woman she had come to see. With the matron seated away by the door and when Phyllis was assured of some privacy, she met Janne's stare.

"You look so young."

The woman's lips parted in mild surprise, but she recovered quickly. "You're American."

"I am, yes."

"All right. I can tell you I'm twenty-five. How old are you?"

Phyllis smiled. "That'll teach me to mind my own business, but Miss Garnes, I've never been very good at that."

"Who are you?"

"My name is Phyllis Bowden and I work for the American Embassy in Oslo."

"Why are you here?"

"You speak English very well. How did you learn the language?"

"My husband spoke English and he taught me."

"He taught your daughter well too."

This time Janne's mouth dropped open in utter shock. "You know...Lisbet?"

"I do."

Her lips trembled, tears pooled instantly in her eyes. With sudden ragged breathing, fat tears slipped down her pale cheeks where a shaky hand tried to wipe them away.

Phyllis reached into her purse and fished out a hanky. She offered it to Janne, who took it gratefully. When Janne was composed, Phyllis cleared her throat.

"I didn't come here to upset you, but to let you know that your daughter is well and safe."

Janne clutched the hanky as if she would never let it go. "Thank you for telling me. She's all I think about since the war ended and we were separated."

She dabbed her eyes with the damp cloth. "What happened to her?"

"I know your circumstances, Miss Garnes."

"You know my husband was arrested?"

"Yes. I also know Lisbet was in jail for a while and then lived with a foster family."

The young woman's expression darkened. "Were they... nice to her?"

Phyllis didn't want to go there, so she didn't. "Lisbet was only with them a short time and then I met her. She's living with me now. I have a very nice apartment in downtown Oslo and..."

"Wait a minute, Miss Bowden, is it? You flew right past my question. Was the foster family good to her? We've heard some horrible things here."

Phyllis' eyes slid to the matron sitting a few yards away and knew their conversation would be overheard. What the hell...

"No, they weren't." Janne gasped, a hand flew to her mouth. "I met her when she had run away and was hiding behind a restaurant across the street from where I live. That's the worst of it."

But Janne was crying again anyway. "My poor baby," she sobbed.

When Sturdy Shoes looked ready to interrupt, Phyllis patted Janne on the hand.

"I know this is unsetting to you, but please hold it together, so I can do what I came here to do. I could get thrown out at any time."

"You're not here officially?"

"No, I'm not, but my boss, the Military Attaché, knows I'm here and supports my efforts."

"All right." Janne blew her nose and blinked several times. "Please go on."

"I'm not sure what's going to happen to you, but I have an opportunity to place Lisbet with a very nice family that my boss knows in Sweden, just outside of Stockholm. The man is a glassblower and his wife..."

"Can't you keep her until I get out of here?"

Phyllis shook her head, tucked curly hair behind an ear. "There's some kind of problem and she's in danger. Either Soviet or British authorities, possibly both, appear to be looking for her...something about your husband. I'm really not sure why, but I've heard he gave her information of some kind. Do you know what they could be looking for?"

"NO, NO IDEA." Her drawn face reflected. "Oskar would never get Lisbet involved in anything bad."

"Maybe he slipped her a note."

"No, I don't think so."

"What happened to her doll?"

Janne looked surprised. "What doll?"

"Lisbet told me her papa ran to a bedroom and handed her the doll called Sonja just before he left. What happened to the doll?"

She shrugged, looked blank. "The house was blown up and probably the doll was too. She didn't take it when we were arrested."

Hmm. A dead-end.

"And Miss Bowden?" She reached over to touch Phyllis' arm. "Why couldn't Lisbet go to my uncle in Bucharest until I can come for her?"

Phyllis' head snapped to attention. Her neck tingled and goose bumps broke out on her arms. "Bucharest?"

"You know, I've only had two visitors since I've been here and I've discussed Bucharest with both of you."

"Who...who was your other visitor?"

"It was a few months ago now and I don't remember his name. Maybe... Joe or John something."

"Joe? Joe Schneider?"

Janne nodded absently. "Possibly. I really don't remember."

"What did he look like?" Phyllis' breaths came in short spurts.

"Well, he was medium height, dark hair and eyes. Nice looking."

"...Was he wearing a fedora?"

"What is that?"

Phyllis' hands touched her head. "It's a dark gray hat of a soft material with a band."

"Yes, I believe he did wear a hat like that." Janne was quick. "You know this man?"

"He's my fiancé."

"Oh. Oh, dear. I hope he's doing fine. He was nice to me."

"Was he looking for Lisbet?"

"He was. I suggested he look for her with my uncle since I had no other place to tell him."

The lump in Phyllis' throat just wouldn't go down. *Oh, man. His mission to Bucharest was to find Lisbet.*

Janne's hand reached out to pat Phyllis' hand. "Are you all right, miss? Your face has gone white. Perhaps you need some water."

She shook her head. "No, thank you, but I probably should go. I want to thank you for your time." Phyllis stood and shifted from the chair. Janne moved toward her.

"Miss Bowden? Will you take her to Bucharest for me?"

"No, I can't. It's...difficult politically there right now and it wouldn't be safe for us to travel." She looked Janne in the eye. "Sweden *is* safe. It would be safe for you too. Perhaps the family who has volunteered to help Lisbet could help you as well. Should I ask them?"

A dejected expression washed over the Norwegian woman's thin face. Phyllis couldn't imagine what she was thinking.

"I really have no choice about anything. I've heard my husband has been arrested and a stranger has my daughter. A kind stranger perhaps, but a stranger nevertheless. I have no idea how long they will keep us here and I appreciate what you are trying to do for me and for Lisbet."

Phyllis took her hand, smiled. "One of these days it will be all right. Please keep faith."

She nodded and brushed straggly hair from her face. "Then I will do as you suggest. Please ask the Swedish family if I can come to them once I am released. I have nowhere else to go and it's a lot to ask, I know."

"I understand they are nice people. Let me handle it."

Janne kissed Phyllis' hand; her eyes filled again. "I'm not used to the kindness of strangers. I'm not used to any kindness at all, so thank you, Phyllis Bowden. Thank you for trying to help me. I appreciate it more than I can ever say."

"I'll be in touch."

She smiled slightly before heading back into the barracks. After seeing Janne inside, the matronly guard escorted Phyllis back to the office. When they passed the sign hung on a barracks' wall, she had to ask, "What does *tysker-tosers* mean in English?"

Without pausing in her step, the woman grunted, "German sluts."

THIRTY-THREE

"I told you I would call when I needed your help."

"Yes, but somehow, I thought we'd be going skiing or having fun, not this."

Phyllis coolly observed John Edelland sitting across the table. With his fine clothes, stately manner and polish, he should have looked better in her eyes. He should have sparkled.

But he didn't.

In fact, of all the men in Arne's Café tonight, he was the least attractive to her. He wasn't the man she thought she knew.

She drained her coffee and signaled to Arne. Gathering her purse and hat, Phyllis prepared to leave.

"Wait a minute, Phyllis. Let's talk about this."

"What's there to talk about?"

"This is major what you're asking me to do. I don't think you realize how much trouble we could get into."

She locked eyes with him. "I can't believe you're saying this, John. With all the people you know in this, your home country, and all the connections you keep telling me you have, it's hard to believe that you can't help me get a passport for Lisbet."

He chuckled. "Well, it's nice that you're finally truthful

about the little girl. The last time we spoke, you practically denied her existence."

"No." Shaking her head, she took a breath. "I lied about who she was for her own protection. Maybe coming clean to you wasn't such a good idea."

"I won't say anything to anyone about her, but what do you plan on doing? Where are you taking her?"

Phyllis leaned back in her chair when Arne brought over a refill of coffee. He smiled sweetly at her and winked before pouring a refill for John. When he left, John chuckled.

"That man has a small crush on you."

"Arne?" She laughed. "Oh, no. We've just been enjoying each other's company. I must eat here three times a week. I've sneaked Lisbet in a few times and she's made friends with Arne too."

"Phyllis, your loyalty is admirable, but do you think you can actually pull this off? Taking a child that authorities are looking for to Sweden with a fake passport isn't for the faint of heart. You need to know what you're doing, how to behave, and other things. Are you really up to this?"

The question of the day. Was she?

"The only thing I am absolutely certain about, John, is that Lisbet will be treated horribly if she stays in Norway. It's not her fault who she is, but Norwegians will always see her as that quisling girl. She's just a little girl. I have to get her out of here."

"And your boss, the Military Attaché I might add, can't or won't help you?"

"I'm not getting him involved. The less he knows about my plan, the better. It could compromise his position, which I would never want to do." She paused, lowered her eyes. "In fact, it may force me to resign mine."

"Phyllis..."

"No. I'm determined this is the best course of action."

His gaze swept her face. He must have found what he was looking for. "All right. Let me make a call. I can help you find someone."

"In the black market?"

"Oh, yes. This is blacker than black. It's quite illegal and I'm sticking my neck out just making a call."

Her eyes softened. "Thank you, John. Thank you for little Lisbet's sake. She really is the most precious child."

"You've become attached, Phyllis."

"I have and I'm not ashamed to admit it."

"You show great character which has made me fond of you."

"Thank you. Now let's pick up your soup so you can get home. I know you've had a long day. I don't want to add to it."

She smiled at him while he waved to Arne. It was going to be all right, like she told Janne. Somehow it would be all right.

THIRTY-FOUR

Phyllis, thought Jay, was something else. She had what the Yanks called, 'true grit' and should have run from the situation instead of coolly making such a dangerous decision without batting an eye.

The black market was flourishing, as she'd told Phyllis before, but to see it up close and personal was something else again. Early one frosty morning, Jay and Phyllis strolled through the open marketplace searching for stall number thirteen. Of course, it had to be number thirteen. The marketplace was a ragtag collection of goods in a back alley not far from downtown Oslo. The rumor was that Norwegian authorities tended to look the other way since it was having such trouble getting the people of Norway the goods and services they required. After the German occupation, there was a pent-up demand and a ready market, but companies and producers were in short supply. Price controls only worked if there was a product to sell, so illegal commodities sold quickly and at high prices.

The old trolley had dropped them off by a building that had been used by the hated Gestapo. It was destroyed in a bombing raid last year. Residential and commercial buildings around it had survived, but the former Gestapo headquarters had been leveled to the ground in a raid quickly becoming legendary. Jay and Phyllis had picked their way carefully through the tangle of wood and concrete that still littered the area before walking into an alley closed at one end.

Phyllis glanced over at Jay. She turned up the collar of her wool coat and tucked escaping curls under her hat. "This isn't my idea of a fun shopping trip."

"Mine either, but let's get what we're after and get the heck out of here."

Phyllis lowered her voice. "I thought people selling illegal goods would look scarier than these folks. I swear I saw that woman we just passed at Arne's last week."

"You probably did. They're ordinary people caught up in extraordinary circumstances."

The corners of Phyllis' mouth turned up. "Kind of like us."

"Yeah, kind of like us."

Hastily erected individual stalls boasted warm coats, silky blouses, pleated skirts and heavy sweaters from Sweden. One man sold leather belts and purses similar to items Jay had seen at a local department store recently reopened. Closer to Phyllis were tables of bread, salami, different varieties of cheeses, chicken and various cuts of beef. Jay couldn't help stopping to check the price for a pound of butter. Normally priced at a dollar, American money, the butter was offered for thirteen dollars. The escalated price made Jay's jaw drop with astonishment. Phyllis tugged her away.

"We can't stop to gawk at everything we see. Help me find number thirteen."

"These prices are terrible."

"You were expecting discount sales?" Phyllis whispered in Jay's ear. "This is what a black market looks like, right? Come on."

The smell of fish was strong in every section of the alley. The kinds of fish that had been impossible to get under occupation were suddenly readily available. Even though the Norwegian government was distributing donated food as fast as it came in, there were still hungry people. It would take time to put needed pounds on the people of Norway.

Jay walked past a man selling milk and brown cheese. Phyllis reached out to yank her back.

"Hey!"

"This is our stop."

"How do you know?"

Phyllis angled her head at a table. "I've been counting. It's either the milkman or the woman over there with the smelly fish. I'm hoping it's this guy. I could use a liter of milk."

Jay's brow rose. "At these prices?"

"No, you're right." She rubbed an eye where a sudden nervous tic had begun and straightened her shoulders. Jay noticed she looked the man directly in the eye using a voice that was whisper soft.

"John sent me. Do you have the item?"

The man was of medium height and definitely not Norwegian. Jay was thinking Finnish or somewhere farther north in one of the Baltic countries until he opened his mouth. With a few missing teeth and a heavy Slavic accent he said, "Here you are." He reached under a table for a small bag. When he passed it to Phyllis, she gave him an envelope stuffed with cash.

"Thank you."

"Da." Turning to another customer, the man smiled and spoke fluent Norwegian. Phyllis tucked the bag in a coat pocket and jolted when Jay grabbed her arm to move her along.

"Let's go."

Jay and Phyllis strode determinedly toward the end of the alley.

"Thanks for chipping in for this. I didn't have enough and didn't want to take any of Helge's money."

"That was nice that she offered."

"A hundred dollars is a steep price."

Jay smiled at her. "Especially when butter is at thirteen dollars."

"I'll pay you back."

"No, I..."

They neared the alley's end when noises increased substantially from where they'd entered. Women screamed, men hollered and footsteps behind them broke into a run. Suddenly, people were running past them flocking to the exit coming up fast. Jay glanced back to see Norwegian policemen moving a few vendors up against walls and heard shrill whistles frightening the rush of people coming toward her and Phyllis. They were in danger of being trampled and had to move out of the way quickly.

Phyllis was tripped by a young man rushing by and stumbled to the ground. Before Jay could reach her, a tall Norwegian man picked her up, grabbed Jay's hand and towed them both through a nearby door. He locked the door behind them and pulled both women towards the front of an empty warehouse. Jay and Phyllis could barely keep up with him until they were out on the street where they were whisked into a waiting car. As the driver hit the accelerator and the car roared off, Jay heard Phyllis gasp.

"John? What in the world are you doing here?"

"Phyllis, Phyllis. What am I going to do with you?" His attention turned to Jay. "Miss Lawlor. How are you this fine morning? It's a bit chilly though, so I'd wear gloves if I were you."

Phyllis' finger moved John's face back to hers. "John Edelland, meet Jay Lawlor."

Jay smiled, offered her hand. "Nice to meet you, Mr. Edelland, whoever you are. And thanks for the rescue. It was getting kinda busy in that alley."

"You said you couldn't come with me today, so why are you here?" Phyllis' eyes turned stormy. "Did you know the place would be raided?"

The man had the decency to look sheepish. "I found out after I gave you the contact."

"So you had to come rescue us."

He shrugged. "It seemed like the gallant thing to do."

She wasn't buying it. "First you put me in danger and

then you get me out of it. How do I know you're on the level?"

"Such a quaint American expression." John's smile was pleasant. He turned to Jay. "Do you have an expression like that in England?"

"How do you know I'm..." Jay shook her head. "Never mind. I don't want to know."

"For two women with tradecraft training, you certainly manage to get into much trouble. Interesting."

Jay's brows shot up into her hairline, but Phyllis folded her arms across her chest. "No, it's not. Take us home, please, and we'll not discuss this little...episode again."

He nodded, smoothed the front of his sleek black topcoat. "I agree. Unpleasantness is best forgotten."

Silence in the car seemed oppressive to Jay and she knew Phyllis was angry, but John was cool and calm. He spoke a few words to his driver and smiled all the way home. When Jay got out first, she turned to Phyllis.

"I'll grab the trolley." Her eyes darted to Edelland and back. "Talk to you tomorrow."

"Okay."

Once out of the car, John spoke again to the driver and escorted Phyllis to the door of her building.

"I need a few minutes, Phyllis, if I may."

"We're not going to talk about today."

"No, we're not. I assume you got what you wanted and so there's no need. I have something else to discuss with you."

"All right."

Inside the old building, Mrs. Lind caught sight of them and shuffled off to her apartment waving at them as she left. "Good day, Miss Bowden. Good day, Mr. Edelland."

"Good day, Mrs. Lind," Phyllis said to a closed door.

John laughed. "I guess she didn't want to stay and chat." He took her hand to walk her over to the enormous fireplace on one side of the lobby. Old World elegance sparkled with the stone hearth, ornate mirror above and crystal chandelier hanging from the engraved ceiling. It was a movie-worthy setting.

"Have a seat, Phyllis. I need to talk to you."

When she was comfortable on a plump sofa, John sat beside her and stroked her hand. His face remained neutral but his knee couldn't keep still.

"What is it, John? I've never seen you...nervous, I guess I'd have to say. You look nervous."

He sat poised exuding a fine picture of a well-dressed man with light hair and attractive features. His eyes seemed to take her in with a look.

"Here's what I came to say—I'm a wealthy man and have come to love you, Phyllis. I have much to offer you besides my love and need to know how you feel about me. Would you consider marrying a Norwegian?"

Phyllis blinked, temporarily stunned by his sincere words. She rubbed her chin, raked a hand through her curly hair. "I'm truly at a loss for words."

His eyes softened. "You must have sensed my feelings."

She shook her head. "No, I didn't...at all. This comes as quite a surprise."

"Maybe it's a surprise, but is it unwarranted? Say you have feelings for me too."

She knew it was a genuine offer. John Edelland was a man who said what he meant and meant what he said. That much was true. But how could he consider asking her to marry him? Did they really know each other that well? Phyllis didn't think so. There were many closed compartments in the makeup of John Edelland, businessman extraordinaire. His offer of marriage was certainly flattering.

She wet her lips and took a deep breath.

THIRTY-FIVE

"I can't marry you, John."

He watched her for a moment as disappointment flooded his face.

"Your being Norwegian has nothing to do with my decision, but remember, I'm already engaged to another man. He's a man I've given my heart to and that's not a small thing for me."

He shifted in his seat when she pulled her hand from his.

"To be honest, I've enjoyed our time together, but I can't return the feelings you say you have. I'm incredibly flattered, but it just wouldn't work."

"Joe Schneider may not be the same man he was, do you know that?"

She nodded slowly and her gaze fell to a pattern in the carpet.

"I realize that, but it's a chance I'm willing to take. If he's in trouble, I wouldn't hesitate to help him."

"I didn't hesitate to help you either."

She smiled. "And I appreciate your help with the contact very much. That was generous of you and I'll never forget your efforts. Because of you, I have a passport to get Lisbet to Sweden. You can take pride in the fact that you had a hand in helping a little Norwegian girl be happy again."

They looked at one another; smiles crept onto their faces.

"Do you have much time left in Oslo?"

"I have a few months left on my contract."

"Could we still see each other from time to time?"

"I don't see why not."

"If you need to talk to me about Joe or anything, you know you can call me, Phyllis."

"Thank you. That means a lot to me."

John Edelland rose, put on his gloves. He moved towards the door, then looked back. "You're unforgettable, Phyllis Bowden. I'll call you next week for dinner. Will Lisbet still be with you? Please bring her if she is."

Rising, Phyllis shook her head. "I don't think so. I've got a small window of opportunity for her and I have to take it."

"You know you can count on me if you're in a jam, as you Americans like to say." He smiled as he said it. "I've got a good track record."

"You're just full of American idioms, aren't you?" But she smiled when she said it.

"I'll see you soon." Tall, handsome John Edelland shook loose his expensive woolen coat, adjusted his hat, and walked resolutely to his waiting car.

"Farewell, sweet prince," whispered Phyllis.

LORRAINE CAME TO TOWN! Funny, perky, sweet and loyal Lorraine Watkins, her best friend from London. Phyllis could hardly believe it when she met Lorraine getting off the military transport plane. It had only been a few months since they saw each other, but it somehow seemed like a century. They grabbed one another as soon as Lorraine left the tarmac.

"Man, it's good to see you, sweetie."

"It's been too long."

Lorraine wiped her moist eyes then laughed. "I just bought these gloves and now they're wet."

Phyllis looped an arm around her friend's waist. "Is that one suitcase all you brought?"

"Yes."

"Good. Let's go home. I can't wait to show you my new apartment and have you meet Lisbet."

They jabbered through the Army base laughing and joking like old times. The rusty trolley rolled to a stop just off the base, so the women hopped aboard to travel towards downtown Oslo. Curious eyes turned towards the Americans as they continued their fast-paced patter.

"We're not going to see Ronnie?"

"Not today. He gave me the day off since you were coming and Nancy is there to fill in for me."

"Nancy?"

"A sweet gal Ronnie hired to help me in the office. These months have sped by with all I've had to do with getting the Office of the Military Attaché back up to speed."

"You mentioned having to notify families of their deceased relatives." Her eyes slid away to look out the window of the trolley. "You still doing that?"

"Yes." Phyllis sighed, glanced out the window with her. "The list never seems to end." She lowered her voice. "Norwegians lost so many loved ones in the camps. My team and I have notified over fifty."

Lorraine gasped. "That many?"

Phyllis nodded, lowered her voice even more. "We expect the number will run into the thousands. There are so many missing people."

"What team?"

"I assembled a team of American and Norwegian pastors, some military, who are doing the bulk of the notifications. It's a sensitive subject."

"I'll bet." A knowing look passed between them.

Trying to catch up on latest events, Phyllis was surprised her street came up so quickly.

"Here's me." She pulled the overhead rope to signal the driver to stop.

Other passengers smiled and nodded as the women made their way off the trolley. When it jerkily pulled away, Lorraine laughed.

"And that's what passes for transportation in old Oslo these days?"

"Hey! We're happy to have it. Beats walking to work every day."

Strolling towards the apartment building, Lorraine filled her in on what her former roommates in London were doing. When she got to their landlady, Mrs. Stewart, Phyllis chuckled.

"I have a new landlady, Mrs. Lind. She's not as nosy as Mrs. Stewart, but that could be because of the occupation. Mrs. Stewart in London had to contend with V-2 bombs falling, but not with any Germans directly. Mrs. Lind had German officers living in her building, in fact, in the apartment I have now."

Lorraine's eyes widened. "You're kidding! In your apartment!"

"Yep. I found clothes and helmets and other stuff that was downright spooky."

"What did you do with it all?"

"I mailed it to my sister in Virginia." Phyllis laughed. "She told me she was scared stiff when she opened the box."

"I wish I could have seen that."

Entering the old building, they saw Mrs. Lind sweeping the floor. The elderly woman looked up from her task.

"Miss Bowden, how are du today?"

"Well, thank you." She nudged Lorraine forward. "I wanted to introduce you to my best friend, Miss Lorraine Watkins. She's from London."

A small smile crept onto Mrs. Lind's lined face. She set aside her broom, wiped her hands on her long skirt and made a curt bow.

"How do you do, Miss Watkins? Will you be visiting Miss Bowden for long?"

Lorraine shook her head, pushed pale hair from her pretty face. "Not long enough, I'm sorry to say. So happy to meet your acquaintance."

"And I yours, tusen takk." She picked up her broom to resume sweeping.

"Come on up. I have someone else for you to meet."

The women climbed up the worn marble staircase bubbling with happy conversation. Helge met them at the door with a bright smile.

"Lorraine, this lovely Norwegian woman is Helge Hansen. She's been helping me with Lisbet while I go to work." Phyllis turned to Helge. "And Helge, this chatterbox is my good friend, Lorraine Watkins. She'll be here for a few days."

"Nice to meet you, Miss Watkins." The women smiled at one another until a little girl shyly peeked around Helge's skirt. With blonde braids draped over her shoulders and pale blue eyes, the girl flicked long lashes at Phyllis' friend.

Phyllis held out her hand. "Lisbet, I want you to meet Miss Lorraine. She's come all the way from London to say hello to you."

Lisbet took Phyllis' hand and moved slightly away from Helge. Dressed in a matching skirt and sweater of bright yellow, Lisbet nodded towards Lorraine.

"Hello, Miss Lorraine."

"Hello yourself, cutie. You're just too cute for words."

Lisbet's face lit up and she bobbed a little curtsy.

"Oh, now, I'm not the Queen."

Phyllis elbowed Lorraine. "It's a sign of respect, dummy. Be nice."

"To someone who's calling me dummy? No way."

Helge laughed, breaking the ice, and everyone went to the living room. After a few minutes of polite talk, Lisbet whispered in Phyllis' ear.

"Sure, sweetie. Go ahead."

The little girl popped up, grabbed her doll and ran back to her bedroom.

"What was that about?" asked Lorraine.

"She wanted to put Sonja down for her nap."

"Who's Sonja?"

"That's her dolly," replied Helge. "They're quite inseparable."

"Have you been out today?" Phyllis asked Helge.

She shook her head. "After what happened a few days ago, I don't dare."

Lorraine turned to Phyllis. "What happened a few days ago?"

"Helge took Lisbet for a walk and was chased by some man, we don't know who. It was scary enough to push me into putting my plan in action soon." She paused to glance toward Lisbet's bedroom. "You know, the one I mentioned to you."

"Sure you want to do this?"

"It's best, Miss Lorraine, for Lisbet's safety."

"Her safety?"

"I don't know what's going on politically, but there's rumors about Lisbet's father wanting to trade something for his life. He's been arrested, I know, and is locked up somewhere."

"He's still alive?"

Phyllis nodded. "So far as I know."

"And her mother?" asked Lorraine.

"We'll talk later when Lisbet's asleep. There's still a few things I haven't told her."

"Maybe the time has come, Miss Phyllis, to tell her what you've learned."

Phyllis sighed, glanced at both women. "I know you're right, Helge. The trip is going to be difficult for her, at best."

"Let's talk about that tonight too. We have many details to go over before it's time."

"And it's nearly time," added Helge with a nod. "Would anyone like something to drink? I've made fresh coffee."

"Please," Lorraine and Phyllis said at the same time.

THIRTY-SIX

"So you've made up your mind? You're bound and determined to go?"

"I am, sir. I'm convinced it's the best thing for Lisbet."

"And the mother, what's her name? Janne? What did she think about your plan?"

"She wasn't in a position to argue about it."

"She must have said something."

Phyllis nodded, shifted awkwardly in her chair. Ronnie's look pinned her in place.

"Janne asked me to keep Lisbet until she was released from that women's camp."

"But we both know you can't do that. Who knows if that will even happen and besides, I've heard rumblings about British or Soviet authorities, maybe both, looking for the girl. If I heard anything officially, I'd have to turn her over to them."

"Not to the Soviet authorities surely."

"Well, no, but to the British certainly."

Phyllis glanced out the window of Lt. Col. Lawrence's second floor office. The day was mildly overcast although the sun appeared to fighting its way through the clouds.

"You still haven't learned why they're looking for her?"

Ronnie shook his head, picked up a stapler on his desk.

"No and the sources I tried got rather peeved about me sticking my nose in where it didn't belong." He rolled his eyes. "So in regards to little Miss Lisbet, the Office of the Military Attaché and the American Embassy are officially not involved." His eyes brooked no nonsense. "Are we clear, Miss Bowden?"

"Crystal, Colonel."

"Have Lorraine come in to say hello before you leave for Stockholm. I gather she's had a pleasant trip so far."

"Yes, sir. She's only been here two days, but she likes Oslo as much as I do."

"And the clothing distribution project? How's that going?"

"Very well, I think. The mayor's office took the ball and ran with it. I'm just supervising now when a new shipment of clothing comes in from America. They're doing most of the work of sorting and distribution and are happy to do it. The Norwegians seem thrilled to receive new clothing. Well, new to them."

"Good work." He picked up a sheaf of papers, glanced at them. "Captain Stevens told me the notifications were all up-to-date, at this time. We both know that more lists will be coming, so it's good you put together that crack team of pastors. They're doing good work with a sensitive job."

"I agree. Mark, Erik and the others are doing a very commendable job. We need to do something nice for them to show our appreciation."

"Good idea. Give me a few ideas before you leave and I'll see what I can do. This office needs to give them a sincere pat on the back."

"Yes, sir. Anything else for me?"

"No, Miss Bowden. Thank you and have a good trip this weekend." He cocked an eye at her. "Be careful, Phyllis. The forest is full of trees."

She nearly laughed. "I will, Colonel, and I'll watch out for the ah...trees."

"You do that." Lawrence turned to the papers in his hand to begin reading. Phyllis gathered her pad and pencil and went back into her office to confer with Nancy. She got busy and didn't notice the time until she glanced at her watch. With nervous resolution, Phyllis slipped her arms into coat sleeves, put on her hat and retrieved her purse from the bottom drawer of the desk.

"Goodnight, Nancy. Have a good weekend. See you Monday."

"Night, Phyllis. You too."

A good weekend. Oh, boy. That might be asking a lot, but she had to try. For Lisbet's sake, she had to try.

BUTTERFLIES DANCED NONSTOP IN PHYLLIS' stomach when she, Lorraine and Lisbet left the trolley for Oslo East Station. The huge gray brick building only served as a reminder that her darling Lisbet was going away. Forever. It was a tough reality and one she wasn't able to choke down with her breakfast. Little Lisbet with her puppy dog eyes held tight to Phyllis' hand making this so much harder. Their conversation from last night tugged at her conscience.

"But why are you sending me away, Miss Phyllis?"

"You're not safe here, Lisbet."

"I don't understand." The little girl's lip quivered and she held tightly to her doll.

Phyllis glanced at Lorraine. "I don't think...um...Norway may not be the best place for you right now, sweetie. But I know a very nice family in Stockholm that would love to have you."

"Where's Stockholm?"

"It's a city in Sweden."

"Oh. Is it far away?"

"Not too far by train, about five hours."

"That sounds far." Long lashes flicked over wary eyes. "I wouldn't see you very often then, would I? Or Helge?"

"No, Lisbet. You'd have a new family, at least for a while."

"For a while?"

She hadn't explained to the little girl about finding her mother in the women's camp outside of Oslo. Phyllis knew it would be too hard for Lisbet to understand her mother was near yet far away. Besides, Janne might never be released for all she knew. Better to keep that information to herself instead of filling poor Lisbet with hope that could ultimately fail.

"Yes, sweetie. They're nice people and already have a Norwegian girl living with them. They want to meet you very much."

Lisbet pouted. "I still don't see why I can't stay with you."

"It just isn't possible, Lisbet. You know I would keep you if I could."

Lisbet hadn't looked convinced.

She still didn't look convinced as they made their way inside Oslo East Station. The place was enormous. The ceiling, surely five hundred meters high, was circular in design with huge windows at both ends. Several rows of tracks ran parallel with long platforms in between. People clustered in small groups to patiently watch and wait. Large signs posted overhead stated destinations with the occasional flashing light to alert passengers of their importance. Smells of dust and, oddly enough, perfume wafted through the vast area. Women in fur coats hurried by with luggage-laden porters hurrying behind them. Businessmen and others strode with purpose to one train platform or another. Rumbles and train whistles could be heard for miles before a train actually pulled in to the station. Once inside, people clamored to get aboard, talking loudly and jostling others around them. Norwegians were polite people but sounds of dropped luggage and raised voices reached Phyllis, Lorraine and Lisbet as they wandered from one platform to another looking for the train to Sweden. She finally waved at a porter in a black uniform and red cap. He stopped, looked at her expectantly.

"Kan jeg hjelpe deg?"

"Engelsk?" asked Phyllis.

He bobbed his head with a smile. "Yes, miss. May I help you?"

"We need the train to Sweden. Which platform is that?"

"This way, miss." He pointed to his right. "What city is your destination?"

"Stockholm."

His head bobbed again. "You'll change to a Swedish train at the border to continue on to Stockholm. Customs officers will come onboard to check your papers at that time."

"Thank you."

Phyllis and Lorraine exchanged a look over Lisbet's head. Customs. Phyllis' gut tightened at the word and knew Lorraine was feeling the same. As the trio began to walk towards their platform, a Norwegian policeman stood by a book vendor intently observing people who passed him. She licked her lips dry the closer they got to the man. Lorraine had seen him too and turned her attention to her watch. Phyllis stalled at the book vendor, pulling Lisbet closer as she watched the policeman out of the corner of her eye.

"Would you like a book to read on the train, Lisbet?"

The little girl beamed with delight. Her twin braids bobbed up and down matching the excitement in her face.

"Oh, please, Miss Phyllis. Can I look?"

Phyllis pushed her closer to the shelves of books and magazines laid out before them. Soon Lisbet found a children's book she liked and Phyllis counted out coins to the vendor.

Lorraine angled her head toward the train platform. "Let's get a move on, ladies. We don't want to miss the train, now do we?" Her eyes widened at Phyllis tucking her wallet back in her purse.

"No, we don't."

"Lisbet," began Lorraine. "Why don't you take a look at the pictures in your book as we walk along? It looks so interesting." She winked at Phyllis who got the message.

"Sure, sweetie." Phyllis raised the book slightly so Lisbet's face was partially covered. "We'll make sure you don't trip, okay?"

The braids bounced again as Lisbet bent her head to pour over her new book. When the women and little girl passed by the policeman, he barely spared a glance in their direction. He paid no attention to Lisbet at all. Once past him, both Phyllis and Lorraine let out collective sighs of relief. Lisbet looked up at them.

"You all right, Miss Phyllis?" Her little head swung to Lorraine. "Miss Lorraine?"

Phyllis nodded. Lorraine choked out, "Fine. How are you?"

Her eyes brightened. "I just love my new book. Why, look at this picture. See the..." Lisbet babbled on for several minutes until Phyllis handed her suitcase to Lorraine and lifted the girl in her arms as a noisy train rumbled into the station. Clouds of smoke bellowed from the smoke stack bringing new smells of steam and burning coal into the stuffy train station.

"What?"

"We need to get on the train in a minute, sweetie. Keep that thought about your book until we get onboard, then you can continue to your heart's content."

Lisbet smiled, clung to her book as the train chugged to a complete stop. People crowded around waiting patiently for the conductor to step down and allow them access. When they were finally onboard, Lorraine found two seats together by a window and a third across the aisle. The seats weren't overly comfortable with thin cushions and the old train was looking her age. It was obvious train travel had worsened in the years of the occupation. Lorraine shrugged off her coat, stuffed their bags on a shelf overhead and helped Lisbet out of her winter coat. She plopped in her seat tugging Lisbet with her.

"Now let me see that book." She and Lisbet bent heads together while Lisbet read the book out loud, once in Norwegian and again in English.

While they were busy, Phyllis took the opportunity to check out fellow passengers in the same car. It wouldn't hurt to be aware of their surroundings. She took her time unbuttoning her wool coat to sweep a casual glance around the passenger car. In front of them was a family of four—a father, mother and two young boys. They were having a lively discussion in Norwegian and Phyllis guessed it was about what they'd do when they arrived at their destination. The boys' hand gestures indicated throwing a ball.

She tuned them out.

In the row behind, an attractive woman with an elegant upswept hairdo gazed with disdain at fellow passengers. When her gaze fell to Phyllis, her disapproving glance at Phyllis' clothing almost made her laugh. Behind the haughty woman was an older man in a dark hat. His beard and mustache were tinged with gray and his eyes were closed beneath metal-framed glasses. An elderly couple in matching red jackets sat the row behind chattering happily.

Phyllis had unbuttoned the last button when she saw him. A young man with blondish hair and a clean-shaven face stared out the window beside him. His woolen suit, white shirt and knotted tie didn't look out of place, but it was the feeling she got while observing him that bothered her. She took her time stowing her coat on the next seat keeping him in view. Just before she sat down, he casually glanced around the passenger car. But there was nothing casual about that glance. The fact that his eyes stayed a beat longer on Lisbet than anyone else made the hair on the back of her neck stand up. She almost put her coat back on.

So he was the one. Okay. At least she knew the game was still on, even on a train out of Norway. She'd worried constantly after Helge told her of that day when a man chased after her and Lisbet, so precautions had been taken to keep Lisbet out of sight. Smiling at Lisbet and Lorraine still engrossed in the new book, Phyllis spied the conductor wending his way down the aisle.

"Billetter, vaer sa snill. Tickets, please," he said to the family in front of them. Lorraine glanced over at Phyllis who dug through her bag for their papers. When the conductor stepped to their row, Phyllis was ready.

"Tickets, please."

"Here you are."

"Thank you, miss." In a crisp, dark blue uniform and matching cap, the older man's experienced eyes checked the paper Phyllis gave him. He punched the tickets with a small tool before handing them back with a tip of his hat.

"Thank you, miss."

Only when he had moved on did Phyllis breathe again. She noticed Lorraine looked nervous too before busying herself in Lisbet's book. One check done. This would be a piece of cake compared to the border crossing where their passports would be scrutinized at length.

Phyllis settled in and tried to relax. Lisbet eventually dozed off and Lorraine read a magazine she'd brought along. For the next hour, as the train headed south to the border of Sweden, Phyllis' mind raced through unsettling thoughts that surfaced.

Where was Joe? Having no idea whatsoever was scarier than if she knew he was still with the Romanians. She couldn't bear the thought that he could be hurt, that he could be dead. She shook her head trying to clear the dread rolling through her like mist on a rainy day.

Oh, please let him not be dead. Her closed eyes filled— they hadn't even started a life together. *Let him not be dead.*

John Edelland had asked her to marry him. She couldn't for the life of her figure that one out. Sure, they'd had some fun times and he had come through with the black market contact for Lisbet's passport, but how could he possibly think they fit together?

Ronnie hadn't bothered her about the passport. Another puzzling thought. He must have known that she'd gotten it off the black market, yet he made no comment about it. Nor had he made a move to stop her from leaving for Sweden with it. He'd babbled about his wife having found a family who wanted to help Lisbet and actively encouraged her to get Lisbet out of town. Maybe he knew something she didn't. That was likely. He certainly didn't tell her everything.

Lisbet was going away. Not only that, but Phyllis was taking her to Sweden where she, more than likely, would never see her again. Even though her heart ached, a big part of her realized that Lisbet belonged with her mother. It was possible that Janne would be deported and to Sweden, if Ronnie could arrange it. And there were telephones and mail, weren't there?

A ragged breath escaped.

"Are you all right, miss?

THIRTY-SEVEN

Phyllis opened her eyes to the mysterious man in the woolen suit from a few rows back. He stood before her with a worried look on his smooth face. A glance at Lorraine with raised brows and shoulders told her nothing.

"Fine, thanks."

He opened his mouth to speak again when the conductor returned to announce the border crossing was coming up in twenty minutes.

The man smiled. "That's my stop. I hope you're feeling all right."

"Thank you."

Instead of returning to his seat, he looked over at Lisbet.

"Hello, little lady. What are you reading?" Lorraine shot Phyllis a look that brought Phyllis to her feet.

"Lisbet, let's see if there's a dining car. Aren't you hungry?"

The little girl shook her head, patted her pretty green skirt. "No, not really."

Phyllis reached over a hand. "Well, I'm hungry. Come with me, please."

Lisbet obediently rose, smiled at the man and took Phyllis' outstretched hand. She walked quickly past the man heading for the next passenger car.

Glancing back, she saw that Mr. Mystery was absorbed in an animated conversation with Lorraine and she was using her wily ways to keep him occupied. Still, his eyes darted back to her and Lisbet before he returned to his seat, reaching for something on the floor. Phyllis didn't wait to find out what. She hurried little Lisbet through a full car before she found what she wanted. Seeing a small closet labeled Porter, Phyllis yanked open the door and pulled Lisbet in with her. When the girl opened her mouth, Phyllis put a finger to her lips.

"What are we doing in the closet, Miss Phyllis?" whispered Lisbet.

"We're, ah, hiding from Miss Lorraine."

Lisbet looked puzzled. "Why would we want to do that?"

That stumped Phyllis for a moment. "Because she, um, likes to look for people. It's a game to her."

Lisbet shook her head. "That's an odd game."

Phyllis shrugged, pulled the little girl closer. "She can be an odd person at times, but she's very nice."

Although she was standing still with Lisbet clutching her hand, Phyllis began to feel light-headed. Smells of ammonia kept her from breathing deeply and even Lisbet noticed a change in her.

"You're breathing funny," whispered Lisbet. She wrinkled her nose. "It doesn't smell too good in here." She looked at their clasped hands. "And your hand is freezing." She looked up. "Are you feeling okay?"

Out of the mouths of babes. Lisbet grabbed the doorknob. "We should leave."

Phyllis' hand shot out to stop her from opening the door. "No, sweetie. Not just yet."

"But Miss Lorraine hasn't found us and you don't look good."

Just as white spots danced before her eyes, the door opened to a surprised porter.

"Miss? Are you and your daughter, ah, lost?"

Lorraine's head popped around the porter and she

reached out for Phyllis. "Come on, slugger. Let's get you out of here before you pass out."

"I'm fine." Phyllis swallowed hard, but took Lorraine's steady hand to walk into the hallway.

Lisbet frowned, straightened her sweater. "She pushed me in there, Miss Lorraine, and said you'd come to find us."

"And I did, didn't I? Now let's go back to our seats. The border crossing is coming up soon."

The porter shook his head as he watched them go. Phyllis turned back with an uncertain smile and let Lorraine lead her back to their seats.

"Where'd that man go?" said Phyllis softly.

"Which man?"

"You know which one."

"Oh, you mean the cute one who wanted my phone number?"

"Funny."

"He got his bag and headed towards the front of the car."

"Was he following us?"

"It sure looked like it, that's why I came looking, but he went to talk to the conductor. Of course, you were about to faint in another tiny closet." The corners of Lorraine's mouth twitched. "Just can't seem to stay away from small places, can you?"

Phyllis rolled her eyes. "The man said he was getting out here. Keep an eye out for him." Lorraine nodded. "Let's get ready to change trains. Then we have the customs check."

Her smirk long gone, Lorraine took her place by Lisbet. She found their coats and was helping the girl into hers when the conductor came back once more. He spoke clearly in Norwegian before repeating what he said in English.

"The train will be stopping at the border crossing for approximately fifteen minutes. If you are traveling on to Sweden, you will continue on the train coming in now. Please watch your step and remember all your belongings."

There was no sign of the mysterious man when the women and little girl made their way to the second train. Even though they were in Sweden now, Phyllis felt no more secure about Lisbet than she had in Norway. She hoped her feelings would change with distance.

A light snow had coated the platform. Lisbet pointed and laughed at the footprints they were making.

"Look, Miss Phyllis," she gushed. "Isn't it pretty?" She stuck out her tongue to catch snowflakes as they fell. "I wonder if Swedish snow tastes like snow in Norway."

She walked between Lorraine and Phyllis swinging hands. People bustled by heading for various platforms and trying to keep their suitcases from being dragged in the snow.

As they boarded the train to Sweden, Lorraine climbed up first, then helped Lisbet who stopped suddenly to look back. Her pale blue eyes softened as she looked around the station.

"What you are looking at, Lisbet?" Phyllis smoothed flyaway strands of the girl's blonde hair.

"Goodbye, Norway." Tears pooled in her eyes before slipping onto her pink cheeks.

Lorraine patted Lisbet's face. "Think you'll miss it?"

"No." She shook her head. "I miss my mama and my papa, but people in Norway weren't very nice to me. I won't miss them." Her face lit up when she looked at Phyllis. "I'll miss you though, Miss Phyllis."

Before she got teary, Phyllis gently pushed the little girl forward. "Get in there, sweetie. There's people behind us wanting to get aboard." Her eyes darted to Lorraine whose eyes had already moistened.

"Sure, Lisbet. Let's find new seats and see about getting something to eat."

Lisbet clapped her hands delightedly and disappeared into the train.

The train to Stockholm began to pick up speed. The nondescript landscape hadn't changed much going from Norway to Sweden; it was still flat, open countryside with plenty of frozen lakes and covered with layers of even snow. The occasional building, usually painted deep red with smoke rising from chimneys, would come into view until the train chugged its way past. Phyllis looked up ahead to more of the same: trees shrouded in white and an enormous sky with thin clouds shredded like strips of paper. It was cold, uninviting and did nothing to warm the chill in Phyllis' heart.

They'd found seats and waited anxiously for the custom agents.

"Look!" Lisbet stood and pointed excitedly out the window.

"What?" Lorraine peered around the little girl. "What do you see?"

"It's a tunnel. We're going into a tunnel!"

Phyllis couldn't imagine why that would possibly be exciting to the little girl, but dutifully looked out where she was pointing. A long, wooden tunnel over a lake was coming up as fast as the old train would go. The A-framed roof, coated with deep snow, pointed high in the air. Before anyone could utter another word, the entire passenger car was plunged into darkness with the continuous rattling sounds of a train going along its track.

Clickety-clack. Clickety-clack.

The train's whistle, enclosed in the long tunnel, had a much louder "woo-woo" sound than when they'd left the border crossing into Sweden.

In the dark, Phyllis grabbed for Lisbet just as Lorraine did. The trio held on to one another, seeing nothing but hearing heightened breathing. Lisbet clung tightly to Phyllis while Lorraine's body pressed from behind.

The darkness was relentless. The kind of intense dark that permeated the bones and was absorbed in the blood. Eyes wide open couldn't see a solitary thing, causing the brain to click into panic mode. Lisbet's sharp gasp echoed in the dark settling in Phyllis' chest where she had sought refuge. The darkness was unending and just when Phyllis couldn't stand it any longer, the passenger car was suddenly bright with sunshine, as if a light switch had been flipped.

Their relief was short-lived. Phyllis blinked to see two subdued men in long black overcoats and hats standing before them. They seemed like apparitions appearing out of nowhere causing her mind more agitation and worry. The men's unblinking eyes stared back before coolly observing other passengers.

The conductor came into the car and the agents spoke to him for a few minutes before going from passenger to passenger speaking softly, utter concentration on their serious faces. They'd check various papers and passports, ask questions and observe. Phyllis' anxiety grew as they made their way slowly to their row in the noisy passenger car. As they neared, Phyllis was ready to jump out of her skin. She sucked in small, even breaths to slow her rapidly beating pulse. Lisbet had settled down with her book and was jabbering to a pale Lorraine whose eyes swept from the men to Phyllis.

Then the agents were upon them.

THIRTY-EIGHT

Up close, one man was not intimidating. He was young, with a clean-shaven face and a white shirt under his dark overcoat. His gaze took in the two women and the little girl with a small smile. The second man towered over the first with black hair and blacker eyes reminding Phyllis of a medieval villain she'd seen in a movie. This one could be a problem. Phyllis stiffened her resolve. Lisbet's future depended on what happened in the next few moments.

"Passports, please," said the young man in Swedish and in English. He gathered Lorraine's passport while Medieval Man took Phyllis' and Lisbet's. The girl watched with wide eyes, curious about what was happening.

"Why are you traveling to Sweden?" asked the second agent.

"We're going to..." began Lisbet.

"I'll talk to the nice men, sweetie. All right?" When Lisbet nodded, Phyllis smiled. "We're traveling to Sweden to shop for winter clothes."

"For a few days?"

"Yes, sir."

Lisbet's wide eyes grew wider, but she kept her mouth closed.

"You know you're not allowed to bring much Swedish krona back to Norway."

"We understand."

The younger man looked up from reading Lorraine's passport. "You have a diplomatic passport."

"I do, yes."

"Where do you work?"

"At the American Embassy in London. I'm visiting my friend here in Oslo."

Medieval Man looked at Phyllis' passport. "You have a diplomatic passport as well."

Phyllis nodded. "I work at the American Embassy in Oslo."

"Who is this girl?"

"She's my niece."

Lisbet glanced up at Phyllis with a question in her young eyes. Phyllis was relieved when she didn't speak it.

The man held up Lisbet's passport for a better look. "And you're all going to Stockholm for shopping."

"Yes, sir." She smiled brightly. "My friend is in town for a short visit and we thought we'd visit Stockholm while we had the opportunity. Norway's a little short on clothing right now."

The younger man nodded, stamped Lorraine's book and handed it back to her. "You're right there, miss. I hope you find what you're looking for."

"Me too."

The second man stamped his books, handed one to Phyllis, but delayed with Lisbet's. He kept looking at it.

"Is there a problem?"

He angled his head down. "I was wondering about this smudge in the corner." Phyllis looked at the passport in his hand.

"I'm not sure. I guess it was there when she got it."

"And when was that?"

"It was issued last week."

After a few minutes that seemed interminable, the agent

handed the passport to Phyllis. "You'd best see about cleaning that up. It could look fake and that would never do, would it?" His question took her aback. She wasn't sure how to answer so she didn't say anything. Lorraine gently squeezed Lisbet's hand.

His eyes never left hers as Phyllis grasped the book. She stared back at him.

The younger agent smiled. "Thank you, ladies. Have a good trip to Stockholm." He glanced at the second agent and waved a hand. "Let's move on."

The man moved away, but Phyllis didn't breathe again until he was definitely busy checking papers of other passengers. Lisbet shrugged and buried her nose in her book. When the customs agents left the passenger car for the next, Lisbet handed her book to Phyllis with a sly grin.

"Will you read my book to me, Aunt Phyllis?"

"I can explain, sweetie."

She shrugged. "Maybe some other time. Let's read."

Lorraine kissed her cheek. "You're a smartie, Miss Lisbet."

She bobbed her head sending the braids in a mad scramble.

Phyllis took her book, opened to the first page. Smiling, she read the title, "*Heidi*? You're like a Norwegian Heidi, aren't you, Lisbet?"

"Yes, but I don't have any goats." She pointed to the goats on the cover.

"Maybe not now, but who knows?"

"Will you get me a goat, Miss Phyllis?"

Winking at the little girl, she chuckled. "I'll see what I can do."

After reading *Heidi* and getting some lunch, Lisbet fell asleep. Lorraine moved to give her more room and was sitting by Phyllis where they were in deep conversation.

"I've been wanting to ask you this since I got to town."

"What?"

"What's happened to Joe?" Lorraine held up a hand. "Don't give me any more stories like you've done with Helge and Lisbet. I want the truth." She locked eyes with Phyllis. "It's bad, isn't it?"

Moisture clouded Phyllis' vision as she nodded solemnly. Lorraine fished a tissue from a pocket to hand over.

"Thanks."

"Tell me."

"...After our visit, Joe went to Bucharest," Lorraine gasped, "and was apparently kidnapped by Communists there."

"For spying?"

"Well, yes. He is MI5, but you knew that."

"Who told you this information? How reliable is it?"

"Ronnie told me. He's been able to get quite sensitive intelligence and I asked if he could find out what happened to Joe."

"So you're sure it's reliable?"

"Yes. John Edelland told me the same thing."

"Edelland? What's he got to do with this?"

Phyllis' lips flattened. "He, ah, asked me to marry him."

"What?" Lorraine's squeak was a little too loud so Phyllis shushed her.

"He checked Joe out with his sources—whatever those are—and came up with the same story."

Lorraine shook her head. "Let me get back to the marriage proposal in a minute. I want to know why Joe was in Bucharest in the first place."

Phyllis glanced at a sleeping Lisbet, ran a hand through her dark hair. She lowered her voice. "I didn't know it at the time, but Joe went to see Lisbet's mother in an internment camp on an island outside of Oslo."

Surprise lit Lorraine's face. "Her mother is still alive?"

"And in Oslo."

"So why," Lorraine whispered, "are we taking Lisbet to a new family in Stockholm?"

"Her mother will likely be deported. Ronnie will try to get her sent to Stockholm, Sweden at least."

Lorraine's smile bloomed slowly. "So...you're hoping to reunite mother and daughter."

Phyllis blew out a breath. "Yes."

She patted her friend's face. "You're really a sentimental slob, aren't you, Phyllis Bowden?"

"I think so. It seemed like the right thing to do."

"But Lisbet doesn't know any of this."

"No. I can't promise that her mother will get out of the camp, much less be deported to Sweden. But she can't stay in Norway."

"Why not?"

"Her mother married and lived with a German officer, Lorraine. That's the height of being a quisling in Norway."

"Quisling?"

"The word is synonymous with traitor, thanks to Vidkun Quisling who was the head of the Norwegian Nazi party. He was arrested, tried and shot."

Lorraine considered that. "What about Lisbet's dad?"

Phyllis shook her head. "No idea what's happened to him."

"And you may never know."

"So I figured if Lisbet and her mother could be reunited, that would be the best case scenario."

"I agree."

Sunlight filtered through a window reflecting off Lorraine's golden hair. She took ahold of Phyllis' hands.

"We had a tough time in London, but I fear your time in Oslo has been tougher."

"I think you're right. I've had difficult assignments to do."

"And without your best friend." She choked out the words.

Phyllis kissed her friend's hand. "But you're here now and I'm afraid this is going to be the roughest part of our journey."

"What is?"

"Saying goodbye to Lisbet."

"Okay. At least I'm here for this." Lorraine glanced down. "And maybe we'll find out together about Joe."

Phyllis began to cry. Lorraine wrapped arms around her as sobs overtook her friend.

"He, um, could be..."

"Don't say it, sweetie. Joe's a tough character and has probably been in rougher waters than this."

"I know but..."

"There are no buts. He will come back to you."

"Lorraine." Phyllis looked up with tears sliding down her face. "He was looking for Lisbet."

Lorraine's jaw dropped. "Looking for...Why?"

She shook her head. "Not sure. Lisbet's mother told me that when I visited. Joe was searching for Lisbet. I don't know why."

"I bet," Lorraine rubbed her chin. "I bet it has something to do with Lisbet's father."

"Her father?"

"Well, sure. It makes sense." Lorraine handed her another tissue. "Didn't you say her father was a German officer?"

"Yes, but—"

"If he's been arrested, which is more than likely, maybe he had something to trade for his freedom or for his life."

"Something to trade..."

"Yes."

"I actually thought about that but what could it be? They took nothing with them when they were arrested."

Lorraine reached into her purse, pulled out a flask. "While you're thinking, sweetie, think about telling me how you've gotten two marriage proposals in two months. That's got to be some kind of record." Her eyes twinkled as she bent back her head to take a sip from the flask.

"What's that?"

"Good Irish whiskey."

"Give me that." Phyllis tipped back the flask and felt the whiskey burn down her throat.

"The John Edelland story please."

Phyllis laughed. "You're so bossy."

"Missed you, sweetie."

"Missed you too."

THIRTY-NINE

Their names were Kjell and Margareta Karlsson. The shy couple smiled awkwardly on the front porch of their home in a working class neighborhood of Stockholm. A wooden swing set sat in the yard by a girl's bicycle with a sprinkling of toys scattered around. Phyllis had knocked lightly on the door and was pleasantly surprised when the couple bounded out to clasp her hand and nod to Lorraine and Lisbet.

"Hello. I'm Phyllis Bowden and this is Lorraine Watkins. I'm hope you speak some English."

"Some." The man flashed a wobbly smile. "Pleased to meet du. I'm Kjell and dis is my wife, Margareta." The man and his wife shook hands politely before turning their attention to Lisbet.

"And this is Lisbet Garnes."

Their faces were full of curiosity when they were introduced to Lisbet, especially when another little girl about Lisbet's age or perhaps younger came out of the house.

"So pleased to meet du," said Kjell. A stocky man with a rugged face and fair hair, Kjell Karlsson's grey eyes fairly twinkled when he gazed at Lisbet. He solemnly bent at the waist and shook her little hand. Lisbet's eyes widened as she watched him.

"Hello."

Margareta was less formal. "May I hug du?" A woman with an open face, short, straight hair and welcoming smile, she resembled the hard-working wife of a hard-working man. Plain blouse and long skirt added to the look as she leaned over to give Lisbet a heartfelt hug. "You're a lovely little girl, aren't you?"

Lisbet returned her smile before glancing at Phyllis for her approval. When Phyllis nodded, she turned to the younger girl standing next to her parents. Pushing blonde hair, streaked with the sun, out of her eyes to peer at Lisbet, the little girl opened her mouth.

"I'm Laila. Wanna see my toys?"

Lisbet looked again to Phyllis.

"Go on, Lisbet. It's all right."

The two girls scampered into the house leaving the adults standing on the porch. Kjell waved a hand inviting Phyllis and Lorraine in.

"The kitchen would be good place to talk," said Margareta as she led them through the community space and into the kitchen. The areas they passed were clean with wooden floors, some furniture and a large wood stove next to one wall. Sewing tools and a skirt Margareta was making rested on a chair. The house wasn't large, but it was decorated nicely and was big enough for a family of four. The sun shined brightly through a window in the kitchen illuminating the entire area with light and warmth. Phyllis, Lorraine and Kjell sat at a round table in the corner while Margareta served coffee. Phyllis curled her hands around the stout cup before tasting the strong brew. She looked around and waited for Margareta to sit down. Happy sounds of the girls playing made them smile.

Everyone seemed to be waiting for her to start the conversation. Phyllis set down her coffee and took a deep breath.

"I want to thank you, Mr. and Mrs. Karlsson, for what you are doing to help Lisbet."

"Iz fine with us, Miss Bowden," began Kjell, "but we need information about her mother." He reached into a pocket to hold up an envelope. "In your letter, you mentioned a problem. Could we talk about that?"

"Not with Lisbet listening in. I haven't told her anything yet."

Lorraine tapped her hand. "Why don't I go back with the girls and close the door, so you can talk."

Phyllis smiled at her friend. What a good friend Lorraine really was. "Yes, please. Everything needs to be known for this to work."

Kjell frowned when Lorraine left to be with Lisbet and Laila. "I don't understand."

"I couldn't go into all that I need to with you and your wife in my letter. I hadn't met Lisbet's mother at the time but I have a pretty good picture now of what is going on." She looked from Kjell to Margareta. "I hope this doesn't change things for you, but if it does, I need to know."

"Please tell us. We know how bad it is in Norway."

"It's not just the cities and the country that are struggling. The people have struggled and are continuing to struggle like no one will ever truly know. In my position with the American Embassy, I've had a front seat to the problems of hunger and housing and clothing shortages. The country is trying to rid itself of Germans and German collaborators, but it will take some time."

"Ja. We know about Quisling and his followers." Kjell sipped his coffee. "What does this have to do with Lisbet's mother?"

Phyllis nervously picked up her cup, swirled the remaining coffee.

"You need more?" Margareta began to rise. Phyllis laid a hand on her arm.

"No, please stay. I, um, need to tell you something."

The couple looked at her expectantly and said nothing.

"Lisbet's mother is Janne Garnes. She is being held at a women's internment camp on Hovedoya Island by Oslo."

"Why?" asked Kjell. "What did she do?"

"She married a German officer and had a child with him." She licked her suddenly dry lips. "That child is

Lisbet." Kjell and his wife's eyebrows rose. "They lived together during the occupation and were apparently happy."

"Where is the man now?"

"I'm not sure, Mr. Karlsson. He may be in prison and has tried to bargain for his release by saying Lisbet has something that can help him."

"What does she have?"

Phyllis shook her head. "Nothing that I can figure out, Mrs. Karlsson, but people were looking for her—another reason she needed to leave Oslo, besides being the daughter of a German officer."

Kjell clicked his tongue. "My country tried to stay out of that horrible war."

"But friends of ours asked us to put up a few of their Jewish relatives when they couldn't hold them all." Margareta looked sad. "Many Swedish homes took in refugees when the Germans went into Norway."

Phyllis waited a moment before continuing. "Lisbet is like one of those refugees. She's had to flee her country for problems she didn't start."

Kjell looked at her thoughtfully. His focused eyes held a serious intent. "You want us to keep Lisbet or adopt her? Your letter said things had changed."

"The situation has changed since the wife of my boss, the American Military Attaché, visited with you. Here's what it is now: Janne Garnes, Lisbet's mother, will most likely be deported from Norway to Sweden sometime this year. The camp is being emptied but I have no idea when and Janne can't stay in Norway." She took a breath. "Would you consider keeping Lisbet until her mother comes for her?"

Margareta gasped. "Her mother is coming here?"

"With your permission. Lisbet's life has been shaken silly and being reunited with her mother is, I believe, the best that could happen for her. If there's a tiny possibility that her mother can meet her here in Sweden, would you be willing to help?"

Kjell and Margareta exchanged anxious looks before turning back to Phyllis.

"What would you expect of us? We were hoping to adopt Lisbet."

"I know." Phyllis' head bobbed. "I know and that is wonderful of you. If you're willing to help me with the situation as it has changed, I can offer you two things."

"What things?"

"Mr. and Mrs. Karlsson, if you will keep and feed Lisbet until her mother comes, my office would be willing to help you with the adoption of another Norwegian girl. There are many like Lisbet who have lost their families and the orphanages are overrun. There's a desperate need for families to take them."

"You would help us find another little girl?" asked Kjell.

"Yes."

"But, Miss Bowden, when her mother comes, what will she do? Where will she stay?"

"That's a good question, Mrs. Karlsson, one that I will have to think about to answer."

Kjell shook his head, tugged on an ear. "Our church can help Lisbet's mother find a place to live in Stockholm and possibly with a job. We're already helping other Norwegians get settled, so we can help one more."

Phyllis nearly broke down and cried. She straightened in her chair and smiled instead. "That would be wonderful if you could help Lisbet and Janne get settled. It's a desperate situation for them in Norway and they can't go back."

The man's brow furrowed deeply. "What about the German husband? He wouldn't be welcomed here."

"I'm not sure, but I would bet money that he's either in prison for a very long time or..."

"Shot," Margareta whispered. "We've heard stories of captured officers. They are not good stories."

The trio at the kitchen table with the sun shining all around exchanged knowing looks.

"Miss Bowden?" asked Kjell.

"Yes, sir?"

"You offered us two things if we helped you. What is the second?"

Phyllis pulled out her purse, looked from Kjell to Margareta. "I will send you money each month to help with food and other necessities until Janne comes and gets them settled. Once she has a job, you know."

Kjell's mouth dropped open. Margareta spoke quickly. "We couldn't possibly accept that."

"Then put it aside for Lisbet and her mother. Give it to them when they move into their own house." She opened her wallet to pull out some money. "I can give you dollars. I don't have any Swedish krona."

"We couldn't..."

"Please." Phyllis pushed the money across the table. "You're doing so much; let me help you help them."

A door opened in the hallway. Lorraine shouted out, "Ready or not, here we come!" Phyllis pushed the money closer to Kjell who picked it up and stuck the cash in his pocket.

"We'll talk more later, Miss Bowden." But he smiled when he said it complimenting the sunny atmosphere of the kitchen. When the little girls tore around the corner with Lorraine on their heels, Phyllis knew it would be all right.

FORTY

They stayed three days. Kjell said he had an extra room Phyllis and Lorraine could use that would be Lisbet's when they left. Every time Lorraine suggested they should head to the train station, Phyllis thought of another reason to stay. Lisbet and Laila had clicked like two peas in a pod and the Karlssons were a good, stable couple who would do right by Lisbet. She'd sent a cable to Ronnie asking for an additional day off this week and continued working with the Karlssons to get things set up.

Finally...she couldn't stay any longer.

After packing her suitcase, Phyllis called Lisbet into her room. The little girl had been playing outside with Laila and she came in wiping snow from her clothes.

"You two having fun?"

Lisbet's cheeks were rosy and her eyes were bright. "Yes! I finally have a sister, Miss Phyllis, and she likes to play, and we'll go to school together and..."

"Lisbet."

The girl's eyes tracked from Phyllis to her suitcase and back. Her eyes widened. "Are you leaving?"

When Phyllis nodded, Lisbet's lower lip quivered.

She sat Lisbet down by her on the bed. "I need to talk to you, sweetie. The time has come for me to leave. You're going to live with the Karlssons and Laila here in Stockholm." She took hold of the girl's cold hands. "This is what we came here for. Do you remember?"

Lisbet nodded her head. Phyllis took off her knitted cap to smooth back the little girl's pretty blonde hair.

"Can you come visit me, Miss Phyllis?"

"Yes, sweetie, I can."

"Helge too and Miss Lorraine?"

"I'll see if I can make that happen."

"Miss Phyllis?" Tears leaked from her eyes. "Will I ever see my mother again?"

"I'm not sure about that, Lisbet, but don't give up hope."

Lisbet threw her arms around Phyllis' waist and hung on tightly. Phyllis bit her lip to keep from crying but her cheeks began to glisten anyway.

"Go get your bag, sweetie. The one you keep Sonja's clothes in."

She rushed into the room she shared with Laila and hurried back. "Here it is."

Phyllis opened the small bag and reached into her pocket. "Look, Lisbet. This is between me and you."

"What is?"

"I'm giving you some American dollars. Do you see? This is twenty dollars, which should help you if you ever need money." She tucked the money inside Lisbet's bag. "Also," she held up a piece of paper. "This is my phone number at the American Embassy. If you should need to call me for any reason, get to a phone and call me."

"Where would I find a phone?"

"Maybe the neighbors have one or maybe the church we went to yesterday. Keep this bag in a safe place, Lisbet. It's for you and for you only. Do you understand?"

"Yes."

They embraced until Lorraine came to the door adjusting her hat. Phyllis and Lisbet broke apart at her appearance.

"Ready to go?"

Phyllis nodded, rose and picked up her suitcase. After

saying their farewells to the Karlssons, Laila and Lisbet, Phyllis and Lorraine began walking towards the train station. At the end of the block, she looked back to see Lisbet still standing there watching. They waved at one another and then Phyllis turned the corner.

"I guess that's it," said Lorraine.

"I guess so," sniffled Phyllis.

"You going to cry all the way to the station?"

"And maybe all the way to Oslo too."

"Okay, sweetie. Here's my hanky."

RONNIE WAS cranky when she finally made it back to the American Embassy. He'd summoned her as soon as she opened the door to the Military Attaché's office.

"Miss Bowden!" She heard him yell before she'd taken the cover off her typewriter. He hadn't even bothered to buzz her on the intercom. Oh-oh. Lt. Col. Lawrence must be mad.

She opened the door to his office and peeked in. "Sir? You called for me?"

That's when Phyllis noticed two men sitting off to the side. They rose when she walked up to his desk and took off their hats. Ronnie rose too, obviously not pleased if the scowl on his face was any indication. She glanced from the men to her boss.

"Sir?"

"These men are from Military Intelligence, Section 5." When Phyllis looked blank, he explained. "Phyllis, they're MI5 from London."

"I see." But she didn't. What could they want with her? If this was about Joe, she didn't have a clue where he might be.

Dressed in black suits, both men had young faces with neatly combed hair and penetrating dark eyes. They looked so similar and nondescript that she knew she'd have trouble picking them out of a line-up. One man took out a wallet with a badge and card to show her, while the other held a small notebook.

"Sit down, please. They have questions for you."

"For me?" she squeaked. When Ronnie nodded, she sat in a chair close to his desk. All three men sat back down when she was seated. No one had taken eyes off her since she walked in and the intensity of the situation made her pulse quicken. Her eyes darted from the men to Ronnie and back.

"I'm Agent Atwater, Miss Bowden, and this is Agent Croft." The first nondescript man motioned to the second one before dipping his head towards her. "I understand you've just returned from Sweden. Could you explain the nature of your trip?"

"I suppose you want the whole truth and nothing but the truth?"

The man nodded with no change in his neutral expression. "Yes, miss."

She looked at Ronnie whose lips had flattened. He definitely wasn't happy about this. Phyllis cleared her throat and began.

"My friend, Lorraine Watkins, and I took a little girl named Lisbet Garnes to her new family in Stockholm."

"Miss Watkins is with the American Embassy in London?"

"Yes."

"Where did you meet Miss Garnes?"

Phyllis glanced back to Ronnie who seemed to be holding his breath. "I met Lisbet when I found her in a bathroom at Arne's Café in downtown Oslo."

"What was she doing there?"

"She'd run away and was hiding."

"What had she run away from?" This man was nothing if not tenacious. The second man said nothing, but continued to scribble in his notebook.

Phyllis took a deep breath and the words rushed out. "Her parents were lost and she was turned over to a man and woman who were supposed to take care of her, but did not. Instead," her fury grew with each word, "the poor girl was whipped daily, called names, starved and chained out in the back yard with a dog. She slept outside in all weather until she got free and ran away. That's when I found her." She paused for breath. "Oh, and for kicks—the man carved a swastika on her head with a lump of coal."

Neither man blinked. "And her parents are?" asked Agent Atwater.

She wet her lips. "Her mother is Janne Garnes."

"Norwegian?"

"Yes."

"Where is she now?"

"She's in the women's internment camp on Hovedoya Island."

Agent Croft scribbled furiously.

"And her father?"

"Her father was a German officer named Oskar something. Janne told me they had married but she doesn't know where he is." She stared at him. "Do you, Agent Atwater?"

He ignored her question.

"Why did you take Lisbet Garnes to Sweden?"

"I told you. A Swedish family has taken her in. Lisbet is what is known as a quisling here in Norway. Do you know what that means?" Phyllis was rewarded with a curt nod from Agent Atwater. "Okay, then you know her life will be worth nothing in Norway. People knowing her story will see that she's ostracized, ignored or spit on if she continues to stay here."

"So you took it upon yourself to take her to Sweden?"

"Yes."

"Why?"

"It was the right thing to do."

"I repeat: why?"

She crossed her arms across her chest and inched forward. "Are you human, Agent Atwater? I just told you that a little girl, not five years old, was repeatedly abused because her father was on the wrong side of the war. Lisbet is an innocent; she doesn't deserve the label 'quisling' because she never collaborated with the enemy. The little girl merely had a father—that's all she knew him to be. Her father. He wasn't a Nazi to her, he was her papa."

Moisture on Agent Atwater's upper lip collected and he discreetly wiped it off before glancing at Ronnie.

"Were you aware of her activities, Lt. Col. Lawrence?"

"I was."

"Did you advise her to give the child up to Norwegian authorities?"

"I did."

Atwater looked back at Phyllis. "So, Miss Bowden, do you understand that you've broken Norwegian law?"

"No, sir. How did I do that?"

"By taking the girl out of the country. The Norwegian government has decreed that, at this time, anyone collaborating with the enemy, meaning Germans, are to be arrested and brought up on charges."

Lawrence interrupted. "Agent Atwater, are you here to arrest my secretary? If you are, you need to know that I will resist her arrest and bring in diplomatic assistance to further my cause." While he stared pointedly at the agent, Phyllis hoped Atwater was reading between the lines of what Ronnie said.

"And I believe you are not the appropriate arresting body in this case. Miss Bowden is an American civilian working on contract for the United States War Department in Oslo. You're British and she's American. In short, you can't arrest an American citizen."

The neutral expression on Agent Atwater's face slipped just a bit. "Perhaps," he began, cleared his throat. "Perhaps this...unpleasantness can be overlooked and charges do not have to be brought against Miss Bowden."

"In exchange for what?" asked Ronnie. He sat up straighter with hands folded on his desk.

"As agents for the British government, we would settle for Miss Bowden's cooperation in this matter."

"What do you want?"

"We want to know what happened to the doll."

Ronnie and Phyllis exchanged startled looks before exclaiming at the same time, "What doll?"

"The doll Miss Garnes had when her father left their house. The day Norway was liberated."

"How would you know about the doll?" asked Phyllis.

"Please answer the question."

She nodded. "Yes, Lisbet had a doll named Sonja. It was her favorite because her father had given it to her. She was holding it when the house blew up and then she and her mother were arrested."

"Did she take the doll with her?"

"No. Why do you want to know about the doll?"

"Do you think the doll could still be in the house?" Atwater persisted.

"No. The house was blown up, destroyed. Lisbet and her mother barely survived before being carted off to jail by Norwegian police." She shook her head. "The doll is gone."

Agent Croft stopped writing in his notebook. Agent Atwater nodded once with a semi-satisfied look on his face. Phyllis interpreted his look to mean he'd partially gotten what he came for. What was all the attention about the doll?

"Do you have anything else to add, Miss Bowden?"

"Yes. Will you quit looking for Lisbet now? She's just a little girl trying to rebuild her life. Please leave her alone."

"That's not my call to make, but I will pass your suggestion on to higher authorities."

"You do that," Phyllis huffed.

After the British agents left the office, Phyllis slumped in her chair, exhausted. Ronnie poured a glass of water and walked over to hand it to her. Phyllis accepted the water gratefully and drank it down with one long swallow. Ronnie plucked the glass from her hand and set it down. With crossed arms, he leaned against the desk, giving her a thoughtful stare.

"What, Colonel?"

He shook his head. "You've been nonstop trouble since I met you, Phyllis. Why is it that I spend more time wondering what you're up to than anyone else in this entire embassy?"

She bit back a grin. "Maybe you're just lucky, sir."

His smile finally leaked out. "What's lucky is that I have a soft spot for you and your shenanigans."

"Shenanigans? That's a bit harsh for what I've been..."

He waved off her protest. "Yes, yes. Stifle your denial. You know I've got your back or else you'd be cooling your heels with more British authorities."

"Sir?"

Ronnie sat down in the chair next to Phyllis.

"Listen. I think I've figured out what's going on here."

"Please enlighten me."

"Now no one has said anything to me." He laughed. "Atwater and Croft were more like Laurel and Hardy—one was the straight man and one was the comic. Croft tripped on the rug coming into my office."

Phyllis' smirk was there and gone.

"And they didn't tell me the true nature of their investigation, but I'd bet my bottom dollar that they have Lisbet's father, Oskar, in custody. Lt. Casey from the OSS told me that several high-ranking German officers stationed in Norway were captured by the British when Norway was liberated. I bet Lisbet's father was one."

"That seems likely, doesn't it? But what's all the interest in the doll?"

"You said Oskar gave Lisbet the doll before he left, correct?"

"Yes."

"I'm guessing here, but I bet he put some kind of intelligence information in that doll. Why else would MI5 be searching high and low for Lisbet?" He stared again thoughtfully. "It's a wonder you and Lisbet weren't nabbed here in Oslo, but they let you take her to Sweden."

"So you think we've been followed?"

"Yes and they believed you'd take them to the doll."

"But Lisbet knows nothing about any of this."

He nodded. "And the doll has apparently been destroyed. Whatever was in that intelligence was what Oskar was trading for his life."

"So...it may not go so well for Oskar if he has nothing to trade."

Ronnie shrugged. "All this is conjecture but it seems likely."

"Wow." Phyllis blew out a breath. "Poor Lisbet. Caught in the middle of a whirlwind."

"I'd say you're right on the money. And Phyllis?"

"Yes, sir?"

"Of course I don't know for sure, but it's possible they know something about Joe. Why else would he have been sent to Bucharest?"

"I was wondering if anyone would mention him."

HE SMILED AT HER. "Don't give up hope. These agents making an appearance today is encouraging."

Phyllis brightened, perked up in her chair. "Think so, Colonel?"

"I do." He waved her off. "Go get busy now. I have more to do than hold my secretary's hand."

"Thank you."

But long after Phyllis left his office, Ronnie stood by the window staring out at the Oslo Fjord and wondering what had happened to Joe Schneider. He'd given Phyllis a spark of hope that he didn't really have. Joe had been missing for too long. If his hunch was right, Phyllis had some tough times ahead of her. Tough times that could upend her life, certainly her career in military intelligence.

Lt. Col. Lawrence squared his shoulders and walked back to his desk. There were many urgent matters waiting for his attention and he needed to get to it.

FORTY-ONE

In a blurry haze, Joe was back on the filthy floor. Dim light from an overhead window revealed an anonymous prison cell with stripes from bars reflecting on his weary face. A young woman sat on an old bed in one corner but her face was obscured. Moving slightly, every part of his body screamed at him to stop because pain shot out from every appendage. With his chest on fire and the smell of antiseptic in his nose, he reached out blindly towards the ceiling, his mouth open in a noiseless shriek.

"No! No!" he choked out. A nurse came running to his bedside.

"Mr. Schneider? Wake up!" She shook him gently and with effort, Joe's eyes blinked open.

Where was he?

"You're fine, Mr. Schneider, but don't toss and turn like that. You'll tear your stitches and everything has begun to heal nicely."

He turned to the young woman with the white cap and long wrinkled skirt. Her short dark hair curled at her neck and her pale face looked worried. About him?

"Where am I?"

"You're in Queen's Hospital in London."

"How...how," he gasped, "did I get here?"

She poured him a glass of water and brought it to his lips for a drink.

"Here's a little water, Mr. Schneider. It'll help you feel better."

With wet lips, Joe blinked again. Hard. "How did I get here?"

"My name's Anne and I'm your nurse. All your questions will be answered by someone else."

"Who?"

"Oh, I'm sure I don't know their names," she smiled brightly, "but there was a very nice pair of gentlemen here to see you this morning. They come every day but haven't been able to catch you awake."

"They come every day? How long have I been here?"

Anne glanced up at the ceiling in thought. She tapped her chin. "Well, let me think. You were brought in probably seven days ago, maybe eight. Oh, it was a big deal." Her pale eyes widened. "Lots of men in dark suits transported you out of an ambulance in the middle of the night. My friend, Edna, the nurse on duty, commented that people were shouting orders and moving fast. Why, she'd barely touched her tea when she was flung into action to help you."

"Brought me in from where?"

She shook her head. "Sorry, I don't know."

"Well," he glanced around the antiseptic-smelling room with the bland walls and scary machines, "what's wrong with me?"

Anne beamed. "Now *that* I can tell you. You have gunshot wounds to your chest and right shoulder, but surgery was conducted right away and you're healing up nicely. So please lie still and let your body rest. You've been through an ordeal, I'd say."

"Have I been in a coma?"

"No, but you've been in and out of consciousness for several days. You do awaken from time to time."

"Why can't I remember anything?"

"You've got a concussion, Mr. Schneider, and your brain needs to heal. The doctor will be in to see you," she glanced

at her watch, "in about an hour." She pulled up the blanket
to his shoulders. "So please get some rest."

He quieted when she left the room wondering why his
mind was such a blank slate. He could remember very little,
just bits and pieces and what he could remember was dark.
Images. A room somewhere. Amnesia? He'd have to ask the
doctor. He fell back asleep to be awakened later when a tall
man in a white jacket and stethoscope in his pocket was
checking his pulse.

Joe's sleepy eyes tracked the man from head to hand.
Had to be a doctor.

"Mr. Schneider? Are you awake?"

Tired eyes made an effort to stay open. "Yes. Are you...
my doctor?"

"I'm Dr. Archer. Do you feel up to talking? If you're too
tired, I can certainly come back."

"No, no, doctor. Stay." He tried to push up on his arms
but the doctor gently pushed him back.

"I can't let you up just yet, Mr. Scheider. Your head has
taken a beating."

"What's wrong with it?"

"You've been hit several times with either a fist or a blunt
object. I'm surprised you're doing as well as you are."

Joe licked his lips. "The nurse said I had two gunshot
wounds."

"Yes." Dr. Archer moved to the other side of Joe's bed,
checking tubes and machines. "It was strange. Someone had
attempted to patch you up wherever you were. Do you
remember getting some sort of medical assistance?"

"No."

"That's just as well. Whoever it was did a bad job. You
were extremely lucky with the chest wound. Somehow the
bullet missed anything vital, which has to be some kind of
miracle, and lodged by a lung. I operated to remove the bullet
and repair the damage. It was a mess."

"And my shoulder?"

"The second bullet went through a muscle on your right
shoulder and went out the back. You'll have both discomfort

and soreness there for some time, probably a few months. I may put your arm in a sling to keep you from overtaxing yourself."

"But I'm going to live?"

"Yes, sir, you are."

Tears pooled in Joe's eyes. The doctor patted his arm. "There, there, Mr. Schneider. You've had a tough time of it, whatever happened to you, but you're going to be all right." He looked towards the door. "I want to let you know that the hospital psychologist will want to begin working with you daily and perhaps as an outpatient when you leave."

"Why?"

"You've been overwrought when you wake up and the nurses have had to sedate you from time to time. You've also been shouting out in your sleep."

"Have I yelled out anyone's name?"

"No, but I'm sure what happened to you wasn't pleasant. The nurse tells me you awaken bathed in sweat most days."

Dr. Archer observed Joe clinically. "Do you know who you are?"

"Of course, I'm Joe Schneider."

"What do you do for a living?"

"I...um..."

"Are you married?"

His eyes squeezed shut. "There's a woman..."

"Do you live in London?"

Joe opened resigned eyes to the doctor. "I'd like to see that psychologist as soon as possible, doctor. I can't remember very much at all." He blew out a ragged breath. "And I want what's left of my life back."

"I'll see if he's available after lunch, but listen, Mr. Schneider."

"Yes?"

"Don't expect too much at first. You're going to be frustrated that your body is failing you, but it's reserving its energy for healing. Your mind has suffered as big a trauma as your body so it's reserving energy too. It may take something special to get your memory back."

"Like what?"

"Oh, it could be anything—a song on the radio, reading the newspaper or talking to a person. Anything can be a trigger."

Joe sighed. "I hope I'm a patient person."

Dr. Archer laughed and nodded. "See you tomorrow. Take it easy."

"Will do."

Joe closed his eyes and slept fitfully until later that day when a short man in a dark blue suit and round glasses shuffled noisily into Joe's section of the large room. He dragged a chair across the floor past the other patients making scraping sounds like nails on a chalkboard until he found just the right spot. He settled onto the chair and looked Joe in the eye.

"You have battle fatigue."

FORTY-TWO

"Excuse me?"

"Battle fatigue. Combat Stress Reaction in official terms. It used to be called shell shock in the first war."

"Well, don't sugarcoat it, doc. I presume you're a doctor. Just give it to me straight."

"I'm Dr. Edward Spearman, one of the psychologists on call at this hospital. You were extremely fortunate to be admitted on my shift."

A small smile crept out on Joe's face. "And why is that?"

The nattily dressed man pulled a pipe out of his pocket. With his bald head and greying mustache, he could have been an actor in a tobacco advertisement.

"They let you smoke in patients' rooms?"

"Sure. I find it relaxes my patients to see a man with a pipe."

Joe chuckled. "So you're one of those funny psychologists."

The doctor smiled with a twinkle in his eye. "That's me —Happy Dr. Spearman." He twirled his pipe. "But I don't have any tobacco right now, so, Mr. Schneider, let's return to you. You've been through an extraordinary event. Do you remember it?"

"Not much." Joe shook his head, ran fingers through his

disheveled hair. "I have nightmares about being in a dirty prison cell."

"Do you know where the cell was?"

"No."

"What else do you remember about the cell? Were you alone?"

"No, there was a...woman sitting on the bed."

"Anyone you know?"

"Her face was obscured." He looked over at Spearman. "Is that important?"

"Probably. She wasn't hurting you?"

"No. She was just watching. I got the feeling she wanted to help me but couldn't."

Spearman nodded, looked longingly at the pipe. "She may be someone in your life that you want to remember. Are you married?"

Joe shrugged. "I don't know."

"Do you have a girlfriend?"

"I wish I knew. It would be nice to know someone somewhere cared about me."

"Indeed it would."

Joe and the psychologist watched one another until Joe rubbed his head.

"Is your head beginning to hurt again?"

"Yes. I have nonstop headaches."

"The nurse will be coming in soon, I'm sure, so let me leave you with a little information, Mr. Schneider."

"About?"

"Battle fatigue."

"The war's over, Dr. Spearman. How could I have battle fatigue?"

"That's when it generally starts, when you're out of the situation causing the stress. The only information we have about you is that you work as a liaison to the American State Department here in London. However, I recognize the symptoms of battle fatigue when I see them. You have chronic headaches and nightmares about combat situations. The nurses claim you can be aggressive and hostile, then fall into a pit of despair. You've lost weight and sleep is difficult. The nurses say you're restless and irritable with most staff who come to assist you in some way."

"Wow, I...ah...had no idea. Do you think I was a soldier?"

"No. From my experience you fought the war another way." Spearman stuck the pipe back in his pocket. "No matter." He rose from his chair. "I'll be back tomorrow, Mr. Schneider, and we'll pick up our conversation then. Rest now."

"Thank you, doctor." Joe yawned and was asleep before the man left the room.

Later that afternoon, Agents Atwater and Croft stood at the foot of the bed looking at a sleeping Joe.

"I thought you said he was awake, nurse."

Anne nodded. "He's been awake much more yesterday and today than he's been all week." She motioned to a chair nearby. "Perhaps if you take a seat and wait, he'll wake relatively soon. If you'll excuse me." And she left.

Atwater shrugged and walked to the chair. He unbuttoned his jacket taking a seat and pulled a notebook from his pocket. Agent Croft lingered by the bed watching the scene in the hospital room. Moisture collected on his upper lip as his gaze fell on Joe's bandages. He swallowed hard.

"I hate hospitals."

"Oh, would you pull yourself together, Croft? This happens every time we have to visit a hospital."

Croft wiped his lip and stuck his hands in his pockets. "Can't help it. Ever since we investigated that poor bugger who'd been tortured, I hate hospitals."

Agent Atwater rolled his eyes. "Go to the bathroom and splash water on your face, then get back here. We have a job to do."

When Croft left, Joe yawned and stretched his arms. When he blinked his eyes a few times, he focused on the man sitting on a chair close by. A man whose unblinking stare made him nervous.

"Hello?"

"Mr. Schneider?"

"Yes."

"I'm Agent Atwater with Military Intelligence, Section Five." He held up his badge for Joe to see."

"Okay."

"Do you know why you're in the hospital?"

Joe shook his head. "Not really. One of the doctors here says I have battle fatigue. Why, I'm not certain."

"I can enlighten you, if you're ready to listen."

"What does Dr. Archer say?"

"He says you can handle it if you want to."

Joe shifted in his bed, pulled up the sagging blanket. "I'm as ready as I'm going to be."

Atwater nodded, looked around the room before lowering his voice. "You're with the bureau, Mr. Schneider."

"What bureau?"

"MI5. You've been an agent like me for the past four years working in various places. Your last assignment was to go to Bucharest to uncover intelligence about a missing girl."

"Why?"

"She has, or we thought she had, information that her German officer father gave her. Information vital to the British government."

"Did I find her?"

"No. The girl's in Sweden now and apparently knows nothing. We believe the information from the German officer was destroyed."

The door opened and Agent Croft stepped in looking calmer. He walked over to Joe's bed and took out his notebook.

"This is Agent Croft." Joe noted the man's flushed face. "Do you have any questions?"

"Why am I in the hospital? What happened to me?"

"Apparently you were kidnapped by Romanian Communists and tortured," Atwater glanced briefly at Croft, who had paled, "and shot. You were held for a month or more until the Soviet handler dumped you out at one of our checkpoint stations."

"Soviets were involved?"

"Yes. Romania is slowly becoming Communist and the Soviets are very much in control of that. Your Romanian contact was undertrained and things got out of hand. The Soviets stepped in to avoid an international incident."

"Since we were on the same side in the war."

"Precisely."

"Guess I have a dangerous job," Joe muttered to himself.

"Mr. Schneider?"

He shook his head. "What happens now?"

"You need to regain your strength and memory before coming back to work. Since you're awake now and talking, I'll be back in a few days to see how you are. You have parents in Manchester. Do you want them to be called?"

"No. They'll just worry. I can visit them once I'm on my feet."

"All right." From the foot of the bed, Croft scribbled another note.

"We've notified your boss here in town of your where-abouts and gave him a cover story for your being in the hospital. When you're released, no one will know anything about this event."

"Thanks, I guess."

Croft cleared his throat and looked at Atwater, who nodded. "In your office, Mr. Henry McKinnon has asked to see you. Is that a friend of yours?"

Joe shrugged his shoulders, glanced wearily around the room. "Your guess is as good as mine."

"Should we notify him that he can visit?"

"No. Not yet." Joe shivered under the blanket. "I've had enough visitors today to last me a while." He blew out a breath and closed his eyes.

Atwater rose. "We'll leave you now, Mr. Schneider, and see you in a few days."

Joe's last conscious thought after the door clicked shut behind the agents was of a vast body of water with fishing boats sailing into a harbor. A woman's laugh floated through the air before landing on his smiling face.

FORTY-THREE

"I don't know how you can be so calm, Phyl. I'd be a nervous wreck."

"I *am* a nervous wreck, Lorraine. Guess you just don't see it."

Jay held up a hand to Arne. "More coffee, please." The man trotted right over with a fresh pot of coffee. He cast an inquiring glance at Phyllis.

"Du all right, miss?"

Phyllis' smile was small. "Sure, tusen takk, Arne." His frown showed he didn't believe her, but refilled their cups and went on to other customers in his busy café.

"This has been one rough week." Phyllis chewed on a fingernail. "First I have to say goodbye to Lisbet and then Ronnie calls me about Joe."

Lorraine shook her head and tucked strands of pale hair behind an ear. "I don't know how you're still standing. When did Henry call Ronnie?"

"This morning."

"What did he say?" asked Jay. Concern colored her tone.

"Just that Joe was in Queen's Hospital in London and had been shot."

"Shot?" Both Jay and Lorraine glanced at one another in horror.

Phyllis nodded, took a sip of her coffee. "The story is that Joe was shot in a hunting accident." She glanced at her disbelieving friends. "Yeah, I know. It's got to be a cover story since Joe doesn't hunt. Well, for animals at any rate."

"Anything else?" asked Lorraine.

"The hospital notified his boss at the State Department with that crazy story. The boss called Henry in to tell him about it, since he and Joe are friends and colleagues."

"Has Henry visited Joe?"

"No. No one is allowed to visit him just yet."

"Well," began Lorraine, "what about you? Can't you visit? You're engaged to the man."

Phyllis shook her head. "He has amnesia, Ronnie said, so he doesn't remember anyone at this time."

"Amnesia?"

She shrugged. "That's all I know."

Lorraine blinked wary eyes. "So all you know is that he's in a hospital with amnesia and he's been shot? That's it?"

"Believe me, Lorraine, when I tell you that I know just about nothing."

Jay patted her arm. "At least he's alive, Phyllis and that's a pretty wonderful thing. You didn't know what had happened to the guy for a long time after he left."

She smiled at her friend. "Right you are and I am happy to know what's happened, it's just..."

"It's just what, sweetie?" asked Lorraine.

"I can't go see him. Ronnie told me not to call the hospital either. I can't do anything but sit at my desk in Oslo and pretend to work. Ronnie finally told me to go home since I couldn't concentrate on the smallest task and couldn't stop crying."

Jay turned to Lorraine. "Thanks for calling me. I'm happy to offer my company to make Phyllis feel even the tiniest bit better." She glanced at Phyllis, whose eyes were on the door. "Maybe we should order some food."

Phyllis shook her head. "Thanks, Jay, but I couldn't eat a thing."

"I know what you mean." Lorraine took Phyllis' hand. "Let's go back to your apartment and kick off our shoes."

"Good idea. I took the afternoon off too." Jay signaled Arne for the bill.

After leaving Arne's Café, the three women made their way across the busy street to Phyllis' apartment building. The day was cloudy with more snow forecast, but for the moment, it was clear. People had bundled up against the cold and climbed onto the old trolley as it squeaked to a stop. As it chugged to a start again and passed them by, Lorraine, Jay and Phyllis stepped carefully along the snowy street. Going inside the ornate old place and on up to her chilly apartment, Phyllis breathed a sigh of relief. She was happy to be home, happy to be with her friends. But sad that Lisbet was gone. Sadder still about Joe.

Joe.

Phyllis went back to her bedroom to change out of her work clothes. Jay and Lorraine puttered in the kitchen, putting together coffee and cookies on a small tray. Lorraine took the tray out to the living room, then got the fire going to warm the atmosphere. She tidied up the place while Jay washed dishes in the kitchen. When Phyllis came back out, the three women settled with their cups of coffee looking tired and saying little. After several long minutes, Phyllis glanced around the room and shivered. Lorraine rose.

"Need your sweater?"

"No, stay," said Phyllis. "I'm fine."

"You don't look fine."

She pushed back strands of dark hair that had fallen in her face. "No, Lorraine. I mean that I'm as fine as I can be."

"Under the circumstances," finished Jay.

Silence fell around them as they watched the snowfall outside on the patio. Fat flakes were already making a chunky layer of pristine white on the outside table several inches thick. Both chairs looked to be draped with fuzzy cloths. One chair hadn't been moved since Lisbet sat in it. Joe had sat in the other chair sipping a glass of wine and whispering sweet nothings in Phyllis' ear. She closed her eyes as the scene played out before her.

"Phyl? You okay?" Lorraine exchanged worried looks with Jay.

She nodded wearily. "I am." Suddenly, she brightened and sat up.

"Now what?" asked Jay.

"I just remembered a conversation Ronnie and I had with two British agents last week."

Lorraine bit into a cookie. "What about?"

Phyllis leaned towards her friends, softened her tone.

"Two agents from MI5 were in Ronnie's office the second I returned from Sweden."

"Really?" Lorraine's eyes widened as she leaned towards Phyllis. Jay scooted her chair closer.

"Can you tell us what you talked about?"

"It didn't seem like a confidential conversation. They wanted to know what you and I were doing in Sweden, Lorraine. They weren't particularly sympathetic with the reasons why I took Lisbet to her new family, but they seemed really interested in the doll she used to have. You know, her old doll named Sonja."

"The one you gave her?" asked Jay.

Phyllis shook her head, refilled her cup to take a sip. "No. Before her father left, he put her favorite doll, the original Sonja, in her arms. The British government thinks there's a reason for that."

"Yes, but," began Lorraine looking doubtful. "Why in the world would they care about her doll?"

"That's what I was wondering too. I told them the house blew up and no one knows what happened to the doll. After the agents left, Ronnie floated out his theory."

"What?" Jay reached for a cookie, frowned at it before setting it back down.

"Ronnie thinks that Lisbet's father, the German officer, slipped some secret intelligence into the doll somewhere. He gave it to Lisbet for safekeeping, maybe knowing he would need the information later." She stared at her two friends. "I agree with Ronnie. I think that's what Oskar did."

Lorraine shivered, smoothed her wool skirt. "He sure put Lisbet in a dangerous situation."

"No doubt."

Jay leaned back in her chair with eyebrows furrowed over disbelieving eyes. "I don't know, Phyllis. Why would he do it?"

Phyllis swirled the cooled coffee in her cup. She rose, took it into the kitchen. When she returned, she had a funny look on her face.

"Uh-oh," said Lorraine.

"What?"

Lorraine tilted her head towards Phyllis. "Whenever she gets that evil look on her face, Jay, something's up." She smiled at the woman with the dark curly hair who smiled back. "You've got that we're-going-somewhere-and-don't-even-question-me-about-it look."

"Exactly right. Grab your coats and hats, ladies. We're going to take a drive."

"Where?" Jay jumped up looking for her coat.

"To the house where Lisbet lived with her parents."

Lorraine took the tray into the kitchen. "How do you know where it is?"

"My assistant, Nancy, and I had to scour Oslo to find families who had lost their loved ones in the war."

"So?"

"I had her find where Janne Garnes had lived."

Lorraine stopped in front of Phyllis, put her hands on her hips. "You want to look for that blasted doll, don't you?"

Jay blinked surprised eyes at them both. "I thought the doll was destroyed. In fact, you said that the house blew up, so how can there be anything left to find?"

Phyllis slipped arms into her coat sleeves, adjusted the hat on her head with the Daughters of the American Revolution hatpin. "Well, I guess we'll find out."

Shrugging into her coat, Lorraine headed for the door.

"We're not going in that rusty old trolley, are we?" She opened the door and looked back.

"Nope. If I can get to a telephone, I'm going to call John Edelland."

"Edelland?" Jay laughed. "The guy who rescued us from the black market caper?"

"And the man who asked you to marry him?" added Lorraine.

"What?" Jay's voice rose a notch.

Phyllis waved a hand at them both. "Calm down, you two. Your jobs are to support me, not create waves. I know what I'm doing. Let's use the phone at Arne's Café. He just got one installed."

She sailed out the door, tugging on her gloves, while her friends grinned at one another behind her back and sailed out with her.

FORTY-FOUR

The shiny black car moved noiselessly down Oslo streets. Lorraine and Jay clucked continuously about the car's merits while Phyllis stared out the window.

"John just sent you this car? Just because you asked him to?" Lorraine shook her head. "Would you get a load of this upholstery?"

"And the shiny chrome." added Jay with eyes wide as saucers. She ran her hand along the leather seat in front, accidentally touching the driver's shoulder. He looked back at her.

"Oops! Sorry."

"That's all right, miss. Nice car, don't you think?" The older man adjusted his cap and winked.

"I think so. Phyllis, what do you think?"

When she didn't respond, Lorraine poked her in the shoulder. "Hey. Where are you?"

Phyllis turned back from the window. "Oh, sorry. I was just watching the neighborhood."

"What neighborhood?" Lorraine glanced out Phyllis' window. "The place has been leveled."

"True but a few signs are still around." She tapped on the driver's shoulder. "Excuse me, but how do you know this is the right street?"

The man slowed the car and adjusted the rear view mirror. "I've lived in Oslo all my life, miss. My bestemor used to live in this neighborhood."

"Bestemor?" asked Phyllis.

"My granny. She always gossiped about the neighbors. Mr. Edelland and I discussed which house you must be looking for and I think it's this one." He pointed out the window.

Phyllis stuck her nose to the glass as Lorraine and Jay pressed hard against her from either side, their noses as close to the window as they could get.

The empty shells of two houses close together looked ready to collapse. On either side were heaps of broken bricks, boards and the remnants of furniture. One bedraggled tree stripped of its leaves and bark leaned precariously toward the house.

"Her house was bombed all right," said Phyllis shaking her head. "It must have been so frightening for little Lisbet and her mother."

The driver stopped the car and Phyllis opened the door. Stepping out, she nodded toward the tree. "Lisbet said there was a large tree on the side of the house where her father put a wooden swing. She said she spent many happy hours out here."

Lorraine and Jay flanked her on both sides. Jay shivered in her wool coat.

"It's going to snow again. Let's do this."

The driver retrieved three shovels from the back of the car. He walked to the women and handed them over. "Mr. Edelland said you might have need of these."

Phyllis took one. "Will you stay and wait for us?"

The man tipped his cap. "I'm at your disposal for the rest of the day. Compliments of Mr. Edelland."

She smiled. "I'll have to thank him personally for this favor."

"He remarked he would be waiting for your call, miss."

"I'll bet," whispered Lorraine with a smirk. She patted

her long pageboy. "Boy, did I pick the wrong day to curl my hair."

Jay laughed and grabbed a shovel. "Let's get to work, ladies. We're wasting valuable time."

They stepped towards the ruined house cautiously. A glance at her feet had Phyllis shaking her head. "I should have thought this out better. We can't do much digging in these shoes."

The driver cleared his throat. "Ah, miss?"

"Yes?"

"Mr. Edelland took the liberty of also putting three pairs of boots in the car. He said you might need them."

Phyllis laughed. "We sure do. Wonderful John! I'm going to buy him dinner tomorrow."

After tugging on the leather boots and lacing them, the women looked from boot to boot.

"Wherever did John get these?" asked Lorraine.

"Probably Sweden," said Jay. "Norway still doesn't have much in the way of shoes, much less boots."

"Ja, Sweden." The driver beamed before heading back to the car.

"Ready?" Phyllis looked at her two friends, who each gave her a thumbs up. "Lorraine, you take that area." She pointed to her right. "And Jay, you start over there." She pointed to her left. "If you see anything at all, give a holler."

Inside the hollowed-out house, the women headed in three different directions. It was a crazy scene of destruction. The roof was entirely gone enabling snow to fall over the remnants of stone, bricks, wood and furniture. Three glass-less windows with rows of bricks overhead still intact revealed heaps of destruction across the street. The wind picked up with the snowfall making their task even more difficult. Sounds of shovels hitting bricks and wood were almost swept away with the wind blowing their breath away as well. The women stumbled constantly over rubble that refused to move.

Phyllis finally gave up on the shovel and had begun

moving bits of debris aside by hand when she heard Jay give a shout.

"Hey! I found something!"

Jay was pointing just past her boots and Lorraine got to her first. She crouched down to pluck wood and rocks aside.

Phyllis picked her way over taking care where she placed each booted foot. She bent down to look at what Lorraine was holding. "What is it?"

"It's a red apron." Lorraine blew out a breath before tossing it down.

"Okay. Well, it's a start." Phyllis swept the hair out of her eyes as she slogged back to her section of the house. She climbed over part of a chair and walked around table legs sticking up like bowling pins.

They'd worked for a few hours finding remnants of Lisbet's former life—a dish here, a sock there—when Lorraine found bits of a ragged rug caught under a pile of bricks. When she tugged on the rug, she noticed a small budge, which encouraged her to tug harder.

"Phyl! Jay! Come here!"

Jay wiped sweat from her brow and lifted her bulky coat to hurry over. "What have you got?"

"Not sure but help me clear these bricks."

By the time Phyllis made her way over, the women had moved crumbling rubble to show a ruined rug covering a bump on the ground. Breathing hard, Phyllis and Lorraine pulled up the rug as Jay reached around to grab what was underneath. By the time she brought out a plastic head with bits of curly brown hair still attached, Phyllis gasped out loud. The doll's body was nearly gone with only part of a torso and one arm left. But her head was still adorned with a lacy pink bonnet, frayed and dirty after months in the weather. Jay's face clouded as she handed the doll to Phyllis.

By this time tears were already rolling down Phyllis' face and not for the ruined toy in her hands, but for the little girl whose life could be summed up by the condition of the doll.

The tattered doll. The tattered country. They were one and the same.

Without moving from the spot, Phyllis pulled off the bonnet and watched unbelievingly when a small piece of folded paper fluttered to the ground. She bent over to pick it up.

"What is it, Phyl?" asked Lorraine. She moved closer to peer over her friend's shoulder. "Names?"

Jay came around the other side. She pointed to the paper. "Looks like English names."

"And Russian names," added Lorraine. She looked at Phyllis. "What are we looking at?"

Phyllis' frown deepened. "I can guess, but I'm not going to just yet. Let me say that it was a horrible thing for Oskar to do to his own daughter. He made her a target for British and Soviet authorities." She shook her head. "Not nice at all."

Lorraine and Jay watched her with their faces etched in curiosity. Phyllis tucked the doll under her arm and wearily made her way back to the waiting car.

FORTY-FIVE

"What are they doing here?" Phyllis dashed into Lt. Col. Lawrence's office the minute she saw the two British agents walking down the hallway. "Colonel? Did you call them?"

Ronnie rose from behind his desk and motioned for Phyllis to take a seat.

"You bet. This is too big for us, Phyllis. It's for the British government to take control of, not us."

"But, Colonel..."

"No buts. The information is way over my pay grade and yours."

She barely refrained from rolling her eyes. "I know that, but still..."

A knock at the door of the Military Attaché at the American Embassy in Oslo stopped her midsentence. Ronnie nodded at the door.

"Let them in, Miss Bowden, and don't go anywhere." He bit back a smile. "You're the one in the hot seat."

She popped up from the chair, smoothed the collar of her blouse and twirled a curl behind her ears. Within five steps, she flung open the door to the waiting agents. Looking as nondescript and bland as before, Agents Atwater and Croft walked into Ronnie's office.

"Lt. Col. Lawrence." He nodded to Ronnie.

"Agents."

"Miss Bowden. Nice to see you again."

Phyllis managed a weak smile.

"Please have a seat, gentlemen and let me know how we can help you—again."

"You called us, Colonel."

Lawrence glanced at Phyllis. "I guess I should turn the show over to Miss Bowden. She's the one with the information you've been looking for."

When the two men turned their attention to Phyllis, she reached into her skirt pocket to pull out a small, folded piece of paper. Atwater nearly quit breathing when she handed it to him. Croft stared as if mesmerized.

"This is it?"

"Yes."

"Where did you find it?"

"I combed through the bombed out house where Lisbet and her mother had lived just north of town."

Atwater's neutral face nearly slipped into astonishment. "But...how did you know where to look?"

Phyllis coyly arched an eyebrow. "You have your sources and I have mine."

"I guess so." Atwater opened the folded paper and gazed at the information written there. His slight flinch was noticeable. Croft's only reaction was his widening eyes.

Agent Atwater tucked the paper inside his pocket, rose and tipped his hat to Phyllis.

"My government owes you a debt of gratitude, Miss Bowden. If this information had fallen into enemy hands..."

"Who is the enemy now, Agent Atwater?"

He smiled. "A very good question indeed." He turned to go with the silent Croft right behind.

"Wait a minute." Both agents looked at her. "You can't just go without telling us something."

"Yes, we can."

"You said the British government owes me a debt of gratitude. Well, I have a couple of things in mind for payment."

Ronnie bit back a smile.

Perplexed, Atwater stepped forward. "What did you have in mind, Miss Bowden?"

"First of all, you owe an explanation to the little girl whose life was in danger because of that slip of paper in your hot little hand." She stuck out her chin defiantly. "What do those names mean?"

Atwater and Croft exchanged a studied look before glancing back at Phyllis.

"All right, although the explanation will give her no comfort." The agent cleared his throat. "These are names of British and Soviet spies that her father had compiled. Oskar Albrecht was a German spy living in Oslo infiltrating other spy rings. His job was to discover his counterparts within the Allied countries."

"How do you know this?" asked Lawrence.

"Oskar was captured by the British while trying to escape Norway. He was imprisoned and tried for war crimes. When he explained his job to British authorities, he asked to trade information for his life."

"What's happened to him?" asked Phyllis.

Atwater glanced at Croft before answering. "This intelligence was not found in a timely manner. Oskar Albrecht was tried and sentenced a month ago. He was subsequently shot as punishment for his crimes against Norway and the Allied powers."

Phyllis sucked in a ragged breath, looked from agent to agent. "He's dead?"

"Yes, Miss Bowden. Anything further?"

Since Phyllis' flushed face stopped her from replying, Ronnie stepped into the pause.

"Agent Joseph Schneider is in Queen's Hospital in London. Miss Bowden is his fiancé. Is there any way she can see him during his recovery?"

At Joe's name, Phyllis perked up.

"I'll pass along your request, Colonel and Miss Bowden." Atwater tipped his hat and with Croft bringing up the rear, left as quietly as they'd come.

Phyllis sank into the closest chair. "Thank you, sir. I was

overwhelmed by what happened to Lisbet's father."

"I know you were, but it was the right time to ask for a favor. You need to see Joe."

She rose, walked over to him with her hand outstretched. "You're too good to be true, Colonel."

He laughed. "Tell that to my wife."

FORTY-SIX

"Where shall we meet?"

"How about that little café across the street from your apartment? You're always there anyway." Lt. Col. Lawrence looked up from the flurry of papers on his messy desk.

"Arne's? We can't meet at a noisy café, Colonel. Or in public." Phyllis glanced about the office, steno pad in hand. "This is a sensitive meeting and will probably get messy with a flood of tears." She plopped on the chair by his desk only to rise again as quickly as she sat. "Oh, I wish Lorraine hadn't gone back to London so soon. She'd know what to do."

Ronnie chuckled. "How about your apartment then? It's quiet and private."

"Yes, but getting past Mrs. Lind might prove to be difficult. I'd just as soon not take the chance."

Phyllis stared out the window while Ronnie buried his nose in his work. "I'm sure you'll figure it out. In the meantime, don't you have some work to do?"

She nodded, heading for the door. "I'll let you know when I think of a place. When is he arriving?"

Ronnie glanced at his watch. "The transport should have arrived by now. You'd better get on move on, Miss Bowden. He should be here within the hour."

"He's coming here?"

"You were busy digging in the rocks at Lisbet's house when I got official notification, so I did the best I could. Figure out what to do with him when he arrives at the embassy." Ronnie picked up a pencil. "Put him in the conference room for now."

"Yes, sir," she said half-heartedly. "Yes, sir!" Phyllis repeated more emphatically with a bright smile. "That's it!"

"What's it?" Ronnie didn't look up.

"I'll bring Astrid and Helge to the embassy and they can meet him in the conference room. I can bring in snacks and water and..."

"Better check the schedule to make sure the room is not being used for an hour."

"Got it."

"And Phyllis?"

She turned back to him. "Sir?"

He pointed the pencil at the door. "Go! I need to get busy and so do you."

Back at her desk, Phyllis picked up a phone. Before dialing, she caught her assistant's attention. "Nancy? Are we caught up on the notification list?"

"Yes, we are. I spoke to Chaplain Stevens yesterday. He's finished the last few names."

Phyllis sighed. "He's had a thankless task, to be sure."

"And there's a new clothing shipment coming to Oslo from New York this week. Should I contact the mayor's office?"

"Yes, please. That clothing is still so desperately needed that it needs to be distributed the second it comes in."

"I'll take care of it."

"Thank you, Nancy." After dialing, Phyllis scanned her pile of letters that needed to go out today. Lt. Col. Lawrence had been busy this morning and her pile was high. She'd probably have to put in an hour of overtime since Nancy had to leave early. While waiting for her party to pick up, Phyllis' mind drifted to Joe. He was never far from her thoughts. What was he doing now? Did he remember her at all?

Before she could get too worked up over Joe's situation,

she spoke clearly into the phone when the call was picked up.

"Jay Lawlor, please."

"One minute."

Phyllis checked her watch and in exactly one minute, Jay's cheery voice filled the phone line.

"Jay Lawlor. How may I help you?"

"If it isn't my old digging partner."

Jay laughed. "Hi mate. What's up?"

"Is Astrid at work today?"

"She is. Why?"

"Lt. Col. Lawrence found one of her brothers, Gunnar. Alive."

"He did?" Jay couldn't contain her excitement and dropped the phone. Phyllis heard a thud as it hit the floor.

"Hey! You there?"

"Should I tell her? Do you want to tell her? How do you want to handle this? Phyllis, I'm so excited that I'm trying hard not to shout!"

"I know you are, Jay, so calm down." Phyllis tapped a pencil on her desk. "Why don't you bring her to the embassy for some reason and I'll tell her when she gets here. Check in at the front desk and have someone take you to the small conference room towards the back. I'll meet you and Astrid there."

"Now?"

"Yes, now. He's on his way here as we speak."

"What about Helge?"

"I'm going to call her on some pretext to meet me here too. Hopefully, they can meet their brother together."

She heard Jay catch her breath. "I know I'm going to cry when I see Astrid."

"Hold it together, sweetie. Let's do this right."

"Phyllis?"

"Yeah?"

"Just the one brother?"

Phyllis swallowed hard. "That's right. Just the elder

brother, Gunnar, appears to have made it. We're pretty sure the other brother perished."

"Oh no. How do you know?"

"The Colonel's source found Rolf Hansen's name on the roll of a labor camp around Auschwitz."

"But no one can find him?"

"No."

"That sounds definitive."

"I think so."

"See you soon."

"Okay."

After calling Helge and notifying the front desk of her plans, Phyllis tidied her desk. Nervous now, she buzzed Lawrence to let him know she was going to the conference room. He wished her luck and she hurried down several hallways to the back of the embassy. Ducking into the small conference room, she checked to make sure water was available as well as cups and cookies. With everything in place, she also checked her reflection in the glare of a bright window. She patted her curly hair, tucked a few loose strands behind her ears and smoothed her lipstick. There was still color on her lips and her brown eyes were wide with excitement. She hadn't had as many high points in this job in Oslo as she'd had lows, so the coming rendezvous was making her giddy.

Looking past her reflection, she gazed at houses along the Oslo Fjord standing like sentries to the boats sailing towards the pier. The sky was bright blue with puffy clouds arched overhead like fuzzy caterpillars. The still water reflected blue and white, an almost mirror reflection. Her smile nearly became a laugh when she actually glimpsed fish jumping out of the water. It was a beautiful snapshot of a placid place in time. A knock at the door brought her back to the moment at hand.

"Come in."

Helge walked in, her face slightly puzzled.

"Hi Miss Phyllis. I didn't think I'd hear from you so soon."

"Sorry about that, Helge. To say I've been busy is not much of an excuse but it's true."

She nodded, took off her coat. The blonde Norwegian woman seemed taller than when Phyllis last saw her.

"Just put that on a chair."

"I assume Lisbet is tucked away in Sweden."

"She is. It went very well."

"Have you heard from her?"

"She writes every week and has asked for your address. Make sure I have it before you leave."

Helge smoothed her long skirt. "Miss Phyllis, why did you call me?"

"I told you." She reached into a pocket. "I need to pay you for the days you watched Lisbet for me."

"And I told you on the phone that you owed me nothing, yet you insisted I come over anyway." She glanced around the room. "Did you plan a party and forget to invite other guests?"

"Have a seat, Helge. I'm not going to spoil the moment for you. Just wait with me...please."

Helge's pale blue eyes narrowed. "I don't like surprises."

Phyllis bit back her smile. "You'll like this one."

The door opened revealing Astrid and Jay. They swept into the room babbling about how the temperature outside had dropped like a stone and more snow was forecast. Helge rose to greet her sister while Jay walked over to where Phyllis was standing. They hugged briefly before turning to watch the Hansen sisters. Tall, blonde and lovely, the girls made an impressive picture. Two sets of blue eyes swung her way.

"There's water and cookies on the table, so please help yourselves."

No one moved.

"Why are we here?" asked Astrid. Her eyes darted to Jay. "Miss Jay? Do you know?"

She opened her mouth to reply when there was another knock at the door. The loud noise reverberated through the room. All eyes turned to see a thin man on crutches hobble into the room escorted by the front desk officer. The officer nodded to Phyllis and left.

For a moment, the silence in the room was absolute as everyone stared at the shaggy-haired man who seemed to be barely there. His thin frame couldn't possibly be holding him up. If not for the crutches, he wouldn't be standing. Scant traces of hair dotted his cheeks and his angular jaw looked pointy by skin stretched taut on a still-handsome face. But his eyes were clear and bright as the man observed them as well. A smile started small and soon consumed his face.

"Gunnar?" gasped Astrid.

She and Helge began sobbing as they flew to him, arms outstretched. They nearly knocked him over in their haste to grab him and hold him close. The crutches dropped to the floor, echoing about the room. Phyllis and Jay slowly shuffled out the door, closing it quietly on the breathtaking familial scene behind them. The friends looked at one another with glistening cheeks.

"Let's leave them alone for a while," said Phyllis motioning down the hall. "There's a small kitchen back here. Let's get something to drink and wait for them."

"What happened to them, Phyllis? Did you find out?"

She nodded, opening a door not far from the conference room. "The Colonel learned both brothers were deported on the SS Donau like their parents, but at a different time. At Auschwitz, they were taken to a labor camp close by where they worked on construction projects." She poured a glass of water for Jay.

"Thanks." She took a sip, watched Phyllis pour a glass for herself. "What about Rolf?"

"They were at the same slave labor camp, but we're fairly sure that Rolf didn't make it. We've heard stories of brutality, malnutrition and torture that would curl your toes. We found Gunnar in a Polish hospital after liberation."

Jay blew out a heavy breath and set down her glass. "Do you think Gunnar knows what happened to his brother?"

Phyllis shrugged, gulped half her water before putting the glass in the sink.

"I don't know, but I'm sure if he does, he will let his sisters know."

"Should we head back now?"

"In a minute. I need to arrange transportation to the girls' apartment."

"Right. You don't want them trying to get him on the trolley."

"No, I'm going to call for a taxi."

"I've seen one or two out on the streets now." She smiled. "I'll split the fare with you."

"Thanks. I'll take you up on that."

Strolling down the hallway, the two women held their heads higher and had a slight spring in their step. With straightened shoulders, they felt taller. It was a good day.

No. It was an incredible day. The kind that makes you glad you are alive.

FORTY-SEVEN

Phyllis arrived at Queen's Hospital after dark, tired and worried. The lobby was deserted except for a woman mopping the floors and an attending nurse who blocked her access with arms folded across her chest and a huge scowl.

Phyllis pulled out all the stops. She was ready to go down on her knees if need be, but after the third rendition of "Please let me see him. I'm his fiancé," each one more pleading than the last, the nurse's scowl faded to a frown and she hesitantly escorted Phyllis to Joe's room. All the way down the hall, the nurse issued dire warnings about bothering sleeping patients, especially one who slept as little as did Mr. Schneider. He refused any sleeping medication so he was only sleeping a few hours at a time and his sleep schedule was a mess.

Standing before Phyllis with her white cap placed squarely on gray hair, the stocky woman's hands fisted on her long white skirt. The expression on her tight face brooked no nonsense.

"You understand what I'm telling you, Miss Bowden? Do not wake this patient for any reason."

"I understand completely, nurse. I'll just sit quietly and wait for him to awaken." Phyllis smiled her best winning smile. The nurse didn't appear convinced.

"Ten minutes, Miss Bowden, whether he awakens or not."

Phyllis' head bobbed repeatedly. "Certainly, ma'am."

She was busting her buttons to peer around the woman to see what she could see. When the nurse finally stepped aside, Phyllis peeked inside the large room. With several patients in attendance, Phyllis glanced back at the nurse.

"Which one is he?"

The woman put her finger to her lips before pointing to a bed at the end of the row. A screen had been erected around it so Phyllis couldn't see anything.

The lights were dimmed and when the nurse left, piercing Phyllis with one more scowl, the moon shining in a window was the only way she could find her way along the row of patients. Stepping softly, Phyllis hardly gave any of the other patients a second look, so focused was she on one patient in particular. With her heart in her mouth and having been away from him for months now, her legs began to shake the closer she got to the screened bed.

Fear tiptoed down her spine as Phyllis crept along the path concentrating on putting one foot in front of the other. It surprised her that her mouth was dry, her pulse was pounding and there was a sudden ringing in her ears. She probably should have talked to Lorraine before coming to see him, but nothing would have prepared her for the assault on her senses as that stark screen grew closer. Suddenly, a patient in the next bed murmured something causing Phyllis to freeze. Nervous eyes darted to the man who tugged on a blanket before settling back in. When he began to snore, she moved on.

Barely breathing, Phyllis blew on her cold hands before reaching to part the curtains in the screen. She stepped inside the small space furnished with a bed, chair and tiny table. Moonlight gave her the first look at the sleeping man. One arm was thrown up over his head giving him a restless look, as if no position was particularly comfortable. White sheets and blankets contrasted with his dark hair but matched his pale face. If it weren't for the circles under his eyes, his appearance would have been washed out entirely. He had the look of a very sick man.

Phyllis' hand flew to her mouth to muffle her gasp. This couldn't be her Joe Schneider. The Joe she knew was full of life and fun, blushing cheeks and flirty eyes. She remembered seeing him off at the train station in Oslo. His gray fedora was tilted at a jaunty angle and his eyes tracked her wherever she went. The dark topcoat over his nice blue suit set him apart from other men at the station with his confidence and poise. When he kissed her goodbye, those full lips wanted to remain on hers forever. She knew that. She felt that.

Looking at him now, she was shocked. His lips were thin and closed tightly against some unforeseen danger. The blanket was askew so she could see bandages covering part of his chest and right shoulder. Fingers of one hand seem to dance to their own tune. The confidence and poise had fled. Whatever he'd been through had drained the life out of him.

Phyllis raked a shaky hand through her hair and licked her dry lips. He needed her now and she knew it, although seeing the task at hand scared her to death.

She could do this.

The space began to move in on her. Moisture collected on her face, dripped down her neck. The outer edges of her peripheral vision began to narrow and Phyllis clenched her teeth. Not now! She couldn't fail Joe. Not after whatever had happened to him. He needed her...

Phyllis rubbed her face hard to stop the coldness beginning to spread through her body. She pinched the underside of her arm to keep herself focused. It helped. Fighting her body's reactions, she stepped to Joe's bedside. One arm hung loosely by his side and she reached over to touch him. He was freezing cold. Phyllis looked around for another blanket and upon seeing none she shucked her wool coat to lay over him. With the warm material close to his chin, Phyllis softly stroked his face. When she laid her hand lovingly on one cheek, he smiled, still asleep, flipping him in an instant from the unfamiliar sick man in the strange hospital bed to her beloved Joe Schneider. She'd know that becoming smile anywhere.

That did it.

Phyllis chucked her shoes and crawled into bed with him. She was gratefully surprised when his arm came around her so she could snuggle close. Kissing his cheek, she snuggled as close to him as humanly possible. Still fast asleep, his body responded by tangling a leg with hers. She hadn't felt this good in months. She sighed deeply, closed her weary eyes and fell asleep.

The stern nurse was surprised when she checked in to tell Phyllis she had to go, but softened somewhat when she saw them wrapped tightly together. Down deep, she realized that this woman was the best medicine Mr. Schneider could have and left as quietly as possible. Her watery eyes told her that she was right to leave them alone.

Joe was in the filthy cell again with light through the bars reflecting on the floor around him. But this time, the woman from the bed was holding him in her arms. Joe took a deep breath, the first one in ages. She was warm and soft and her scent filled his senses as if he were knee deep in a field of flowers. Wanting a good look, Joe reached out to cup her chin. His eyes blinked open and for a moment he couldn't get his bearings.

He was in a hospital bed but a warm body clung to him. With their legs tangled and his hand curled around her chin, he knew this was the woman from his dreams. She opened sleepy eyes to stare back at him.

"Joe. It's me."

That voice, that familiar voice. Recognition washed over him as if he'd been doused with a bucket of cold water. Her pretty brown eyes twinkled with the grin that soon consumed her lovely face. Could it be?

"Phyllis?"

His whisper-soft question was her undoing. Tears flooded her eyes and ran down her cheeks.

"Don't cry. We'll work it out," he said softly.

"You...sniff...always say that."

"Because it's always true."

Tears filled his eyes as their lips met in a lingering kiss full of remembrance and love.

He had a million things to tell her but knew it could wait. He felt like a whole man for the first time in months and savored the taste of it with his entire being. Joe wrapped Phyllis tighter and held on like his life depended on it. He knew it did.

They melted into one another with fluid happiness dripping from every pore.

"Sleep, sweetheart. It's not even light out."

Phyllis kissed his chest, closed her eyes and fell contentedly asleep, her contentedness expressed in the sweet smile on her relaxed face. All their time together came rushing back chapter and verse causing him to remember one of her little eccentricities. She would place her hands underneath him as they spooned closely together. Joe sighed, placed his chin on Phyllis' head and drifted back to sleep. Morning would be soon enough to talk and talk...and talk. For right now, he just wanted to be.

AND SO BEGAN a new routine for Agent Joe Schneider. Both of Joe's doctors, Dr. Archer and Dr. Spearman, approved Phyllis to stay with him at night even though the night nurse soundly disapproved. With Phyllis by his side, Joe began eating and sleeping more regularly and he finally gave in to the physical therapy his doctors had ordered. Up until Phyllis' arrival, Joe hadn't seen the point and refused to leave his bed except for visits to the restroom.

Four days after she'd arrived, Phyllis and Nurse Anne had gotten him in a wheelchair, something Anne had been encouraging him to do. The clunky metal frame with wooden seat wasn't exactly comfortable, but Phyllis wheeled him out into the courtyard to get a bit of air. It was chilly so they bundled up against the cold. Just to see the rosy patches in Joe's cheeks was enough for Phyllis and she closed her eyes to turn her face up towards the sun.

"Isn't it a beautiful day?" she asked him.

Joe watched her closely as her cheeks warmed with the bright sunlight. "It is now."

When she opened her eyes and turned to him, Joe wore a big grin.

"You look so much better than when I first arrived, Joe."

"How did I look?"

She grimaced. "Horrible. Like you'd about given up."

"I had. I've been here nearly two weeks and my memory had failed me."

"Because of your ordeal?"

"That's what Dr. Spearman told me. He calls it battle fatigue."

She crouched to tuck the blanket around his legs. "I don't even want to imagine what you went through."

He ran a finger gently down her cheek. "And I don't want to think about it ever again, so we're even."

"But," she began hesitantly, "aren't you supposed to talk about it? Isn't that part of your therapy?"

"Listen to me." Her eyes snapped to his. "I will discuss it at length with Dr. Spearman."

"You'll continue with him?"

"Yes."

"Even after you're released from the hospital?"

He nodded.

"Good. I've been worried that you'd stop."

"No, but I don't want to talk to you about it, Phyllis. Is that all right? There's so many wonderful things that can be in our future, I don't want to wallow in the past."

She considered his request. Taking his hand, she kissed his palm. "I'll say yes to your request for now. But if a problem develops between us that stems from the kidnapping, then I reserve the right to see Dr. Spearman with you so I can understand what's happening. I don't want this 'battle fatigue' thing to ever come between us."

Joe's smile stretched across his face. "How'd you get so smart?"

"My mama raised me right?"

"And then some."

She rose to kiss his smiling lips, pausing to study his face.

"What?"

"You have color in your cheeks and your eyes are so bright."

He arched an eyebrow playfully. "The better to see you with, my dear."

They laughed and she steered him towards a large tree in the middle of the courtyard. With the severe hospital buildings all around, the tree was the only bit of greenery in a sea of white. Benches had been built around the tree with chairs parked in various places. Joe and Phyllis weren't the only visitors to the courtyard today. As the sun climbed higher in the sky, several more patients were wheeled out to catch the rays and breathe in some fresh air. When she parked him under the enormous tree, she nodded at other patients not far away.

"Did Lt. Col. Lawrence give you much time off?"

"He gave me a week but I've already called him for more. I have an assistant now who can and has stepped into my shoes when need be."

"Glad to hear you aren't leaving him in the lurch."

She bent to kiss his cheek. He smiled up at her.

"What was that for?"

"As much as I admire and respect the Colonel, I'd leave him at any time if you needed me."

With watery eyes, he glanced down at the folded hands in his lap. "I don't deserve someone as good as you."

Phyllis laughed, smoothed his wavy hair. "Probably not, but I think you're stuck with me. Remember we got engaged?"

That made him smile. "I do remember something like that happening. Your pushy landlady, Mrs. Lind, is to blame for that. How shall we punish her?"

"By inviting her to the wedding?"

He shook his head. "I'm a mess now, honey, and you know I am. How can you even consider marrying me?"

She lifted his chin. "Don't think you're going to weasel

out of marrying me, Joe Schneider. You know we'll work it out."

He grinned. "You always say that."

"Because it's always true."

The next day Joe was discharged from Queen's Hospital. His chest and shoulder wounds were healing nicely and all stitches had been removed. Joe and Phyllis moved into his flat in London by Covent Gardens and concentrated on his rehabilitation and recovery. She'd finally talked him into calling his parents and they were due for a visit soon from their home in Manchester, some three hours north of London. In the meantime, Phyllis called her former room-mates at the row house at Seven Addison Bridge Place and talked to Mrs. Stewart, the landlady, as well. Calls from other friends, a visit from Agents Atwater and Croft, plus dinner at home with Henry and Lorraine all buoyed Joe's spirits. He was feeling pretty good after a home visit with Dr. Spearman from the hospital.

Phyllis was still concerned about Joe's weight loss and pale pallor, but he appeared to be rebounding until his parents walked in the door. She realized there was much more going on between Joe and his father when the man looked Joe up one side and then the other before saying, "You don't look any worse for wear. Why in my day..."

And the man hadn't even taken off his hat.

FORTY-EIGHT

A few minutes later when Michael Schneider finally took a breath, Phyllis jumped into the pause.

"Let me take your hats and coats, Mr. and Mrs. Schneider." The man turned inquisitive eyes toward her, eyes that Joe had obviously inherited. Thick in build with graying hair and robust face, Joe's father straightened his shoulders and gave her his full attention.

"I don't believe we've been introduced." It came out like he didn't want to be either.

Joe pulled himself up to face his father. "Michael and Mary Schneider, this is my fiancé, Phyllis Bowden." He glanced at Phyllis. "Phyllis, these are my parents."

She smiled, extended her hand. "So pleased to meet you, Mr. Schneider, Mrs. Schneider. Come into the living room. I'll bring out coffee."

Joe's mother, petite and shy, found her voice. "Joe? You got engaged?" She beamed at Phyllis. "It's a pleasure to meet you, Miss..."

"Phyllis. Please call me Phyllis."

"Phyllis it is then." A smile stretched across her attractive face. Taking off her hat revealed gray hair twisted neatly in a knot on her head. The No Trespassing sign parked above Michael Schneider's head didn't extend to Mary Schneider.

She actually looked excited and reached over to give Phyllis a hug.

Michael harrumphed. "Mrs. Schneider. You forget yourself," he said brusquely.

Mary waved him away. "Oh, pooh, Michael. It's not every day that our only child gets engaged." She stood on tiptoes to kiss Joe's cheek before taking Phyllis' arm to walk toward the kitchen. "Let me help you with the coffee." Leaving Joe and his father to stand stiffly looking at one another.

"Want to sit down, Dad?"

"Might as well. We're here."

Phyllis glanced back at Joe and Michael. They sat in seats not particularly close and she sighed wondering if their physical distance mirrored their personality differences. Mary caught her sigh.

"Don't worry about them, dear. They'll work it out or they won't."

"Has it always been like this between them?" Phyllis reached for the coffee pot.

"Since Joe joined the service." Mary peeled off her gloves. "Where's your coffee?"

"Over there." Phyllis pointed to a cupboard by Mary's head. She wasn't sure what to say so she said nothing. Mary opened the coffee container then patted Phyllis' arm.

"Joe has always looked up to his father, the big strong bobby, but Michael thinks Joe tried to best him by going into MI5. It's been push-pull since then."

"Sorry to hear that."

Mary shrugged. "So am I, believe me. So am I." She brightened. "But with you on the scene, perhaps they'll call a truce."

Phyllis reached for a measuring cup and dipped it into the coffee. She hoped so too.

In the living room, silence coated the room like frost. Joe's eyes wandered from his father's piercing stare to the radio over to the side. He'd moved the chairs to be closer but maybe Phyllis wanted more of a conversation grouping. He needed to ask her about that. Just as he was thinking about changing the wall color from pale yellow to blue maybe, Michael loudly cleared his throat.

"Joe."

"Sir?"

"We received a call from Queen's Hospital about you." He paused. "Some nurse said you'd been injured."

"That's true."

"What happened to you?"

Joe hesitated, wondered how much to say, but knew whatever he said would be wrong.

"I was on assignment, Dad, in Bucharest."

"Romania? Why?"

Joe shook his head. "You know I can't say."

"How did you end up in the hospital?"

"It all went south. I was shot."

"Where?"

Joe laid a hand on his chest. "My chest and shoulder."

"You look all right now."

"I'm recovering, that's true."

Michael swung his gaze towards the kitchen. "Where did you meet this woman?"

"This woman has a name: Phyllis." His eyes narrowed. "We met here in London."

"Also on assignment."

"Yes, sir. You know it's what I do."

His gaze continued. "Does she know what you do for a living?"

"She does."

"And it's all right with her?"

Joe didn't answer right away. His father fixed him with another pointed stare before pushing.

"What aren't you saying?"

"It's all right with Phyllis that I'm in MI5, but it's not all right with me. Not any longer."

Michael leaned forward, a tense frown on his face. "What are you saying? That you're quitting?"

When Joe didn't respond, his father pushed again.

"You're going to give up after getting hurt one time? Why it won't be the last and..."

"Dad." Joe threw his hands up in the air. "Don't get worked up. Nothing's been decided. I'm just thinking about the future and my options. For one thing, Phyllis is American."

"American?" he snorted. "I thought so. Funny damn accent, I told your mother when we spoke to her on the phone." Michael pointed at Joe. "But your job is your job. You stay with it even when the going gets rough."

Joe refrained from any reaction. His dad was serious and it wasn't a good time to rile him up. He raked a hand through his hair. "Dad, I haven't made any decisions. I'm on sick leave right now and I'm weighing my options."

"You owe a debt to your country, son."

"I've paid my debt to my country."

"Joseph..."

Michael was rising from his seat when Mary hurried in with a tray, Phyllis hot on her heels.

"Coffee!" she chirped. "Fresh and hot and just what we need to take the heat off in this room." She eyed Michael, who promptly sat back down. "Would you care for milk and sugar?"

"You know how I like my coffee, Mrs. Schneider."

"Yes, but Phyllis doesn't and she's pouring you a cup."

"Oh." His eyes strayed to the young woman next to his wife waiting for his instructions. "One lump and a dash of milk, please."

When everyone had coffee and the women were seated next to their men, Michael looked at his wife. "Did you know that Miss Bowden is American?"

"Yes, I did. Phyllis told me in the kitchen."

His gaze swung to Phyllis. "Will you be going back to America?" He looked at his son. "Will you be going with her?"

Joe and Phyllis glanced at one another. Phyllis said, "We haven't had a chance to talk about it, Mr. Schneider. I'm working for the American Embassy in Oslo right now."

"Norway?"

"Yes, sir. Joe and I just got engaged before he went on the Romanian assignment and my short time here with him has been spent on his rehabilitation."

"Dad, Phyllis and I need to discuss a few things."

"But you're going back to Oslo?" Mary's look was one of concern.

"Yes," Phyllis nodded. "I will have to in a week. That's all the longer my

boss would give me."

"Will you be going too, Joseph?" asked his mother.

Joe smiled at Phyllis, brought her hand up to his lips for a kiss. "I'll go anywhere she asks me to."

While Mary beamed at the happy couple, the look on Michael's face wasn't pleased. "What about your job?"

Joe shrugged. "We haven't made any decisions."

Phyllis smoothed her skirt, looked over at his parents. "Joe's recovery is number one on the agenda right now. We can decide things later. We don't want additional pressure on him because he needs to heal, inside and out."

Michael looked at her sharply with that comment, opened his mouth to say something when Mary interrupted. "Perhaps everyone should drink their coffee." When he glanced at his wife something shifted on his face and he took a gulp of his cooling coffee.

Later after dinner and with the chilly atmosphere between Joe and his father still prevailing, Phyllis decided to call it a night.

"I've made up the bed in the guest room for you and Mary," she remarked to Michael after she brought him fresh towels. Taking the towels from her, Michael's mouth dropped open.

"But you aren't...married," he sputtered in shock.

Mary came up behind him and took the towels. "Thank you, Phyllis, dear. I believe my husband and I will go to bed now. It's been a long day." She skewered Michael with a withering look, took his hand and half dragged him into the guest room.

Joe's pallor was paler than ever and she knew he was fading.

"Let's get you to bed."

"Aren't you worried about being branded a 'scarlet woman' by my father?"

She laughed, tugged on his arm. "He's challenging, for sure, but my reputation is not the most important thing in my life right now. You are."

Joe swung her around to face him. "Am I really, sweetheart?"

"Always and forever."

"We could find a preacher tonight if you want."

"I think what you need to do right this minute is get some sleep. We can worry about my reputation after you've rested."

"Phyllis..."

"Joe." She rested her hands on her hips. "A lousy piece of paper doesn't mean squat to me in comparison with your health, but if you seriously think we should, I'll get my coat."

He sagged, headed for the bedroom.

"That's what I thought."

"You called my bluff." Joe gave her a wan smile.

"I've got your number, buddy. You're exhausted. Let's get you into bed."

Sometime in the middle of the night, Joe woke up with sweat beaded on his cold face and arms reaching out towards the ceiling. He'd been back in the filthy cell with an angry face pulling back a fist when he woke himself up, a desperate cry escaping his lips. Phyllis immediately wrapped her arms around him. At first he pushed her away until his eyes opened. His fearful look chilled her to the bone.

"Phyllis?"

"I'm here. It's okay," she soothed as she pulled him back towards her, rubbed fingers over his sweaty brow and down his chilly cheeks. "Sh...you're okay."

When he'd calmed somewhat, she whispered, "I'll get you some warm milk." Shuddering, Joe nodded. Phyllis slipped on a robe and made her way to the kitchen. Noticing a light in the dining room, she stuck her head in to see who else was up.

"Mr. Schneider?"

With tousled hair, Joe's father blinked wary eyes at her. "Was that Joe I heard?" Sitting at the table, his stare hardened as he twirled a spoon in his nearly empty cup.

"Yes, it was."

"May I ask you something, Miss Bowden?"

"Only if you'll call me Phyllis."

His look softened. "All right...Phyllis. How bad is he?"

She sat down across the table from him. "He won't tell me what happened, but I know it was bad. I've been told from his doctors that he was tortured and beaten, besides being shot. His physical wounds aren't the ones I'm worried about."

Michael looked down, curled both hands around his cup. "What are you worried about?" he asked softly.

Phyllis swallowed hard. "I'm worried about the battle fatigue he's suffering from. I've been told his condition is difficult to treat and he could suffer the rest of his life."

Joe's father looked up startled. "Forever?"

"Yes, sir. Forever."

"And you still want to marry him?"

She smiled. "With all my heart."

Michael returned her smile. "Then I'm happy he has you. Sometimes men act a little...difficult because...they don't understand. Joe has always tried to act tougher than he is; it could be in reaction to me."

Phyllis reached over to lay her hand on Michael's. "Joe looks up to you and brags about what a good police officer you were. He has nothing but respect for you and I hope you feel the same about your son. He's been a loyal soldier to his country and has paid a high price for it."

"So he told me but I didn't know what he was saying."

They looked at one another for a moment.

"Thank you, Miss...Phyllis. I'm happy we met."

"Me too." Phyllis rose. "But I have to get Joe some warm milk now. Excuse me."

Michael chuckled. "He's been a sucker for warm milk since he was a kid. It kept the monsters under his bed away."

She nodded in understanding. "I'm hoping it will do the same for him now. He has different monsters."

"Monsters are monsters."

"I'll get him a big glass."

FORTY-NINE

"You can't be serious!"

"Why not?"

"Let's talk about this, Joe."

"Okay, so talk."

"You first."

The next day after his parents left, Joe and Phyllis walked down the street where a man was selling ice cream from his three-wheeled vehicle. Close to a park with leafless trees and chilly temperatures, the scene was clogged with noisy children chattering nonstop in queues around the man selling ice cream. Parents hung back on the periphery to watch the action and smile their approval.

"Little early for ice cream."

Phyllis tucked her arm in Joe's. "Everyone is ready for spring. Can't say that I blame them. It feels like it's taken forever for better weather to come around."

"And it's not here yet."

She laughed. "Let's get some ice cream and pretend."

Joining the throng of happy children shrieking and giggling was good medicine for the ailing Joe Schneider. All that happiness spread around like melted butter coating him inside and out. After getting their cones, Phyllis and Joe sat down at a park bench to watch the children frolic and play.

"I'm giving serious thought to resigning, Phyllis."

She looked at him. "Really? I didn't know."

"I brought it up with my father, who gave his standard speech about finishing what you start and not giving up with the going gets rough."

"What did you say?"

"Nothing really. I have no defense."

She watched him lick his ice cream cone. "Joe, maybe you should wait a while to decide anything. You've been through a terrible experience and this might not be the best time to make life-changing decisions."

"I've been thinking about making a change since I met you, Phyllis. When we were together in Oslo, I knew the time had come."

"I didn't want you to leave."

"I wish I hadn't."

They exchanged a knowing look.

Phyllis tossed her half-eaten cone, wiped her mouth with a napkin. "So what do we do now?"

"Has Lt. Col. Lawrence mentioned when he wants you back?"

"In a manner of speaking."

He frowned. "That's cryptic."

When she didn't respond and looked away, Joe swallowed the last of his ice cream cone and licked his lips.

"Phyllis."

"What?"

"You're not good at this."

Her eyes widened. "Not good at what?"

"...Holding back on me. I can tell when you're not telling me something."

"How in the name of King George would you know that?" she huffed.

He laughed, leaned over to kiss her pouting lips. "Because you can't keep a neutral face." Joe chuckled, took her hand. "So tell me already."

She blew out a breath. "All right. So you're a better spy than me."

"That's for sure."

"Ronnie called late last night after you went to bed. You know the Office of Strategic Services was disbanded."

"Yes, I knew President Truman was dissolving the organization."

"Well, he's starting a new international spy agency in Washington, D.C. called the CIG, the Central Intelligence Group."

"And?" Joe prompted.

"Ronnie wants me to apply for a job."

"In Washington, D.C.?"

"Yes."

"With the CIG?"

She nodded. "He says the new agency will be hiring many of the former OSS personnel and it would be good for me to be back with my family."

"Is that what you want to do?"

She shrugged. "I feel good about the work I've done in Oslo and got the ball rolling for many improvement projects."

"And Lisbet?"

"Ronnie said her mother was deported to Sweden and the Karlsson family has promised to help Janne get on her feet. Lisbet's with her mother now."

"That's wonderful news."

"It is."

"...So I repeat: is going to Washington what you want to do?"

She considered his question, then laid a hand on his cheek. "I want to do what is best for us. I love my career in diplomacy, Joe, but I love you more. Since things are changing and if you're quitting MI5, would you consider coming with me?"

"Without thinking twice." He didn't even hesitate. Joe knew he owed his life to this woman and didn't want to lose her. "If America is where you're going, it's where I'm going too."

"Even after what your parents said?"

"We can always fly back to see them. Living in London three hours away, I've only been back to visit a few times yearly."

She took his hand. "Maybe we can do better and they can visit us as well."

"Sounds like a plan." He tilted her chin for a lingering kiss. "A kiss seals the deal."

They strolled slowly back to his flat. Mothers walked by keeping an eye on their babies sleeping in prams as they chatted. His neighborhood was brimming with enthusiasm as shopkeepers swept their sections of the sidewalk and placed placards with today's lunch specials out for all to see. Tall trees along the street looked ready to bud and the Union Jack was proudly displayed above a few awnings. People in flats above the shops were busy washing windows. Indeed. It looked like everyone had spring fever.

Phyllis leaned over to speak softly in Joe's ear. "Ronnie also mentioned that a Soviet spy ring has been discovered operating in Canada. They've been sending American atomic secrets to Moscow."

"Why did he tell you that?"

"I'm not sure."

Joe glanced around before lowering his voice. "Maybe he's got an idea what you're going to be working on in Washington with the new agency."

She smiled, stopped at the door of his building. "Sure you won't miss this, Agent Schneider?"

"I'm sure." Joe laughed, opened the door for her. "Maybe we should pack up my flat."

"Now?"

"I'm as ready as I'm going to be and besides, I could use the exercise."

"You *are* feeling better."

His flirty eyes had returned and a raised eyebrow wiggled playfully. Oh, yes, Joe Schneider had definitely come back to her. She kissed him with all the thankfulness she was feeling and knew their plans would somehow work out.

. . .

IN A WEEK'S TIME, Joe and Phyllis managed to pack up his flat and store some things they would collect later. Mrs. Stewart and Phyllis' former roommates from the row house at Seven Addison Bridge Place had a small engagement party for them. It was a low-key event and Joe managed it well without becoming too tired. Henry and Lorraine came over for a last quiet dinner with just the four friends. Henry had proposed to Lorraine the night before and he was grumpy since she still hadn't given him an answer. Lorraine winked at Phyllis and responded that a good southern girl takes her time with anything important.

Phyllis was saying goodbye to London again, but this time Joe was coming with her. Again her life was about to start on a new adventure and she welcomed it with all her heart. Why? Because any new adventure would include Joe and she couldn't imagine facing whatever the future had in store without him.

With London in the rearview mirror, Phyllis and Joe caught a military transport plane to Oslo arriving late one cool evening. Taking a taxi to her apartment, Joe paid the driver to bring up their few bags for them. With the driver in tow, they'd just managed to cross the tiled floor of the old, elegant lobby when Mrs. Lind stuck her head out her door.

"Miss Bowden? Velkommen hjem!"

"Thank you, Mrs. Lind. It's good to be home." To Joe's confused look, she murmured, "She said 'welcome home'."

"Oh."

The landlady hurried over to the couple as quickly as she could. The colorful scarf belted at the waist of her long white skirt had loosened and the older woman twisted it with knotted fingers. "Iz good to see du."

Phyllis smiled, gave her a brief hug. "Yes, I've been gone a while, that's true. I hope you haven't rented out my apartment."

"No, miss." She shook her head. "Iz just as you left it. I've been checking."

"Thank you."

Mrs. Lind turned her focused attention to Joe. "This iz your forlovede?"

"Um..."

"I mean," she looked off in the distance searching for the word.

"Fiancé?" suggested Phyllis.

"Yes!" she beamed at them both. "Yes, your fiancé. You are well, Mr. Schneider?"

He took off his hat and smiled at her. "You remembered my name, Mrs. Lind. Thank you, I'm well."

"Good, good." She waved her hands. "Go on with you now. Have a good evening."

"Thank you, Mrs. Lind."

Joe nodded to the driver and they hiked up the four flights to Phyllis' apartment because the elevator still wasn't working. Who knew if it ever would work again? By the time they arrived, Joe's face was flushed and the hair on his forehead was wet with perspiration. He needed to rest.

"Just set them down anywhere." Phyllis instructed the taxi driver and paid him. When he was gone, she looked around for Joe. He'd gotten a glass of water from the kitchen and was sitting on the living room sofa with his feet propped up on the coffee table.

"Comfy?"

"Now, yes." He patted the place next to him. "Take a load off, sweetie."

She tucked in close and patted his arm. "We've been here before."

"It was such a short visit and seems so long ago, but I can still remember what you were wearing that last night we were together."

She blinked surprised eyes. "You can?"

His handsome face broke into a smile. "You wore a flowered rayon dress, gray as I recall, with a white sweater." His hands moved up to her hair. "You'd worn your hair swept back with these beautiful combs. They had," he scrunched his eyes in thought, "pink crystals on them."

Phyllis laughed. "I can't believe you remember those. They were my favorite and they're called brooches, Joe."

"Do you still wear them?"

She shook her head. "No."

"Why not?"

"...I gave them to Lisbet."

Joe gently brought her chin up for him to kiss her lips. "Softie."

"When it comes to Lisbet, you bet."

He thought that over. "We both have a connection to her, you know."

"I do know. She's the reason you went to Bucharest. It's crazy, Joe."

"What is?"

"That you went looking for a little girl and I found her in the bathroom of Arne's Café."

"Small world."

"Dinky."

"I need to call her before we leave for Washington."

"Do it then. I'd like to say hello myself."

FIFTY

Phyllis and Joe went to the American Embassy in Oslo the next morning. Lt. Col. Lawrence was happy to see her and thrilled that Joe was alive and in one piece. He came out of his office in his crisp military uniform as soon as he heard them come in.

"Miss Bowden! Mr. Schneider! Welcome back to Norway!" Ronnie was as ecstatic as a proper military man could get. He oozed excitement with a smile bright enough to light the office. He hugged Phyllis, then grasped Joe's hand with a firm grip. "Can't tell you how glad I am to see you, Agent Schneider. I heard what happened."

"Thank you, Colonel. I can't tell you how glad I am to be back. You can thank your secretary here for help in my recovery."

"Phyllis is excellent at everything she does, so I'm not surprised she helped put you back together."

"She did indeed, sir."

"Come into my office and take a seat."

Phyllis glanced around her office. "Where's Nancy?"

"She's running a few errands and should be back shortly."

They walked into the Colonel's office and took seats by

his desk. Streaks of sunlight shone through his second floor window.

"Is she working out for you, sir?"

Ronald Lawrence's smile bloomed. "She's worked out nicely, Miss Bowden, but she's not you."

His brows drew together over teasing eyes.

"No one is, Colonel."

"So what's the plan?" Ronnie looked from Phyllis to Joe.

"Plan, sir?"

"I assume you've been making plans."

"Well, um..."

He interrupted her. "It's been a long war and you've both seen your share of action." Ronnie's eyes softened. "You know how much I appreciate you, Phyllis, but it might be time to go home. You can continue the fight from there, if you like."

"The fight, sir?"

"Your work with the new agency will be similar to what you've been doing here and in London. Lt. Casey in General Donovan's office called me about you."

"About me?"

"Yes, he said a woman with your initiative and smarts would be most welcome in the new organization. There's a cold war brewing with the Soviets that we all saw coming. Our alliance in the war was short-lived, I'm afraid. It's apparently business as usual with them."

"Sir, if I may."

He waved a hand. "Please."

"Joe and I are getting married."

"I know that. Congratulations."

"He's also leaving MI5."

Ronnie's gaze swung to Joe. "Is that true?"

Joe nodded. "I'm going wherever Phyllis is going."

"That doesn't mean you have to leave the service."

"I think it does." Joe looked at Phyllis. "I've done my bit for King and country and I want to move on."

Lawrence's smile was sly. "There are organizations in

Washington that could use a clever man like yourself, Agent Schneider."

"We'll see."

His attention went back to Phyllis. "Can you make sure Nancy is up to speed on all the projects before you leave? How much time can you give me?"

"I'm at your disposal, Colonel. We're not in a huge hurry. My sister's last letter said that our father has been doing well with his new medications."

"Good, good. Glad to hear that. Give me two weeks then. That should be enough time to put in the paperwork with this job and your new one."

"And we need to pack up my apartment."

Ronnie grinned. "We've been through a lot together, Phyllis. I'm going to miss you."

She returned his grin. "I'm not gone yet, sir, and I promise to keep in touch."

"Good deal."

THE WEEKS FLEW by with everything that needed to be done. They had met Phyllis' friend, Jay, for dinner a few times and Jay had promised to visit them in America. During one of their dinners, Phyllis was surprised when Astrid, Helge and Gunnar joined them for coffee at Jay's request. Gunnar looked so much better than the last time she'd seen him when he had walked in the door at the American Embassy. The tall Norwegian had added a few pounds and no longer needed his crutches. His sisters were obviously delighted with his company and grateful to Phyllis for her help in finding their beloved brother.

Getting Nancy ready to assume control of the office of the Military Attaché went smoother than Phyllis had antici-pated. Petite Nancy might have been small, but she took over like a champ and Phyllis knew she was leaving Lt. Col. Lawrence in good hands. While sorry to be going, the future in Washington with Joe looked bright enough that she bought a new pair of sunglasses to wear once they arrived. She smiled at her tiny joke.

The evening before they were to leave Oslo was bittersweet. She had had a nice talk with Mrs. Lind, who was very sorry to see them go. Phyllis thought about saying she would visit, but wasn't sure she could carry through that promise. Then they headed over to Arne's Café for one last meal. She was truly sorry that she'd probably never see the feisty Norwegian proprietor again. He had charmed her thoroughly and his café had been the scene of so many wonderful happenings in her life in the scrappy city of Oslo.

Joe laughed at a small joke Arne made in broken English before turning his attention to the warmed bowl in front of him.

"This farikal looks great. What did you say is in it?"

Phyllis spooned food from her bowl. "It's lamb and cabbage stew. Good, don't you think?"

He shoved another bite in his already stuffed mouth. "Mmm," he mumbled chewing noisily. Joe was looking better. In the weeks she'd been with him, his face looked fuller and he'd had to loosen his belt a notch. Symptoms of his condition had lessened, but Phyllis knew they might never go away.

"How are the nightmares?"

He shrugged, stuck his spoon back in the bowl. "Better."

"Is that the truth, Joe?"

"Yes and no."

"Which is it?"

He looked towards the door. Arne was saying goodbye to a customer laughing about some funny exchange between them.

"Joe?"

"They're shorter in duration, Phyllis, but are still terrifying. You know that."

She nodded, pushed meat around in her bowl. "I do, but..."

"But Dr. Spearman gave me the name of a good doctor in Washington so I plan to continue treatments."

"Good. I was afraid you'd stop."

His warm eyes roamed her face. "Not when I've got such a great gal on the hook. I don't want to run her off."

She laughed. "Good to know."

They ate in silence for a few minutes until Joe finished his bowl of stew and signaled Arne for another. After the frizzy-haired proprietor had brought Joe a new bowl of stew, Phyllis smirked at him.

"Apparently the nausea is gone."

"Apparently." He blew on his spoonful of food before eating it. When he swallowed, Joe spoke up.

"I heard you talking to Lisbet again this morning."

"Yes."

"How is she?"

Phyllis' face beamed. "She's so happy, Joe. She and her mother found a little place not far from the Karlssons. You remember me mentioning them, don't you?" When he nodded, she continued. "They're a great family and offered to help Janne find work."

"Where's she working?"

"She's learning the craft of glassblowing. Mr. Karlsson found her a training position where he works."

"You're kidding."

"No. Women do all kinds of things in Sweden and I guess Janne is getting good at it." She stirred her stew. "Lisbet's in school and seems well adjusted."

"You miss that little girl, don't you?" He laid a hand on her arm.

"I think I always will. She was a delight and..."

"And you saved her life, Phyllis. You probably saved her mother's too. I don't know what to say about Oskar."

Phyllis shook her head. "It's not for us to judge. What happened is what happened. What's important now is for Janne and Lisbet to go forward with their lives."

"It sounds like they're well on their way."

She tapped his hand. "I need to visit the ladies' room. I'll be right back."

After using the facilities and freshening up, Phyllis left

the bathroom to stop abruptly with the unusual scene in front of her. Sitting at the table with Joe was none other than John Edelland, debonair businessman and the charming Norwegian who had asked her to marry him several weeks ago. It seemed a lifetime now. Her steps slowed as she walked over since she had no idea what to expect. Both men rose from their seats when she returned to the table.

She smiled at the attractive man watching her approach. "Hello, John. Nice to see you again."

"Hello, Phyllis. You're looking lovely as usual." His grin was mischievous.

When she slipped into her chair, the men sat back down. She picked up her cup of coffee.

"I must say I'm surprised to see you, yet I probably shouldn't be, should I?"

He shrugged. "I happened to be in the area and thought I'd get a bowl of Arne's farikal."

"It's good, isn't it?" said Joe.

She looked warily from John to Joe. "I assume you've been introduced."

"Yes. Mr. Edelland here..."

"John, please."

"John," he corrected, "has been kind enough to tell me a few things about what you've been up to here in Oslo while I was gone."

Phyllis tried for nonchalance. "Well, a girl has to stay busy."

John bit back a smirk.

"I'll say." Joe pushed back his bowl and reached for his cup. "But the black market, Phyllis? Really?"

Her eyes darted to Edelland with his dark suit and neatly combed blonde hair. "What have you been telling him?"

"Just bits of this and that. Nothing to worry about, Phyllis." John held up a cup to signal Arne for a refill. Arne raised eyebrows at the two men with Phyllis, poured them fresh cups and left.

"What are you really doing here, John?" asked Phyllis. "You weren't just in the neighborhood."

Edelland chuckled, smoothed his tie. "I didn't want you to leave without saying goodbye," he said sincerely. "And I wanted to meet Mr. Schneider." He turned to Joe. "I've heard so much about you."

Joe grinned. "All good, I hope."

"Only the best."

Joe looked from John to Phyllis. He wiped his mouth with a napkin and rose. "I'll be right back, Phyllis. John, if you'll excuse me."

"Certainly."

They watched him walk to the bathroom. When he went in, John turned to Phyllis. "He's a wonderful man."

"I have to agree." Her eyes narrowed. "Why are you really here?"

"I was serious when I said we needed to say our goodbyes."

"How did you know I was leaving? How did you know Joe was with me?"

John opened his mouth to reply, but Phyllis held up a hand. "Never mind. It's not necessary to know that. Just tell me one thing."

"If I can."

"Do you know what happened to Joe in Bucharest?"

Edelland sipped his coffee.

"John?"

He laid a hand on hers. "Phyllis, you don't want to know. Just be thankful that you have him back and make your lives as happy as possible. You both deserve it after what you've been through."

She smiled at him. "What about you, John Edelland?"

"What about me?"

"Will you be all right?"

He chuckled softly. "Phyllis, you have been a shining light in my life for however brief a time we were together. A light that I will remember always."

"Thank you."

"Who knows?" He shrugged a shoulder. "Maybe we'll

see each other again sometime. I may have business in Washington, D.C. in the future."

Her jaw dropped. "How in the world do you know that I'm..."

Joe tapped Phyllis on the shoulder. "Ready to go? We have some packing to finish tonight."

She jerked her eyes from Edelland to Joe. "Sure, sure. Let's get the bill from Arne."

"Please," said John. "Let me pay. It's your final night here in Oslo and I'm happy to have caught up with you once again. And met you, Mr. Schneider."

Joe reached out a hand. "It's been a pleasure, John. Thanks for keeping my girl company while I was gone."

"It was truly my pleasure." Edelland locked dark eyes with Phyllis. "A real pleasure." He rose when Phyllis did and extended his hand to her. They lingered shaking hands until John nodded to her and they both smiled.

After Joe and Phyllis left the café and crossed the busy street, Joe opened the door of the apartment building for her.

"You don't have anything to ask me?"

He shook his head, waited for her to enter the lobby. "No, I don't."

"Joe..."

He held up a hand. "Look. Whatever happened between you and Edelland is none of my business."

"But..."

"I saw how he looked at you, Phyllis. I can guess the rest."

"It was all on his part. He has or had feelings for me that weren't reciprocated."

"Okay."

"I'm serious."

He pressed his lips to her hand. "Sweetheart, neither of us needs to talk about what happened after I left Oslo. We don't have to talk and we don't need to. Let's just let it go."

They began walking up the marble staircase putting their feet in the well-worn path.

"But I need to explain him to you."

"No, you honestly don't."

Phyllis and Joe argued back and forth until they reached her door. Inserting the old skeleton key, Joe looked back at her.

"Let me just say that I trust you, Phyllis, and my trust doesn't come easily. There are very few people in this world that I would risk with my life and you're one of them. In fact, right now, you're the only one."

"Joe."

"So the past is the past and we are moving forward." His eyes twinkled as he pulled her into the apartment shutting the door with a thud. "Besides, the future looks much more promising than the past."

He tugged her into his arms. "Don't you think?"

"Indubitably."

Joe laughed, shut off the light before brushing back her hair to kiss her neck. "Think we can find your bedroom in the dark?"

"I think we could find it in total blackness with no road map."

"Let's do it then."

FIFTY-ONE

THE TRIP HOME

A transport ship was heading from Oslo to New York the very next week. Phyllis and Joe were on it.

So much had happened to the couple that they were weary with effort and looking forward to several days at sea and away from the world. Lt. Col. Lawrence had informed them of a military transport plane leaving the same week, but they'd decided to breathe in the sea air for a relaxing if somewhat unnerving trip back to the States.

Leaving Oslo, the ship had to travel around the tip of Norway and out into the North Sea before heading west to Scotland and across the Atlantic Ocean for home. The problem with their route was that the British had mined the strip of water between Norway and Scotland with contact mines in 1940. The U.S. Navy employed a minesweeping ship to escort them through the North Sea where the weather was very rough and freezing. So the trip was bound to give them a case of nerves hoping the minesweepers did their job successfully.

Bundled up against the cold, the couple stood at the railing one late afternoon watching the unexpectedly calm water. With the unpredictability of the North Sea, Phyllis and Joe went topside only a few times daily. Joe spent much of the time resting as Phyllis hovered and read a book.

Although chilly today, the still green sea contrasted sharply with billowy dark clouds threatening to let loose with a vicious storm at any moment. They watched the coast of Scotland fade in the distance.

"What's the first thing you want to do when we get home?" asked Joe.

"...Um, I'm not sure. See the family, I suppose." She glanced at him. "Why?"

"I think we should buy our wedding rings."

Phyllis smiled. "Are you in a hurry?"

"Well, I think your family will be expecting to see them."

Her brows furrowed over confused eyes. "...Why...what are you saying, Joe?

"I think we should be married by the time we reach New York."

"You think we should..." She trailed off still not understanding.

Joe turned to Phyllis taking her hand. "Do you still want to marry me, Phyllis Bowden?"

She smiled. "Of course, I do."

"Then let's do it."

"What? Here? On board ship?"

Joe chuckled. "Yes. The captain is able to marry us, so why not?" When she continued to have a perplexed look on her face, Joe tried again.

"Phyllis, my feelings for you aren't going to change no matter if we were married in Norway, London or on board a ship in the middle of the Atlantic Ocean."

"But it's a more colorful story to marry at sea," she finished.

"Exactly."

A slow smile spread across her face. Joe gently tucked flyaway strands of curly brown hair behind her ear. "There hasn't been a woman in my life who compares to you, sweetheart. I would be thrilled if you would do me the honors today."

"Today, Joe?" She glanced down at her clothes. "I'm not

wearing anything special. I didn't bring anything appropriate."

"Does it really matter?"

"Maybe not to you, but I'd like to be married in a nice dress."

"You didn't bring any?"

She rolled her eyes. "Well, of course, but not anything special."

Joe leaned forward to kiss her lips. "Wear the dress," he murmured, "and it will become special."

Her smile returned. "What a smoothie, you are, Joe Schneider. Okay." She stepped back. "You round up the preacher and I'll put the dress on."

And so they were married on the ship's bridge with the captain officiating and surrounded by crew and fellow passengers. In a rayon dress with colorful flowers and white sweater, Phyllis stood by Joe, handsome in his slacks and jacket, reciting wedding vows. The short ceremony had just finished when the heavens opened and the ship was pelted with sheets of driving rain. The temporary calm disappeared with sudden rough movement of the buffeted ship. The crew had to disperse to their duties and wedding guests hightailed it back to their cabins. Joe took Phyllis' arm to help her from the slightly tilting bridge along an equally unbalanced corridor. When they reached their cabin, Joe took Phyllis in his arms.

"Ready to go home, Mrs. Schneider?"

"You bet, Mr. Schneider, but..."

He put a finger to her lips. "No, buts, Phyllis." He winked at her. "We'll work it out."

She kissed his finger, smiled at him. "You always say that."

"Because it's always true."

"Joe." She sighed, shook her head.

"Come on in, Mrs. Schneider, and tell me all about that Soviet spy ring in Canada."

"Joe!"

"Just kidding." His eyebrows lifted playfully and he chuckled closing the cabin door snugly behind him. Music spilled out into the corridor dissipating in the ocean with the sounds of the storm bearing down on the small ship in the middle of the vast ocean.

A LOOK AT BOOK THREE:
WASHINGTON SPIES

AN INTERNATIONAL SPY THRILLER BROODING WITH SUSPENSE—HISTORICAL FICTION SET IN THE MIDST OF THE COLD WAR.

1947, Washington DC

Phyllis Bowden is finally working for the Central Intelligence Agency—a goal she's aspired towards her entire life. But working as a secretary, Phyllis *dreams* of field assignments similar to the one she had on her last placement in Oslo.

Her wish is answered when the Cold War sets in, and a major Soviet spy starts stealing atomic secrets. Sent on her first espionage assignment for the CIA to the Oak Ridge Laboratory in Tennessee, Phyllis is tasked with locating and picking up a contact capable of bringing down the infamous Soviet spy.

Sources try to influence her—some for her success, others for her failure. With overt actions, it won't take much to turn a cold war into a real one.

Will Phyllis Bowden make the right choice when faced with a decision that could erupt into a political explosion?

AVAILABLE MARCH 2022

ABOUT THE AUTHOR

SJ Slagle began her writing career as a language arts teacher. Her initial interest was children's stories, and she moved on to western romance, mysteries and historical fiction. She has published 24 novels, both independent and contract and contributes to guest blogs. Her first historical novel, *London Spies*, was awarded a B.R.A.G. Medallion in 2018. She was given the Silver Award with the International Independent Film Awards for her screenplay *Redemption*, and she conducts publishing symposiums in her area. *Oslo Spies* is second in her trilogy about a young woman in military intelligence. She lives and works in Reno, Nevada.